The Dog Sitter Detective Plays Dead

ANTONY JOHNSTON

Allison & Busby Limited
11 Wardour Mews
London W1F 8AN
allisonandbusby.com

First published in Great Britain by Allison & Busby in 2025.

First Edition

ISBN 978-0-7490-3176-3

Typeset in 11.5/16.5 pt Sabon LT Pro by Allison & Busby Ltd.

By choosing this product, you help take care of the world's forests.
Learn more: www.fsc.org

FSC
www.fsc.org
MIX
Paper | Supporting
responsible forestry
FSC® C171272

Printed and bound by
CPI Group (UK) Ltd, Croydon, CR0 4YY

In memory of Kim

CHAPTER ONE

The mist closed around me like a chill, opaque shroud. It had no form yet blinded me with grey shadow, ethereal wisps swirling as if lit from within. A cold, clammy scent passed lazily through the air, disorientating me. I couldn't turn back; there was nothing for me there. I must keep going. I walked on, slowly stumbling through the intangible, infinite veil.

A shape formed before me in the endless grey, indistinct but moving closer. Now it was a silhouette, tall and approaching fast, faster than any normal man could walk. I felt an urgent pull to move forward, to meet it, but every instinct in my soul told me that would end in disaster. I rallied my strength and veered away, resisting the pull, desperate to escape a terrible fate – now! *Now!*

'Morning, Gwinny,' said the postman, barely missing me as he bicycled out of the mist. 'Can't see your hand in front of your face this morning. ''Ow do, Lily,' he added to the elderly Jack Russell terrier I held on a taut lead, as she continued pulling towards him. Whether to steal a fuss or bite his ankles I couldn't be sure, hence my keeping her away.

'It really is quite a fog,' I said inanely. As if he hadn't noticed.

'Aye, and'll likely stick. Tends to, around here.'

With that he was gone. I stepped back onto the path, eager to take Lily home. This *Draculania* business was messing with my head.

I was in Yorkshire for a film role, my biggest part since re-emerging from retirement. I'd given up acting at fifty to look after my father, who was becoming very ill. When he died a decade later, I discovered that we'd collectively burnt through his entire savings, which weren't inconsiderable. He left me a house in Chelsea – in theory worth plenty, but in practice falling to pieces and needing lots of expensive work before anyone would consider buying it. My own flat was being rented by a young couple who'd recently had their first child. I didn't have the heart to evict them and take it back.

So back to work I went, despite my grey hair and failing joints, and began scrabbling around for roles. I was helped in this endeavour by my best friend, Tina, a more famous and successful actress than I would ever be, who put in a good word every now and then; and my new agent, 'Bostin' Jim Austin, who had a mind as shrewd as his Brummie accent. It was Bostin Jim who'd put me forward for this part in *Draculania*, a mid-budget modern take on Stoker's classic. The 'take' was a full gender swap, so I played Dr *Jacqueline* Seward, protégé of Dr *Abigail* Van Helsing and friend to *Lady* Godalming . . . you get the idea. I was playing ten years younger than my age, but that was simple enough with make-up and a wig.

It was a decent screenplay. Very atmospheric, hence my phantasmagoria on the moors that morning. Lily, the Jack Russell terrier so eager to greet the postman emerging from the mist, belonged to the actress Viv Danforth. Viv was of the acting generation before mine and had taken me under her wing when I was young. She'd retired years ago, returning to her native Yorkshire to buy a converted farmhouse in Hendale, so when I learnt the film would be shooting on location in the area I called her and offered to visit.

Although it had been almost twenty years since we'd last met, we immediately picked up where we left off, trading showbiz gossip and laughing at old war stories. Some changes couldn't be ignored, though. Mentally Viv was still sharp, but physically she'd grown frail. She managed to live independently after her husband, David, had passed away, but I could tell it wasn't easy. Especially with a dog to look after.

Lily was eleven years old, an age at which even terriers begin to slow down. The last dog my father owned was a Jack Russell called Rusty, who predeceased him by four years, so I was very comfortable with the breed. Thank goodness, because despite her age Lily still needed regular walks and Viv struggled to keep up. Me being me, I offered to help while I was in the area by taking Lily on the moor before and after work each day.

Normally I'd charge for that sort of thing. You see, the other way I've been trying to make a living since realising I was broke has been by dog sitting. That all started at Tina's aborted wedding, which is a whole other story involving a dead Italian, two Saluki hounds, an olive oil empire and me having to solve a murder because the police couldn't.

But now things were looking up. This small-but-notable part in a feature film meant I could afford to do a freebie, especially for an old friend like Viv. Besides, the decades of living in London hadn't blunted her Yorkshire frugality and if I'd tried to charge she might not have let me walk Lily at all. That would have been a shame, because the dog and I were both enjoying it, even if she didn't have quite the same verve and energy as when she was younger. Tell me about it.

My phone buzzed as we passed through the final field gate onto the road leading back to Viv's house. Signal around here was terrible, almost non-existent on the moors proper, and when I looked at the screen I saw it was notification of a voicemail. Somebody must have tried to call me while I was out of range, walking Lily. Most likely someone from the film, so I decided to check it after I dropped the dog off at Viv's.

But as I neared her farmhouse, the morning mist began to lift at last. Through the thinning wisps of grey, I saw the unmistakeable pulsing blue lights of an ambulance.

CHAPTER TWO

The ambulance crew wouldn't let me ride with Viv to the hospital, partly because I wasn't family (despite her having no family nearby) but mostly because of Lily.

I didn't want to leave the dog in the house by herself. As far as I knew she and Viv had never been apart for any length of time, and no matter their age Jack Russells are prone to destruction when bored. Leave her alone for too long and there might barely be a house worth returning to. That left the neighbours, all at least a quarter of a mile away. So I bundled Lily into my rusty old Volvo and tried to find someone who'd look after her.

'I'm off to work, no dogs allowed—'

'You're joking, I've already got three kids—'

'I don't even know who that is, we only moved here in the summer—'

'You've already got hold of it, why can't you look after it?'

So much for Yorkshire hospitality.

These summary dismissals left me in a pickle. By now it was gone eight, and I was supposed to be in hair and make-up by eight-thirty. If I set off now at top speed I could probably make it. But what about Lily? What about Viv, for that matter?

The voicemail had been from the ambulance medic, informing me that Viv had fallen in the kitchen. A nasty bump on the head and a suspected broken hip, which at her age is never good news. Fortunately, it hadn't completely incapacitated her, and while Viv was stubborn, she wasn't stupid. The moment she'd found herself on the floor she'd pressed the alarm pendant she wore about the house.

But I knew how these things went, having accompanied my father on many emergency hospital visits of his own. The immediate focus would be on getting the patient stable and in a bed, followed by finding a relative or neighbour to bring her a bag of fresh clothes, medication, reading glasses and so on. Given their attitude to Lily I didn't trust any of them to handle that, so I said to hell with it and called Steven McDonald, the film's producer. I could have called the director, but she might have actually picked up and I didn't have time for that. Steven never answered calls.

'It's Gwinny,' I said after the voicemail beep. 'I'm going to be late to set today. My friend has been rushed to hospital, and I need to check on her. I'll be in by noon.'

I ended the call, then immediately silenced my phone

so he couldn't call me back and deliver a stream of invective. I was confident it would be fine, anyway. My first scene was due to start at eleven, but we'd been shooting here for almost a week already and every single day had been delayed thanks to our capricious star.

I fed Lily some kibble, and while she scoffed it I packed a bag of clothes for Viv. Her phone was still charging on her bedside table, so I packed that and the cable too. Then I loaded the bag in the car, with Lily following. She sniffed the air and wagged her tail.

'Don't worry, you're coming too,' I reassured her.

What choice did I have? There was no chance Viv would return home today or possibly even this week. I could have looked up a local kennel, but they weren't cheap, and I didn't yet know how long it would be required. At least Lily knew me, and the shoot was here in Yorkshire for at least another five days. After that, I'd think of something.

The terrier continued to follow as I collected a dog bed, more food and bowls, a couple of toys and her favourite sofa cushion, which Viv had pointed out to me. Lily was already in her coat, as I'd put it on this morning to go out in the cold, misty weather and hadn't yet had a chance to remove it.

'Up,' I commanded, holding the boot open. Lily could still just about manage that height, and dutifully jumped inside. I clipped her in safely, collected Viv's keys, locked up the house and set off for the hospital.

Lily wasn't permitted inside, even though I tried to explain she was in fact Viv's dog and would be valuable as emotional support. So, I had to take her back to the car and leave her in the boot, on top of her favourite cushion and under a blanket. I cracked open a rear window, mostly for air as there was little chance of overheating on this grey day, then hurried back inside the hospital to where Viv lay in a bed. She looked worryingly frail and thin in her nightgown.

'What a nuisance,' she said, typically stoic. 'Slipped on a wet kitchen tile, and now here I am. Good thing I'm retired. If I was doing that film with you, some jumped-up pretty young thing would already be lobbying for my part.'

'Less of the young and pretty if they wanted to replace either of us,' I joked.

Viv grinned, then winced. 'Don't make me laugh, it hurts.'

'Sorry. How long will you be in here for?'

'No idea. Not sure if anything's actually broken, yet.'

'You mean they haven't X-rayed you?' I said, horrified. 'Let me find a doctor. It's outrageous, people our age should take priority, you might have multiple fractures or—'

'Guinevere Tuffel, hush and sit down,' Viv said, sounding uncannily like my mother. 'There's a queue for the machine, and I'm not going anywhere. I won't keel over if they don't see me in the next five minutes.'

'No, you already did that,' I grumbled, and held up the bag I'd packed. 'I assume you'll be here overnight, so I brought you this.'

'Thank you.' She smiled, then hesitated. 'Where did . . . I

mean, did you ask any of the neighbours about . . . ?'

I shook my head. 'Lily can stay with me for a while. We've got another week of shooting here, and you should be back home by then.' Unless she really had broken her hip, but I didn't want to make that concern real by voicing it. If she was still in hospital by the time we finished filming in Hendale, Lily might have to go into kennels after all.

'Let's hope. Thank you, Gwinny. You'll be fine with Lily; she's a good judge of character.'

'How so?'

'She hates the neighbours for a start. But she likes you. What more proof do you need?'

I laughed. 'That might explain why they weren't exactly falling over themselves to look after her. I'd have had more luck flogging double glazing. But don't worry, Lily will be fine with me at Hendale Hall.'

She shivered. 'Horrible place. I don't know why you can't do it all on a sound stage.'

'I've told you, it's for publicity. The producer's convinced that filming *Draculania* at the home of the Hendale Vampire is grist for the marketing mill. It had better be, considering how much they must be paying for the location.'

'But what about the Hendale curse? Do you know the legend?'

'The Viscount mentioned it when he gave us a tour. Something to do with India?' I stopped Viv before she could launch into a recap of the story. 'I'm sure they'll give us a proper brief on it before we do any interviews.

You relax and let the doctors sort you out, while I get Lily settled in at the Hall.'

'Do they have their own dogs?' Viv asked. 'She gets on all right with big breeds, but you'll want to keep her away from other terriers.'

I thought for a moment. 'Now you mention it, I haven't seen any. I'll have to ask the Viscount. He might be able to help walk Lily, too.' I sighed quietly.

Viv, sharp despite her pain, picked up on it. 'Be easier if your fancy fella was here, wouldn't it? The ex-copper, I mean. He could walk her for you.'

'Birch,' I laughed. 'Alan Birch. He's anything but fancy, and I wouldn't call him "mine" either. At least, not yet. We're getting there.'

'What do you mean, "getting there"?'

'Well, you know. Holding hands, cuddles in front of the telly.'

Viv winced again, chuckling. 'Ow. I told you not to make me laugh. "Holding hands"? What are you waiting for, an arrest warrant? Oh, or is he into that sort of thing?' She smiled wickedly. 'Does he still have the handcuffs?'

'You're insufferable,' I said, but appreciated that she was still able to make jokes from a hospital bed.

'Seriously, Gwinny, don't hang about. Your father may have lived to a good age, but most of them don't. Believe me, I know.' She did; Viv's husband passed away less than two years after they moved to the Dales.

'Don't worry,' I reassured her. 'Birch is as fit as a fiddle, and we're making progress. Slowly but surely.'

'Less of the slow and more of the sure. Before it's too late, you hear?' She smiled and took my hand. Her bones felt thin and delicate, like a bird's. 'Now go and be fabulous for the camera, and I'll let you know the moment they have my results. Thank you for looking after Lily.'

I gave her hand a gentle squeeze and stood. She was right, I had to go, both to get to set and because I didn't like leaving Lily in the car. I didn't like leaving Viv here unattended, either.

'So long as you're sure,' I said, looking around for a doctor again. Still nothing.

'If anything goes wrong, I'm in the right place for it, aren't I?' she said with a grim smile. 'Go on, and mind the bloodsuckers at Hendale. The flesh-and-blood kind, I mean.'

CHAPTER THREE

The fog threatened to return as I sped along the Dales' roads, throwing the Volvo around corners to hurry back to Hendale Hall. Luckily, I'd made this journey twice a day for the past week, so knew it well by now. Even if I hadn't, reflective signs tied to lampposts pointed to *DRA – LOC*, ensuring production vehicles wouldn't get lost.

Every time I scraped a hedge or clattered over a pothole Lily grumbled in the back, and the car grumbled along with her. But they both held together until I finally crested Hendale itself to begin the descent to the estate, an extensive woodland park.

I was a few minutes later than I'd promised Steven, and production security at the gate waved me through. I drove under the avenue of oaks, around the lake and onward through the larch wood. Mist clung to the ground, forcing me to drive slowly and casting alternating shafts of light and shadow through the trees.

As I passed the old wooden gatehouse I saw what might have been creatures of the undead, shambling through fog to seek revenge upon the living, but it was only the carpenters and set decorators building a fake graveyard and crypt in preparation for our night shoots. Easy mistake to make, though.

Vampire legend aside, it wasn't hard to see why Hendale Hall was our chosen location. The house was a seventeenth-century pile, a grand old building with spires, a tower and an ivy-covered west wing, surrounded by the park yet standing proud above it all. Forty bedrooms, half as many bathrooms, five different reception rooms, three dining rooms, two libraries, one ballroom, a grand staircase and more all made it a perfect setting for *Draculania*.

There was one more factor, though, that separated Hendale Hall from the many other big old houses around the country featuring spooky legends and alleged hauntings: the twenty-second Viscount Henning (full name Henry George Fitzroy Samuel de Finistere Henning, apparently) desperately needed money to keep the place afloat and so regularly hired it out for use by films, TV, fashion photographers, weddings, corporate functions, grand balls and anyone else who'd pay. He'd even made the bedrooms available to our cast and crew for a small additional fee, which producer Steven had jumped on eagerly as a way to save time and money. I was one of those staying at the Hall, hence my driving to and from Viv's place to walk Lily. I could have had a production driver take me there and back every day, rather than use my own car, but that seemed wasteful.

I sympathised with the Viscount to an extent. If there had been room to swing even half a cat in my own house I'd have hired it out to finance the constant cash injections it required. But I was still embroiled in clearing the place of my late father's things, which was slow going. Half the time I couldn't bring myself to do it; the other half I couldn't decide what to keep or throw out.

We'd been warned that Viscount Henning was a taciturn fellow who resented having to hire out his ancestral home to people like us, but we hadn't seen that side of him at all. In fact he was quite enthusiastic about our film. I often spied him hovering at the edges of the set, watching the actors, particularly our glamorous leading lady, or chatting with crew. If that's what it took in return for us getting the run of his house, nobody was complaining – least of all us older women, as the Viscount was something of a silver fox.

I manoeuvred around the wide, green wall erected in front of the visitors' car park at the side of the Hall. It hid the production vehicles and trailers that formed our temporary unit base and acted as a giant 'green screen', which would help the special effects people remove it from exterior shots.

I found a parking spot, hopped out, opened the boot and clipped Lily on-lead. She immediately jumped out and dropped to the ground for a wee.

'There you are,' said a woman's voice behind me. 'Chloe's been having conniptions, wondering where you are. When did you get a dog?'

I turned to see two people smoking by the 'tradesman's entrance' at the side of the house. I don't know if that was the door's real use, but our crew's nickname for it had stuck. Smoking was forbidden inside the Hall, so those who indulged had to come outside for breaks. They were an odd couple: an older woman in formal Victorian dress and a handsome young man in jeans and T-shirt.

The woman was Ruby Westcott, dressed as Dr Abigail Van Helsing, and even in her grey-wigged costume as the distinguished doctor she remained glamorous. Ruby and I were the same age and had met early in our careers when we shared a storyline on *Casualty*. We'd also both had our native accents – mine London, hers Bristol – hammered out of us at drama school. But that was where our similarities ended. Ruby had continued working, while I'd retired to care for my father. I was five-foot-nothing, while she was five-seven even without heels. Most obviously, I'd foregone the surgeon's knife while, at some point during those ten years we'd lost touch, Ruby had 'a little work' done. It was good work, no question, but she now had fewer wrinkles than when she was forty, which I couldn't get used to.

The young man was Yash Rani, who played Luke Westenra in our gender-swapped production. The advantage of natural youth meant that even in a ratty old T-shirt, jeans and mud-stained trainers he looked like a pop star waiting to be mobbed by adoring fans. I'd never met Yash before this job; a decade ago his career had barely started. But he was a renowned and respected rising star, having moved easily from soap operas to the West End and films. What he was doing on a gig like *Draculania* I couldn't fathom, but I wasn't complaining about the positive effect it would have on our box office.

'Didn't Steven mention anything?' I said to Ruby, picking out dog supplies with one hand while holding on to Lily with the other. 'I called and left a message to tell him I'd be late.'

Ruby exhaled a cloud of smoke. 'I can't believe you've gone and bought a dog in the middle of shooting. Never took you for the furball-in-a-handbag type, Gwinny.'

'No, it's not like that at all. Lily belongs to Viv Danforth. She lives nearby, on her own these days, so I've been walking her dog. But this morning she slipped, so now she's in hospital, and—'

'Gwinny!' called a voice. 'For God's sake, where have you been? Christ, you're not even in costume. What the hell is that?'

I turned to see Chloe Churchill, our young director, alternately sputtering with rage and reeling with bewilderment at the sight of Lily and me. Chloe was another rising star, a young and diminutive Black woman whom you wouldn't think formidable, especially with the voluminous pink bum bag she wore everywhere. But she was loud, self-assured and perpetually frustrated by the idiocy of everyone around her – in other words, born to be a director and no doubt destined for great success. First, though, she had to cut her teeth on jobs like *Draculania*.

'That,' I said, following her horrified gaze, 'is Lily. She's Viv Danforth's dog, but Viv has been rushed to hospital, so I'm looking after Lily in the meantime, and I've just come from there myself. The hospital, that is—'

The terrier chose that moment to lunge at Chloe's ankle, her teeth bared. 'Lily, *no!*' I shouted, pulling her away. So much for Viv's insistence about her being a good judge of character.

'You're lucky Little Miss Sunshine is sulking in her trailer,' said Chloe, 'but she could change her mind at any moment, so you need to get into make-up stat. And don't you dare bring that thing anywhere near my set.'

Little Miss Sunshine was the on-set nickname, though never in her presence, of Juliette Shine, the American star playing Draculania herself, which primarily reflected her reputation for tantrums. While Ruby and I were perennial supporting actors, Juliette was a Hollywood diva who'd starred in dozens of films. But she'd always fallen short of an Academy Award, and in recent years her star began to fade. No doubt that was why she'd agreed to take this role an ocean away from home, and unfortunately it showed. Oh, she was wonderful when the camera rolled, during those precious moments between the calls of '*Action!*' and '*Cut!*', but every other moment was more prickly than precious. Steven the producer had promised Juliette that *Draculania* would herald her career comeback, but she made no secret of her disdain for having to slum it in Yorkshire with the likes of us.

Ruby thought that was why Juliette made a habit

of delaying shooting almost every day, but I suspected our star was simply nervous of her first leading role in years. Nevertheless, her antics risked extending the time we'd have to spend here at Hendale Hall, which made everyone *else* nervous. For my own part, I'd been hoping to spend my birthday next week at home in London. Every morning Juliette spent sulking in her trailer made that prospect increasingly unlikely.

'I told you she'd be trouble,' said Ruby, stubbing out her cigarette in a sand-filled planter beside the door. 'Bloody Americans. Unprofessional, that's what it is. Wouldn't be so bad if her acting didn't resemble boiled ham.'

Other than a nod of greeting to me Yash hadn't yet said a word, merely wearing a wry smile as Ruby and I talked. Now he broke out into coughing laughter.

I rolled my eyes. Ruby had originally auditioned for the role of Draculania, and made no secret of her thoughts on Juliette being cast instead.

'I'm sure you'd have been wonderful in a cape,' I said, 'but Juliette is brilliant, too. When she can be bothered to come to set.' I turned to Chloe and indicated the dog equipment. 'Which likely won't be for a while yet, so give me ten minutes to get all this up to the bedroom and settle Lily in.'

'Absolutely not,' said Chloe, taking everything from my arms and dropping it all back in the Volvo's boot. 'I want you in make-up and wardrobe. If we're still delayed after that, then you can sort out your mutt.'

Lily, no doubt sensing this animosity, let out three

24

high-pitched barks at Chloe, who retreated nervously.

'Fine,' I said, slamming the boot closed. 'You can explain to everyone why I've got a dog with me, then. Come along, Lily.' I strode off towards the trailers, with the terrier in tow.

Ruby jogged after me, lifting her skirts. 'I'll take her while you're in make-up,' she said. 'Tell me about what happened with Viv.'

I summarised the morning's events. Like me, Ruby had known Viv for years and moved in the same circles. She and her ex-husband had even acted alongside Viv in Stratford for a few seasons.

'Poor thing,' she commiserated. 'Is it really serious?'

'I don't know. They hadn't X-rayed her when I had to leave, but if she's broken something she'll be in there for days. In the meantime, Lily's staying with me.'

'What, here at the Hall?'

'Why not? She can stay in my room while I'm filming, and the estate's perfect for walks when I'm not called. You'll like that, won't you, Lily?'

The terrier barked in response, and we continued on through the trailers.

Filming on location is expensive. Not that such things should be an actor's concern, but producers make sure everyone knows it. So does the director, because whenever a show goes over budget it's them who takes the blame.

In a studio, everything can be controlled. Weather and light are all faked, sets are built to accommodate camera movements, power is plentiful, and last-minute needs are easily found nearby because the production is surrounded by filmmaking infrastructure. Not to mention that everyone and everything is in the same place.

By contrast, on location all of those pros become cons. You're at the mercy of real weather and daylight, you have to fit crew and equipment into places not built for them, power must be supplied by generators and batteries, support is miles away, and if you didn't bring someone to set with you, getting them there at the last minute is time-consuming and expensive.

All of which explained why there were only half a dozen trailers at *Draculania*'s unit base: production, special effects, hair and make-up, wardrobe, the euphemistically named 'honeywagon', aka toilets, and a single talent trailer, for Juliette Shine. Other departments like rigging and electrical operated out of equipment trucks, and the remaining vehicles were production cars waiting to drive everyone around.

On the way to hair and make-up we passed Juliette's trailer. The blinds were drawn over the windows, as usual, and all was quiet inside.

'Ready for dressing at last, Gwinny?'

'Needles' Lloyd, the wardrobe manager, popped his head out of the costume trailer as I walked by. If you hadn't known what he did on set, it wouldn't take long to guess; Needles' bright red glasses and spotted bow tie might conceivably belong to a director, but the ever-present measuring tape around his neck was a dead giveaway.

'In a moment, darling,' I replied. 'Make-up first.'

'My, you really are running late. Was he worth it?'

'Chance'd be a fine thing. See you in a tick.'

Ruby and I walked on to the hair and make-up trailer, where I passed her Lily's lead and suggested she walk the dog around rather than standing and waiting. She did, and I prepared to mount the trailer's metal entrance steps.

'Stepping on!' I called out. Nobody wants to be the reason an actor gets poked in the eye with a mascara brush, or jabbed with a needle, in the case of wardrobe, when the trailer wobbles.

'It's just us, Gwinny!' called a voice from inside.

I entered to find Fi and Pri – Fiona and Priya, that is, but they came as a pair and went by abbreviations – taking a tea break.

'We were starting to think you'd been taken ill,' said Fi.

'Close, but it's not me.' I removed my coat and sat in a chair before a brightly lit mirror. The other actors would have been in here hours ago, when I should have been with them. The ladies' next appointment wouldn't be until this afternoon, when Yash Rani would be made up as Draculania's young victim Luke Westenra.

I recounted the situation with Viv once again, partly to make conversation but also with an ulterior motive. Hair and make-up is the nexus of all gossip on a film set. We actors spend hours in those chairs, often first thing in the morning when we're trying to purge the real world from our minds to get ready for filming. I knew that explaining the truth about Lily's presence to Fi and Pri would spread it around the crew faster than anything I could do.

'Ooh, I love Jack Russells,' said Fi, wrapping a bib around my neck. 'We had one at home when I was a girl. Right little tearaway, he was. Couldn't leave him alone for five minutes without him destroying a pair of Mummy's shoes or chewing through a pillow. We loved him to bits.'

That was fairly typical of a Jack Russell owner. My father's attitude towards Rusty had been similar, amply demonstrated when the dog decided the insides of Daddy's favourite cushion would look much better on the outside and spread all over the lounge. I was furious, but my father merely tutted and put Rusty on his lap while I hoovered it all up.

I hoped Lily might be better behaved, especially given her age. There wasn't much of mine to destroy in my room upstairs at the Hall, but it also contained plenty that *wasn't* mine and I could hardly afford to replace anything valuable. This role wasn't badly paid, but it was the first proper job I'd had in a while, and in the meantime I was treading water financially.

Still, I must remain grateful. Without this role I'd be doing even worse, and naturally I hoped it would lead to bigger and better things. I was under no illusions of landing a first-ever leading role at my age, but it was perfectly possible to make a living from good supporting characters. *Draculania* was hardly BAFTA bait, but it promised to make an impact and be seen by people in the industry.

Buoyed by my own internal pep talk, I took out my phone and, after a moment's hesitation searching for the right app, made a video call. Right about now DCI Alan Birch, retired, would be either out walking his dog Ronnie or preparing to have lunch. He'd recently shown me how to make video calls, and I was enjoying feeling like part of the modern world.

'Ma'am,' he answered, looking a little flustered. 'Sorry, wasn't expecting you to call. Not the best time.'

Judging by the scene behind him Birch was at home in Shepherd's Bush, but he didn't seem to be preparing lunch; over his shoulder I saw his glass cabinet of police commendations, which meant I was looking at the lounge. His bristly moustache and lovely blue eyes filled the screen.

'Sorry for the surprise, Birch. I'm in make-up, so I thought I'd say good morning. Wait, afternoon. You know what I mean. Hello, Ronnie,' I added as Birch settled back on his couch and the big nose of his pet black Labrador loomed into view, sniffing at the screen. These video calls with Birch had become a regular feature while I was away filming, but no matter how many times it happened poor Ronnie couldn't understand why he could hear my voice but not smell or see me nearby. Birch had tried holding the phone up to his face while I cooed at him but the Lab looked right through the screen, unable to connect the flat miniature image with me. On one occasion he'd tried to eat the phone. Like most Labs, he was adorable but not overly blessed with brain cells.

For a while I'd wondered if Birch suffered a similar deficiency when it came to reading people. Apparently, he'd been a good policeman and done the Met proud in his career, but it had taken the former detective much too long to realise I was attracted to him. Even when I wasn't especially subtle about it.

Partly this was due to his wife, Beatrice, having passed away shortly after he retired, which left him somewhat rudderless. I'm not sure Birch would have coped without Ronnie to keep him engaged. When we first met he was still in mourning, despite several years having passed since Beatrice's death. Nevertheless, we became good friends and even solved a couple of murders together, which had perked him up no end. But no matter how much I batted my eyelashes, it took him far too long to get the hint and finally take my hand.

Since then, we'd been . . . I'm not sure what people call it these days. Stepping out? Dating? I hesitated to think of us as 'lovers', because the most I'd got out of him so far were cuddles on the sofa. Not that I didn't enjoy them, mind.

'Viv had a scare this morning,' I continued, once again relating the morning's events. I left out the frantic rush to set and being almost bodily shoved into hair and make-up.

'Glad all seems well. Good of you to take the dog, of course. So, um . . . filming today? Yes, of course you are, wouldn't be in make-up otherwise. Silly question.'

I laughed, earning a *tut* from Pri as she worked on my eyebrows.

'Yes, first it's one of the confrontation scenes. That should be fun, watching Juliette chew every inch of the scenery. Then I get to watch her take dessert, in the hypnotic seduction scene.' At least, I hoped Ruby and I would be allowed to sit in and watch. Juliette might be insufferable, but there was no questioning her talent. 'What about you, Birch? Getting ready for lunch with Ronnie? *Escape to the Country* this afternoon, followed by a walk?'

'Yes . . . I mean, yes. Absolutely. Nothing special. Definitely a perfectly normal day.'

It obviously wasn't, but I wracked my brains in vain to think what it could be. As far as I could remember, today wasn't the anniversary of his wedding to Beatrice, or of her death. Ronnie's adoption day? Possibly, although I saw no reason Birch would be shifty about that. Something to do with his policing? He remained in touch with old colleagues, both those who'd retired like him and younger detectives still working at Scotland Yard.

But he clearly wasn't going to tell me, and I was already getting none-too-subtle off-camera hints from Fi to wrap things up so she could get to work on my lips.

'I'll leave you to it, then. I have to be on set soon anyway. I'll call you later.'

'Right you are, ma'am. Look forward to it. Break a leg.'

I smiled at that. It had taken months for me to get him out of the habit of saying 'Good luck', but it had finally stuck, and the boyish satisfaction on his face when he got it right was adorable.

'Wait, Birch, what—' I stammered, as he fumbled with the phone to end the call. But it was too late, and the screen went black.

'Why does he call you ma'am?' asked Fi, reaching for a lip brush. 'Sounds like he's talking to a schoolteacher.'

'Oh – more like a superintendent, actually,' I said, distracted. 'It's an old habit from his police days. Birch is a man of routine.'

'Likes you to boss him about, does he?' said Pri. 'It's always the butch ones, isn't it? Remember that wrestler, Fi, with the thighs? Oh, the stories we heard . . .'

They nattered away, but I wasn't listening. I didn't care about the secret kinks of film stars, because after a lifetime in showbiz little surprised me. I was busy thinking about what I'd seen when Birch ended the call. He'd manhandled his phone, searching for the right button, and the phone had tilted this way and that, changing the camera angle . . . so that in the last split-second I could have sworn I'd seen someone in the room with him.

Not just anyone, but my best friend.

What on earth was Tina Chapel doing at Birch's house?

CHAPTER FOUR

Tina's presence at Birch's home preyed on my mind all through wardrobe, distracting me from Needles chattering about this and that while he and his assistant clipped and clamped my Dr Seward costume over me.

Don't be fooled by elaborate lacing and fastenings on period film costumes. Much of the time they're for show, with the clothing actually held on by hidden Velcro, studs and zips, not to mention the odd well-placed safety pin, for ease of getting in and out. Accurate pieces with real fastenings are used for close-ups or on-camera removal, but unless there had been drastic overnight script revisions, Dr Seward was blessedly free of bedroom scenes.

'. . . so then Dracula settled down with a charming husband and adopted three children, and they all lived happily ever after.'

Somewhat to my surprise I was now fully dressed in bodice and skirts, facing a mirror while Needles stood ready to place my hat.

'I'm sorry, what? Three children?'

'Did I finally got your attention, duck?' he said. 'You've been spaced out since the moment you stepped inside. What's up?'

'I'm sorry, it's my friend Viv. Took a fall, rushed into hospital. That's why I have her dog. Actually, Ruby has her at the moment. Ask Fi and Pri; I told them all about it. Now, I'm due on set or I'll suffer Chloe's wrath.'

That wasn't what I'd been thinking about at all, but it would satiate Needles' desire for gossip. I held my head still while he fixed the hat with a pin.

'I hope your friend's all right,' he said, giving me a final once-over. 'Now don't let me keep you. I've got to get ready for young Mr Rani, anyway.'

I detected a twinkle in his eye. 'Your favourite part of the day?'

'Oh, hush.' He grasped my shoulders, turned me around, and marched me to the door while his assistant held it open. 'You know you're all my favourites. I'll see you later.'

I stepped down from the trailer and had a moment of panic. Everything was suddenly grey and dim. Objects swam in and out of my vision. I could hardly see the other trailers, and couldn't make out Ruby or Lily at all. Panic gripped me. Was I having a stroke?

Then I heard the terrier's unmistakeable high-pitched bark nearby and I turned to see her emerge from the grey on her lead, with Ruby following. The morning fog had returned with a vengeance, thickening even now before my eyes.

'Time to move,' said Ruby. 'Juliette just swanned past on her way to set at last.'

'Are you sure it was her, in this fog?'

'Unless the Hendale Vampire has started walking by day I don't think anyone else is likely to be striding around in a collar and cape, do you?'

I couldn't argue with that. Ruby handed Lily back to me and we rushed inside the Hall via the tradesman's entrance. Luckily today's scene was all waist-up, so period-accurate shoes weren't required. Under my skirts I wore a comfortable old pair of tennis shoes, while Ruby wore athletic trainers. Hard soles are the *bête noire* of sound recordists, and actors often spend all day on our feet, so unless they'll be in frame everyone on set tends to wear trainers or plimsolls.

Hurrying along the corridor we passed Viscount Henning, wearing tweed and Wellington boots as if he was about to partake in a different kind of shooting. Although filming had taken over most of the Hall, there were some sections that remained out of bounds. On the upper floors these included the Viscount's private chambers, the upper wing bedrooms, the roof and access to the tower – these last two more for public safety than privacy, we'd been told. On the ground floor there was an off-limits section branching off this corridor, from where the Viscount now emerged. I'd glanced down there once or twice but saw nothing scandalous: a few small rooms, most of them lined with books. Viscount Henning lived here alone – his ex-wife was somewhere in Scotland, and there were no children – so it was natural he'd want to maintain some privacy while the Hall was hired out. I'm sure I would have felt the same way.

'I say, where's the fire?' he asked cheerily as we dashed past.

'In the library,' I replied with a smile, then realised my mistake when I saw his horrified expression. 'No, not actually a fire! Sorry, I shouldn't have said that. We're about to start filming in the library, that's what I meant. Got to run!'

26 INT. WESTENRA MANOR LIBRARY - DAY

Van Helsing and Dr Seward stand at a READING DESK, cluttered with research books and papers.

Van Helsing reads an old manuscript on vampires, while Dr Seward watches.

VAN HELSING

It's as I feared. Luke's condition bears all the signs of the vampire! You were right to summon me, Jacqueline.

DR SEWARD

I can scarcely believe it. In fact, I hoped you'd tell me I was wrong. How can the vampire of Carpathian legend truly be here in England? What evil design draws it to Master Luke?

VAN HELSING

To create another! The vampire's curse may be transmitted, like a disease. But we can fight it! There are precautions we can take --

Draculania SWEEPS into the room, arrogant and contemptuous.

                    DRACULANIA

        Your 'precautions' have already failed,
                    Doctor.

                    VAN HELSING

        Draculania! But you -- how? -- you may
        cross no threshold without permission!

                    DRACULANIA

        Very good, Doctor. And that is how you know
                the boy will be mine.

                    DR SEWARD

        In the name of God, why? What purpose does
                this evil serve?

                    DRACULANIA

        You cannot understand the loneliness of
        immortal existence. That is the true curse of
                    my kind.

                    VAN HELSING

        You are the curse upon this world,
        Countess! While I draw breath, you shall not
                    prevail!

        Dr Seward draws a CRUCIFIX from her coat and
        holds it up.

                    VAN HELSING

        Yes, Jacqueline -- the vampire is
        vulnerable by day! We have her!

        Draculania HISSES and backs out of the room.

**When we arrived in the library, notwithstanding
that I still had a dog by my side, I immediately relaxed.**

Some actors freeze up in front of a camera, or can't contain the sweeping gestures more suited to a stage. But I relish the self-control and focused concentration required to remain still, knowing the tiniest movement will be magnified by the camera and seize an audience's attention.

Juliette was already there, finding her mark on the set while Chloe spoke with the cinematographer to get her lighting right.

Dozens of crew members crammed into the small room, bustling around now that something was finally going to happen because our star had deigned to emerge from her trailer.

Fi and Pri hurried in after us, but instead of making a beeline for Juliette they walked to 'video village', the bank of screens and headsets where producers and crew monitored filming in real time. I was confused by this until I saw Juliette standing there, talking to Steven McDonald.

Realising my mistake, I looked back to the set and recognised the person standing on the mark as Angela Viste, Juliette's stand-in. Angela was a statuesque Scandinavian working her way up the showbiz ladder, thirty years younger than the Hollywood star but with features and a silhouette similar enough that in full costume and low lighting she was a dead ringer. Angela even had naturally long dark hair, so she didn't have to wear a wig for the part like Juliette did.

Fi and Pri fussed around the star, doing quick touch-ups to her make-up and hair. Juliette must have been in full Draculania make-up and costume the whole time she was holed up in her trailer, or I'd have seen her when I was in wardrobe. Right on cue, Needles and his assistant hurried in to check and adjust everyone's costumes.

'Has Seward suddenly adopted a dog?' he asked cheekily, but he had a point. I needed to find someone who could look after Lily while we shot the scene.

'Would you mind holding her?' I asked him. 'Only for a short while. Once the scene's done I'll put her in my room upstairs.'

Needles looked like I'd asked him to sew up his own mouth. 'Not me, duck. Think of the shedding! No, someone else will have to take it.'

'I'll take her,' said Angela, stepping off the set and holding out a hand. 'They're done with me here. You didn't have a dog before, did you?'

Yet again I explained about Viv as Angela crouched down to Lily's level and stroked the terrier's head. Lily looked pleased as punch, licking her hand all over, then yapped the moment Angela took her hand away.

'If that dog barks during a shot I'll put it down myself!' She yelled from across the room. 'Get it out of here.'

Angela giggled. 'I think she likes my hand cream.' She offered her fingers again and the terrier licked them gratefully, then let herself be led away. As I watched her happily trot away beside Angela, I actually felt a pang of jealousy. But so long as Lily was happy, that's what mattered.

'I'm ready,' Juliette declared, already using the low-register voice she'd chosen for the role. It was a brave choice, given her face and voice were so well-known, but it worked to give her lines an ominous, unsettling tone.

I joined Ruby to take our starting positions behind a reading desk as Drs Van Helsing and Seward. The desk was covered with old books, ribboned scrolls and loose papers, to show Van Helsing's research. They wouldn't stand up to even mild scrutiny, but they didn't have to. There were other versions, known as 'hero' props, for close-ups where the page of a book or writing in a letter might need to be read on-screen. Not that Ruby or I would ever see them, because much of the time when you see a close-up of an actor's hand, it's not theirs. It's much cheaper to hire a specialist hand performer, with impeccably trimmed nails and carefully maintained skin, to do those shots while the principal actors film scenes featuring their faces.

In the meantime, we had to act as if these were important materials, filled with revelations about the true nature of the vampire we faced. Ruby stood at the desk and took the topmost sheaf of papers in one hand. The prop manager stepped in to hand her a reading glass, which she positioned over the papers as he retreated out of shot. I stood at her shoulder, peering down at the materials, and we both adopted serious expressions of concentration, readying ourselves for the moment. When the shooting calls began, I heard them faintly, as if from a distance much greater than the ten feet away they really were.

'Rolling.'

'Sound.'

'Draculania, scene twenty-six, take one.'

'And . . . *action*!'

The last was Chloe. Ruby continued studying the papers. We'd rehearsed this: a moment of Van Helsing reading, then she'd lower the props to the desk and deliver her first line.

Except she didn't. Ruby continued gazing down at her reading glass, until Chloe eventually shouted, 'Van Helsing, go,' at which point Ruby dropped the glass, startled.

'Shit! Sorry, sorry, I didn't have it.'

Even at this distance I heard Chloe sigh. 'Keep rolling, reset and go again!' She called out. Ruby retrieved the glass and re-adopted her starting position. I hadn't moved anyway. The clapper loader called take two and the director hissed, '*Action*!'

Ruby studied the papers, then after a moment lowered them and the glass.

'It's as I feared,' she said. 'Luke's condition bears all the signs of the vampire. You were right to summon me, Jacqueline.'

'I can scarcely believe it,' I replied. 'In fact, I hoped you'd tell me I was wrong. How can the vampire of Carpathian legend truly be here in England? What evil design draws it to Master Luke?'

To my surprise, Ruby burst out laughing.

'For God's sake, I haven't even entered yet,' yelled Juliette from behind the camera. 'Can you get through your own damn lines without corpsing?'

'Sorry, sorry, sorry,' Ruby said, sniggering. 'But that's what they call him in *Star Wars*, isn't it? Master Luke. Can we drop the "master" bit, and just call him Luke?'

'Balls, you're right,' said Chloe. 'OK, "Luke" only from now on. Got that, Gwinny?'

'Fine,' I said, annoyed that the request was phrased as if it was my fault rather than the screenwriter's.

We reset, went again, and in take three I called him 'Luke'.

'To create another,' Ruby replied in answer to the question. 'The vampire's curse may be transmitted, like a disease. But we can fight it! There are precautions we can take—'

'Your "precautions" have already failed, Doctor.'

Juliette stepped into view, her cloak sweeping around her. For this shot she'd have her back to the camera, then later we'd shoot the scene again from another angle with the camera on her. Nevertheless, she looked fabulously imposing, and put her all into the performance.

'Draculania!' cried Ruby, as we both reacted with shock to the vampire's entrance. 'But you – how? – you may cross no threshold without permission!'

Juliette smiled sympathetically, as if humouring children. 'Very good, Doctor. And that is how you know the boy *will* be mine!'

'In the name of God, why?' I pleaded. 'What purpose does this evil serve?'

'You cannot understand the . . . loneliness of immortal existence. That is the true curse of my kind.'

42

Nobody spoke.

'Ruby, for God's sake!' cried Juliette.

'Oh, that was me!' Ruby seemed to break herself out of a daydream. 'Sorry, everyone, my head's not here today—'

'That's it, I'm done,' said Juliette. She turned on her heel, rubber soles squeaking on the hardwood floor, and stormed out. 'I'll be in my trailer. Let me know when you amateurs figure out how to do your jobs.'

I thought that was a bit rich, considering the number of times we'd had to wait around for Little Miss Sunshine, but I was no less annoyed by Ruby's behaviour. I'd never seen her like this before.

'Everyone take fifteen,' Chloe called out. She stomped off set herself, presumably following Juliette. I was surprised she didn't tear a strip off Ruby first.

'What *is* going on with you?' I said quietly as the crew began standing down: covering camera lenses, lowering boom mics, wondering aloud if craft services had any pastries left.

'Lay off, Gwinny, I'm fine,' Ruby insisted. 'Mind your own business, will you?' Without another word she, too, walked off set.

Fifteen minutes. I doubted the break would be that short, but it was still enough time to install Lily in my bedroom. I turned to ask Steven if he saw which direction Angela had taken, but he wasn't in video village, so I hurried out to find her. Ahead of me Ruby walked back down the corridor, towards the tradesman's entrance and unit base.

I crossed the main entrance hall, guessing Angela would have taken Lily outside. Bill, the special effects supervisor, was working with his crew to prepare the hall for a future scene. I ignored them and exited the main doors into fog that had returned with a vengeance. Now even the trees on the far side of the paved area were barely visible, despite only being thirty feet away.

A scream pierced the mist, immediately followed by high-pitched barking. It had come from my right. I rushed towards the sound and found Angela staring into the fog, in the direction of the trees. Lily strained at the end of her lead, snarling in the same direction.

'What's the matter?' I said, taking the lead from Angela.

'There – in the trees, I saw – oh, never mind.' She glared at me and made the sign of the cross. 'You wouldn't believe me anyway. But there's evil abroad in this house, and I can't wait until we're done here.'

I peered into the trees but saw nothing. 'Maybe it was the Hendale Vampire,' I joked, then regretted it when I saw the look of horror on her face. 'Oh, I'm pulling your leg. You can relax for now, anyway. We're on another break.'

'Already? That was quick.'

'Yes, and for once you can blame Ruby.' I explained how filming had been cut short. 'It's not like her; she's normally word-perfect. A bad day all round, it seems.'

Angela shivered and rubbed her arms against the cold. 'The fates told me as much this morning. I can see you're sceptical, but – is that the right word?'

'Yes,' I reassured her. She spoke it so well that it was easy to forget English was Angela's second language. It was equally easy to overlook her physicality, too, but having seen her in wardrobe it was hard for me to believe a Viking maiden like Angela could be so scared of her own shadow. If I were a creature of the night, I'd have thought twice about taking her on for fear of being thumped in the mouth. But she looked genuinely spooked, and once again I reflected that we were all letting the atmosphere of *Draculania* get to us.

She shivered again. 'Ever since we arrived here, I've seen nothing but bad omens.'

I took Angela's hand and squeezed it. 'Darling, I've been on far worse sets than this in my time. It'll all blow over, you'll see.'

If only I could have known how soon I'd be proven wrong.

CHAPTER FIVE

Halfway up the stairs with Lily's dog bed, favourite cushion, toys, food and bowls clutched in my hands, plus her lead wrapped around my wrist, I belatedly wished I'd asked Angela to stay and help me carry it all. I couldn't see the floor past everything in my arms, and one trip would send me tumbling back down to earth.

I made it to the first floor without dropping anything or falling over my own feet, though, and placed it all on the ground to fish out my room key from my handbag. Lily promptly sat on her bed with a toy bone in her mouth and chomped away noisily. I sighed, pushed the door open, and dragged the bed into the room with her still sitting on it. Lily was much more amused by this than I was. Leaving her there, I stepped outside and pushed everything else in with my feet.

I positioned her bed in a corner along with the toys and cushion, and placed the food and bowls on the dresser. Finally, I closed the door, flopped onto the bed, and breathed a sigh of relief.

Or rather half a breath, before the door flew open to reveal a red-faced Steven McDonald.

'Where have you been?'

'A friend was suddenly taken to hospital.' I pointed to his phone, clutched in his hand as always. 'Haven't you checked your voicemail?'

'What? Oh.' He looked at the phone, tapped a few things on it, then ignored it again. 'Lucky for you that Juliette was late as well.'

'For all the difference it made. Are we still shooting the bedroom scene today as well? At this rate we won't have to fake the night lighting.'

'You leave Juliette to me; I know how to handle her. So be ready and – what in God's name is that?'

With a start I realised that I'd been so focused on Steven's outburst I forgot about Lily for a moment. Long enough for the old dog to prove she still had plenty of get-up-and-go in her by getting-up-and-going directly past Steven's legs and through the open door, trailing her still-attached lead.

'Lily, *no!*' I cried, but it was too late. Jack Russells aren't the most biddable dogs at the best of times, and the combination of Lily's age plus unfamiliarity with me as her handler made her even less likely to do what I said. I should have asked Viv what obedience training she'd done with Lily, but I suspected the answer would have been, 'What's obedience training?'

Steven recoiled as the dog ran past him, and again

when I gave chase, making no effort to help retrieve her. Typical.

Lily had stopped a few doors down the corridor to sniff at someone else's bedroom. Thank goodness for canine curiosity. I slowed down to avoid alarming her and quietly called her name as I approached, ready to stand on her trailing lead. 'Good girl, Lily,' I said gently. '*Come* . . .'

She turned to face me, yapped twice, then ran away to the far end of the corridor, past the shuttered entrance to the tower and around the corner.

'Rats! Lily, stop!'

I gave chase, thankful for the tennis shoes underneath my costume, but even at Lily's advanced age I could never match a Jack Russell's speed. I could keep her in sight, though, and hope she got distracted. As I turned the corner I heard a yelp – from a human, not a dog – and saw Zayn Patel jump out of Lily's way. Zayn was Yash Rani's stand-in, a young actor new to the business. I was sure he'd eventually go on to bigger and better things, but we all have to start somewhere.

'When did that thing arrive?' he said.

I hurried past in pursuit. 'Long story, I'll tell you later.'

'Hey, have you seen Yash? He's not in his room,' he called after me. I remembered that they'd been placed in adjacent rooms along this part of the corridor.

'Maybe he's already in hair and make-up,' I called back. 'You should be, too.'

Lily stood at the top of a flight of stairs, poised to

go down but with her head turned towards me. 'Lily, *stay . . .*'

Maybe I didn't imbue the command with sufficient conviction. Or maybe Lily was just a mischievous little sod. Either way, she barked again before barrelling down the stairs at top speed. To her this was a fun game of 'Explore the new environment while playing keep-away'.

Hurrying down the stairs after her, though, I worried the game was about to turn serious. Running around the first-floor corridor was one thing, but down on ground level the house was set up for filming. Many rooms, like the library, were teeming with crew and equipment, with bodies and cables in constant motion. A small, nimble dog could easily find itself somewhere it shouldn't be and get trampled, not to mention that Chloe and the rest of the crew wouldn't take kindly to a loud, furry ball of energy scampering between their feet.

It occurred to me that Viv probably hadn't acted since she moved to Yorkshire, and this was the first time Lily had seen a set. No wonder she was determined to explore.

I reached the foot of the stairs. Lily was nowhere to be seen. All I could hear was the low, murmuring hum of crew conversation throughout the house. It was effectively in stasis, waiting for Juliette Shine to be coaxed out of her trailer once again.

Then I heard the unmistakeable sound of scampering feet on hardwood flooring and saw Lily dash out of a reception room into the hallway. I didn't even want to know what she'd been up to. She was starting to slow down at last, her age finally catching up with her. I knew the feeling, and decided that instead of chasing I would try enticing.

'Lily, *come*,' I said cheerily, crouching as low as I could in the Victorian costume. She eyed me warily, and I wished I had treats in my pocket. Or that I even had pockets so I could pretend there was something in them. '*Come*, Lily.'

She took a delicate step forward . . . then someone opened the front door, letting in a gust of chilly air and all the scents of the estate.

Obedience was forgotten, overruled by the temptation of the outdoors. I was suddenly besieged by visions of Lily worrying the Viscount's deer, or even the swans that made a home on his lake. Panicking, I scrambled to my feet and resumed chasing after her, shouting her name as I ran to the main door—

And nearly crashed into Viscount Henning himself, who stood in the open doorway with Lily in his arms, laughing as the Jack Russell enthusiastically licked his face.

'I say,' he said between licks, 'a new addition to the crew, what?'

'Her name's Lily.' I reached to take her from him. 'She belongs to a friend who's been rushed into hospital and has been leading me a merry old dance for the past five minutes, so thank you, Your Lordship. I was dreading chasing her around the estate.'

'Jack Russell, eh? Any good at ratting?'

'I don't expect she's ever been trained. She's something of a house dog.'

He smiled. 'Instinct's bred in, though, isn't it? If she fancies a run at the vermin, let her out with my blessing. Thorn in my side.' He was still wearing the tweeds and boots in which I'd seen him earlier, but now they were muddy. 'I didn't catch your name.'

'Gwinny Tuffel, Your Lordship.' I lowered Lily to the ground, keeping a firm grip on her lead, then offered my free hand. 'I play Dr Seward in the film.'

'Call me George, please,' he said with a chuckle. '"His Lordship" is for grand balls and mayoral dinners. Certainly don't feel like it when I'm mucking about in the south bog.' That explained the mud, then. 'Still, always delighted to meet a pretty lady with a dog. Carry on, Gwinny.'

He was being polite, of course, but I blushed all the same. The Viscount – George – was around my age and well-preserved. Whether this was thanks to a life of country air, good genes, or simply being able to afford the best in life was up for debate, but it worked. Thick grey hair topped his deeply lined face in boisterous waves, and his easy smile belied a firm jaw.

He swept past me, heading for his private area on the ground floor. I considered taking Lily back upstairs, but still doubted Chloe could persuade Juliette back out of her trailer in the next five minutes. Now Lily and I were downstairs anyway, I decided a quick walk couldn't hurt. We stepped back out into the fog.

CHAPTER SIX

The Hall's immediate surroundings were paved, like a reverse oasis of gravel and tarmac in the estate's wooded land. A full perimeter walk with Lily would only be around a quarter of a mile, but after the exertion of our chase through the house that should be plenty for two ladies of a certain age.

As the door closed, I heard Steven shouting angrily at someone. I glanced back to see him stalking through the entrance hall, his phone clamped to his ear.

'No, you listen to me,' he said, 'and understand who you're dealing with. I was told that insurance had been arranged . . .'

That was all I heard before the door shut. Out here the air was cool and crisp, muffling the sound of my shoes and Lily's pattering paws.

We crossed the house frontage and turned a corner to pass the east wing, where the library was situated. A combination of lights, soft box diffusers and blackout cloths stood outside its window, all mounted on scaffold and stands weighed down with sandbags, ready to simulate whatever time of day was required and control the light level of each shot. As we neared, some crew chatting by the rig nodded and waved, as many at Lily as me. Something told me they didn't think this would be a short break, either.

We continued on, turning another corner and arriving at the rear of the house. Hendale Hall sat in acres of woodland but kept a formal garden area at the back, a typically English affair with neat pathways, parallel flower beds, tall hedges and stone fountains. Personally I preferred something a little wilder, but it was a delightful place to spend a quiet moment. Unfortunately, today it was almost completely hidden from view by the fog. We walked on past the rear entrance to the Hall, unable to see much of that either.

Neither could Chloe, it seemed, as she emerged from the fog at speed and almost tripped over Lily's lead.

'Gwinny, what are you doing with that bloody dog again? I might have to call you back at any moment.'

'Oh, nonsense. Lily needed a walk, and after that debacle so did I. You and I both know Juliette will take her sweet time to emerge from her trailer.'

The director's mouth set in a determined line. 'We'll see about that. I did two seasons of *Emmerdale*, so I know a thing or two about dealing with prima donnas. Were you going that way?'

I supposed I was, as unit base was around the next corner of the house, so we continued together.

'What's next for you after this?' I asked. 'I know it's hardly Shakespeare, but it should be a good stepping stone.'

'I'm considering offers. I've already turned down a few that were macho, bloke-y trash. I want to keep elevating women in the business. That's why I took on *Draculania*. Juliette might be a pain in the arse, but it'll be worth it to counter the male-dominated image of the Dracula legend in people's minds.'

I couldn't argue with that. The script, for all its camp, did a good job of showcasing the contrast in public attitudes between male and female experts. Van Helsing and Seward, in particular, struggled to be taken seriously in this version, something Peter Cushing never had to worry about when fighting evil.

'Do you know what's got Angela so spooked? She insists there's evil afoot.'

'No idea,' said Chloe. 'I haven't worked with her before, but she came recommended by a friend, and she's a good match for Juliette. Beyond that I don't really care.'

Somewhat harsh, but then like all directors Chloe had a lot on her plate. Worrying about the spiritual fears of her cast was a luxury for which she didn't have time.

We rounded the corner and walked through unit base, past equipment and transport vehicles, towards the production trailers. A sound cut through the fog; an impact, like a grip dropping a piece of metal dolly track. I hoped nobody was damaging Hendale Hall's lovely wooden floors. Part of the contract with any location filming is an agreement to leave all property as it was found, and make good on damages.

Chloe was so focused on rescuing the day's shoot, I don't think she even heard it. Without looking at me she said, 'Put that dog in your room and get ready for set. I'll have Sunshine out of there in five minutes.'

She split off towards talent trailer one, which was an ironic moniker as there was no trailer two or three. Juliette was the only actor famous and expensive enough to warrant one, while the rest of us made do with our bedrooms when we needed a break. The Hollywood star had even been given her own suite at a nearby inn, rather than having to stay in the Hall.

I veered off towards the wardrobe trailer, where Needles sat on the steps reading a well-thumbed paperback of *Dracula*.

'Seeking inspiration?' I asked.

'More like staving off boredom,' he said resignedly. 'Honestly, I've never known a woman slow down a shoot so much. And I've worked with some divas, believe me.'

I could have told him a story or two about some famous faces who were much worse than Juliette, but now wasn't the time.

'Could you pass me my phone?' I asked him. 'I want to check up on my friend in the hospital.' If we'd wrapped the library scene properly, I would have already been back here to change out of my costume and retrieve my handbag, but now I was stuck in be-costumed limbo.

Needles retrieved my phone, but before I could use

it Lily suddenly dashed behind me, tugging at the lead.

'I say, where is everyone? Can't move for cameras and people one minute, the next it's a ghost town. Oh, hello again, Lily!'

George stepped out of the fog and bent down to fuss the terrier, who stood on her hind legs and pawed at his muddy Wellingtons.

'*Juliette, open this door right now or I'll break it down!*'

George, Needles, Lily and I all turned in the direction of Chloe's yell. I could just make her out in the fog, hands on hips at the door of Juliette's trailer and easily identified by her pink bum bag. She looked like a petulant schoolchild, even though it was the star on the other side of the door who was acting like one.

'I'll try calling her,' said Needles, taking out his phone. 'She'll answer for me.' We all watched patiently as he dialled her number, so we also saw his embarrassment when Juliette in fact didn't answer, and the call went straight to voicemail. 'Well! Julie, duck, for heaven's sake pull yourself together and let Chloe in. You're doing a fabulous job, and there's no need to hide yourself away like this. *Mwah.*'

Chloe continued to hammer on the trailer door. I approached, seeing concern on her face despite the frustration.

'She swore to me she's been clean for ten years,' Chloe said quietly. 'If she's back on the booze, I swear . . .'

I tried to reassure her. 'Despite everything, I haven't seen anything to make me think Juliette's drinking again. Perhaps she took a sleeping pill and zonked out?'

'During a fifteen-minute break?'

To Chloe the idea was ludicrous, but I'd known stars do worse. It's the director's job to care about 'making the day', slang for actually filming everything on the schedule, a rarer achievement than one might assume, and an actor's job to care about their image and performance. Of course, good performers are also conscious of the schedule, but in my experience, the further up the ladder an actor gets the less that concerns them. After all, what's the director going to do? Find someone else to play their part for the last two weeks of the shoot?

'What's all the shouting?' asked Angela, walking from the direction of the house. 'Shouldn't we be back on set by now?'

'Not until we can coax Juliette out,' I explained.

'Someone must have a key, what?' said George. I braced myself for Lily to lunge at him again, but instead she stood at the foot of the trailer steps, staring up at the door and sniffing the air.

'That's a good idea,' said Chloe, unzipping her bum bag. From it she took a set radio and called for security.

Lily's sniffing suddenly turned to a low growl, and when I bent down to reassure her she pulled her lips back from her teeth. Never a good sign. I started to worry that she could smell something bad and had visions of finding Juliette inside, drunk after all and lying in her own vomit.

'What if something's happened to her?' said Angela,

echoing my thoughts. 'I tell you, there's something not right in this place.' She turned to George. 'Your ancestors were cursed, weren't they?'

The Viscount chuckled. 'My dear, this house is four hundred years old. You don't last that long without a few curses and scandals along the way.'

'Scandal? What scandal?' Fi and Pri had come out of their trailer to see what the fuss was all about, and naturally their hunger for gossip couldn't let George's flippant remark go.

'No, no, I'm talking about history,' he said. 'This house has plenty of it, with the vampire and all that.'

'Shouldn't you be doing Yash's make-up?' I asked Pri. 'Assuming we ever shoot that scene.'

'Still waiting for him to come by,' she said. 'He doesn't need much anyway; he's got amazing skin.'

'What's all the shouting?' Now it was Ruby's turn to emerge from the fog and join the crowd clustered round the trailer door. 'I was smoking at the tradesman's entrance and heard the commotion,' she explained.

Before I could reply I heard the approaching jangle of metal, and a tall black-clad figure approached. The mist parted to reveal Walter, the head of set security, his utility belt festooned with radios, keys and who knew what else.

'What's the – Ms Churchill, I mean – how can I help?' he asked, taking in the motley crew standing around the trailer.

'Juliette won't open the door, and she's not answering her phone,' said Chloe. 'You have the trailer spares, don't you?'

Walter reached down to the half-dozen key rings clipped to his waistband and unhooked one. 'Right here, but – well, I mean, they're – if someone locks themself out, you know – are you sure? What if – she could be indisposed—'

'I don't care if she's playing naked Twister with Donald Glover. Open this bloody door!'

Chastised, Walter mounted the metal steps to Juliette's trailer and inserted the spare key. Or at least, he tried to. It wouldn't go in.

'What the—' he grunted. 'Sorry, Ms Churchill, it won't go – must be – hang on, let me see . . .'

He took a small torch from his belt and shone it at the lock.

'That explains it – key's already in, you see – locked from the inside.' He shrugged. 'No way in.'

'Rubbish,' said Chloe. 'Pull the door off if you have to.'

'I don't suppose you have a crowbar on that belt of yours?' I half-joked.

Walter looked terrified of doing anything of the sort. 'In theory, but – the property damage – I'd need authorisation—'

'I'm the director!' said Chloe, offended. 'What more authorisation do you need?'

'Mine, actually,' said Steven, striding up to join us with phone in hand as always. 'I can't get hold of Juliette either, it's ridiculous. Walter, go ahead and do whatever you need to open it.'

The security head radioed for a crowbar, and we

waited. Chloe continued knocking on the door and calling out for Juliette, while I circled the trailer with Lily, trying to look in through the windows. I'm not the tallest person, so I had to stand on tiptoe, but it didn't matter anyway. Every window was firmly closed, and the blinds all fully down, as was Juliette's habit.

I made it back round to the front as a second security guard arrived, carrying a crowbar. Chloe stepped down from the trailer to let him past, and he carefully placed the crowbar's hook in position to prise open the door. Then he looked to Walter, who looked to Steven, who nodded confirmation for them to go ahead . . .

'Party at my place, huh? Wouldn't be the first time. What are you all doing here?'

As one, we turned to see Juliette Shine walk out of the fog. Upright, perfectly sober and still in full Draculania costume.

'Where the hell have you been? You said you'd be in your trailer!' Chloe sounded furious, but underneath the anger I detected concern and relief that her star hadn't done something stupid.

'I changed my mind. Took a walk to clear my head.'

'You didn't answer your phone!'

'I left it in my trailer when I came to set, and it sounds like I made the right call. Now get lost, all of you. I'll see you there in five.'

Chloe wasn't happy about her star giving directions like that, but swallowed objections for the sake of keeping Juliette happy and making the day. Perhaps the director's work on soaps had shown her the reality of set hierarchy, where the amount of power someone wields often has more to do with their box-office draw than their job title.

The crowd dispersed, with everyone mumbling agreement to be on set, or in Fi and Pri's case, grumbling that they'd been cheated of gossip.

Something felt off to me, but I couldn't put my finger on it so I turned to leave with the others. Lily resisted, though. She continued to stare at the trailer door, her ears pinned back, and her lip curled. Now she started barking, too.

'What's up, girl?' I said, crouching to fuss her. Every muscle in her body was taut. Surely there couldn't be rats in there? They were a perennial problem in old manor houses like this, but modern trailers were practically hermetically sealed. Besides, we'd only been here a few days.

'Holy crap, shut that dog up, will you?' said Juliette, pulling at the door handle in confusion. 'And who locked the damn door?'

'It's locked from the inside,' I said, realising that was what had felt off. 'We assumed you'd locked yourself in. Why do you think we're all stood outside?'

'Because it's my trailer, and you have no right to come in without my say-so. Why would I lock it? I never lock it. Besides, I'm out here, not in there.'

'Walter!' I called out, as a chill spread through my bones. Lily continued her high-pitched barking, and now I knew she wouldn't stop until that door was opened.

The head of security returned, along with everyone who'd begun to leave, intrigued that the crowbar was needed after all.

Juliette turned to Walter. 'Did you lock my trailer?'

'No, Ms Shine – locked from the inside, you see – I was just saying—'

'So open it! And for God's sake, Gwinny, I'm gonna kick that dog if it doesn't shut up. Gwinny? Gwinny, are you even listening to me?'

I wasn't. I was staring at the base of the trailer door, where the cause of Lily's alert pose and incessant barking had finally become clear.

Blood seeped under the door, dripping onto the top step.

Juliette followed my gaze down, saw the pooling blood and cried out. She backed down the steps, stumbling in her haste. George caught her, and she gratefully batted her eyelashes at him, but like all of us he was focused on the blood.

Walter took the crowbar from his staffer and once more mounted the steps, being careful not to step in anything. He wedged the crowbar between the door and frame, then levered with all his strength. The door bowed, bending outwards, allowing more blood to gush out through the gap and stain his boots. He didn't notice.

Ruby did. 'Oh my God, is that real?' she whispered.

The door gave way, springing open with a crash. Walter stumbled back, gasping in shock.

I scooped Lily into my arms to keep her under control, and at last she stopped barking. I stepped up to look inside the trailer, my gaze following the blood trail to its source.

Yash Rani, the handsome young actor playing Luke

Westenra, lay on the floor by the kitchen area. His glassy eyes stared wide-eyed at the ceiling, and blood trickled from his mouth, but that was nothing compared to what Lily had smelt with her keen canine nose.

A wooden stake had been hammered into Yash's chest.

CHAPTER SEVEN

Everyone pressed into the door with me, to peek inside and see the body. For a tense moment nobody spoke. The grisly scene was enough to hypnotise everyone looking in.

Then a sharp and acrid scent swept over us, breaking the spell. Everyone began to talk, scream and move at once.

Chloe immediately called the police, while Steven tried frantically to stop her. Fi and Pri yelled, 'He's dead!' in unison at the top of their lungs, as if there had been any doubt. Juliette tried swooning into George's arms, but he was too busy pushing past me into the trailer, muttering, 'Bloody hell, bloody hell, bloody hell,' over and over. Angela began to hyperventilate, and in between breaths squeaked about the presence of immortal evil on set. Needles, meanwhile, whipped out his phone and got busy taking photographs.

I put out a hand to cover his lens. 'Darling, please.

No need to be a real-life vampire for social media.'

'To hell with social media,' he said with a glint in his eye. 'The papers will pay for these. None of us is earning a fortune from the show, are we? Especially not now.' He followed George inside, snapping away, and before I knew it I was being swept along by the tide of everyone else rushing in after them.

George made his way through the trailer, methodically throwing open every door and cupboard he could find, shouting, 'Show yourself, you swine!' Presumably he hoped to find a killer playing sardines. Considering whoever it was had been strong enough to hammer a stake into poor Yash's chest, I admired his bravery.

Steven, Chloe and everyone else rushed to the body, shouting at one another not to step in the blood while simultaneously trying to get as close as they could. What a strange sight we must have made, with several of us in Victorian period costume.

I could see it was already too late for the police to get anything useful from the scene. People had touched things, accidentally kicked kitchen items lying on the floor (presumably knocked over in Yash's last moments) and generally left evidence of themselves all over the place. Then again, how much difference would it make? Most of us had been inside Juliette's trailer several times already, to go over lines or discuss scenes.

Angela crouched over the body, but the sight of Yash seemed too much for her, and she quickly covered her eyes with a hand. I had a hard time looking at him myself. The acrid smell was worse up close, and apart from the sight of his ruptured chest there was a discolouration to his skin, an unsettling darkening of his features.

Needles was right about getting paid. Yash's death put the whole production in jeopardy. I felt bad worrying about my own job security while staring down at a young man whose life had been snuffed out in its prime, but naturally it was on my mind. Would the production insurance cover something like this? Would that depend on the manner of death? My first thought had been that this was a terrible accident, but the more I looked the more I doubted that.

It surely took serious strength to embed a stake in someone's chest, a fact emphasised in our screenplay by having Van Helsing use a hammer to drive the stake through the vampiric Luke Westenra's heart. Now someone had enacted the grisly scene for real. But how? The trailer had been locked from the inside, and Juliette's keys were still on the inside of the broken-open door. Even if someone had a second set of keys, the first set being in situ would prevent them being used, as Walter had found. So how could Yash's killer have left the trailer and locked the door behind them? It was impossible.

Putting aside the how, *why* would anyone kill Yash? He was a young rising star, not even born when old hands like Ruby and I began our careers. What possible reason could anyone have to murder him?

Come to that, what possible reason could he have had to be in Juliette's trailer?

An affair, perhaps? It's common enough. Actors

spend days, weeks, sometimes months in unnaturally close proximity, being passionate and playful and seeing one another at our worst and best all at once. It's a heady cocktail, especially when you consider that most actors are also attractive and charismatic. Age makes no difference. I've seen *ingénues* fall for leading men in their sixties; young bucks in a clinch with grand old dames; and, sometimes, those same young bucks taking a nightcap with the older leading men – or a producer. Many a handsome young actor lives in the closet or swings both ways, and in showbiz affairs there's always an element of power play going on. For many that's part of the attraction.

So it was possible Yash and Juliette had been sleeping together. But as she stood over the body with the others I saw fascinated disgust, not the grief of a lover. Then again, no matter how much her star might have faded, Juliette was a fine actress.

George had finished his search and now stood with the crowd. 'Anything?' I asked him.

He shook his head. 'First priority upon breaching, clear all potential rabbit holes. But whoever it was has scarpered.'

His clipped cadence reminded me of Birch's police manner, and I guessed the young Viscount had at one time been a soldier. A noble tradition, and a tradition of nobles.

'Oh, God, someone will have to tell his family,' said Chloe, and I mentally added her to my list of possible affairs. Sleeping with the director was also a time-honoured tradition, and while the scenario normally involved a male director and female star, a gender-swapped tryst would be appropriate for *Draculania*.

'The police will do that,' I reassured her. 'Does anyone know if Yash was married? Does he have children? We don't want them being even more upset by horrible pictures on the news.' I directed this last at Needles, who had the decency to look sheepish, though made no move to delete the photos he'd taken.

'He didn't have children,' said George. Everyone turned to him in surprise. 'It came up when we discussed India,' he said with a shrug, and I remembered that during the initial tour we'd learnt of the Hennings' old association with the subcontinent.

'Whoever did this must be covered in blood,' I said, 'which at least puts all of us in the clear.'

'Unless they changed clothes,' said Needles. 'I'll keep an eye out for anything dodgy coming through wardrobe.'

'I doubt the killer would be careless enough to hand them over for washing.'

'They might say it's fake blood,' Chloe pointed out. 'Plenty of it around on this show.'

'Can the police test blood to see if it's real?' asked Angela.

I nodded. 'Yes, but trying to keep track of it all on this set will be a challenge. It puts me, Ruby and Juliette out of the frame, though. You all saw us change into our costumes, and there's no way any of us could have got in and out without your help again.'

'You seem real keen to prove your innocence, Gwinny,' said Juliette. 'How do we know you didn't do this? It was your dog who found him.'

'Lily smelt blood, that's all,' I protested. 'Of course I didn't do this. Yash was a full head taller than me, for heaven's sake. Do you really think I could have a—'

'What the hell's that?!'

Everyone turned to see Chloe pointing and staring in horror at something further back in the trailer. We followed her gaze to the dressing mirror, where two words had been scrawled in blood-red letters:

Hendrick Lives

CHAPTER EIGHT

Looking closer, I saw that it wasn't blood; the words had been written with a dark crimson shade of lipstick. If whoever wrote it was hoping for a shock effect, though, they'd succeeded.

I turned to Juliette. 'Your handiwork?' I asked.

'No way,' she said, shaking her head. 'I don't even know what that means.'

Someone did, though.

'What the – is this someone's idea of a joke?' George choked. Tears of outrage welled up in his eyes, and now I remembered where I'd heard the name before. Hendrick Henning was the so-called Hendale Vampire, the ancestral Viscount around whom the house's notoriety centred. No wonder George was upset.

'That's it,' he cried. 'Out, all of you! Get out!'

He began to herd people past Yash's body towards the door. Needles snapped a few last photos while being pushed towards the exit. Lily yapped excitedly and thrashed around in my arms. It was all I could do to hold on to her.

'This trailer is my property,' insisted Steven, jabbing a finger in George's chest. 'Don't think you can push me around, mate!'

'Technically it's the hire company's property,' I said to him. 'Regardless, I think it's a good idea if we all clear the crime scene now. Don't you?'

'What do you mean, crime scene?' he said as we made our way outside. The fog was finally lifting. 'This was some kind of terrible accident. Yash tripped and fell.'

I almost laughed. 'Onto a stake that happened to be lying around, point up? With enough force to drive it through his ribcage? Pull the other one, it's got garlic on. I know a murder when I see it.'

'It's not murder! Don't you dare say anything like that to the police. They'll shut us down.'

I returned Lily to the ground, keeping a firm grip on her lead.

'Surely we're going to be shut down anyway?' said Ruby, lighting a cigarette. 'Steven, one of your principals has been killed. This may be a story about the undead, but I hardly think you can resurrect Yash to run through his scenes.'

'We'll re-cast,' said the producer. 'We can re-shoot the Luke scenes we've filmed so far.'

'Don't you have insurance?' I asked. 'Surely it's better to shut it down and take the compensation.'

'What are you talking about? You can't buy publicity like this. Everyone will be talking about *Draculania* now. Remember what I said – not a word to the police!'

With that he turned and walked away, dialling someone on his phone. I hoped it was his insurers, but it was more likely the casting director.

Ruby sighed. 'He's an arse, but he's not wrong. This will delay us, but replacing Yash will be simple enough. All his scenes were set here.'

She was right. Every Luke Westenra scene was scheduled to be filmed here at Hendale Hall, either within the house or in the grounds, such as the fake graveyard and crypt under construction at the old gatehouse. We'd filmed several scenes already, but so far only interiors. Re-shooting those with a new actor wouldn't take long.

I looked for George, hoping to ask about the words on the mirror, but he was nowhere to be seen. 'What on earth do you think that message was about?' I asked aloud.

'Isn't it obvious?' said Angela. 'The Hendale Vampire killed him and left his mark.'

'Oh, dear. I know this is a shock, but there's no reason to start believing in fairy stories.'

'But I told you I saw something in the woods!' she cried. 'You even said it could be the vampire!'

Ruby and the others turned to me with surprised expressions.

'It was a joke,' I protested. 'Don't you see? This is clearly the work of a flesh-and-blood person, throwing us off the scent by getting everyone to talk about the family curse rather than looking for the real killer.'

'What curse? What vampire?' said Fi and Pri together. I was grateful they didn't remember, to be honest. I hadn't been paying full attention myself when George regaled us with the story on our first day.

'Hendrick Henning,' said Angela. 'The thirteenth Viscount. It's why we're filming here . . . ?'

'Why don't you remind us all,' said Juliette. I suspected she secretly wanted a refresher, too, so we gathered round as Angela told the story.

'Two hundred years ago the thirteenth Viscount Henning was called Hendrick. He fought with the British Army in India, then returned home and locked himself away in Hendale Hall. Nowadays we'd probably say he was traumatised, suffering from PTSD, but in those days nobody knew what that was. His wife had died giving birth to their son Simon, so his younger sister Helena cared for the boy while Hendrick was fighting abroad. Now he was back, she travelled to India herself. There she fell in love with a local Indian dignitary and wrote to Hendrick saying she wanted to marry him.'

Pri raised her eyebrows. 'I can guess how well that went down.'

'That's right,' said Angela. 'Hendrick forbade it and demanded she return home at once. Helena did . . . but brought her lover with her. Hendrick flew into a rage and said he'd kill the man if he didn't leave immediately.'

'You keep saying "him" and "the man",' Ruby pointed out. 'What was his name?'

'Oh, I know this one,' I said, remembering part of the tour at last. 'His name was never recorded, because it wasn't deemed important.'

'Of course,' said Pri sarcastically. 'He was just an Indian; how could he be important?'

Angela continued, 'Whatever his name, he swore to Hendrick that if he – I mean the Indian man – died in Hendale, the house would know only misery and its dead wouldn't rest.'

'I remember now,' said Chloe. 'He did, didn't he?'

Angela nodded. 'Helena and the Indian were both found dead of malaria the next morning. Hendrick ordered the bodies burnt so the disease couldn't spread, then went mad with grief and climbed the tower while a storm raged. He cursed the heavens and renounced God – and at that moment a lightning bolt struck him. Simon saw him fall, as a swarm of bats flew away into the storm.'

'How very Gothic,' I said, looking up at the tower. It was the highest part of the house, two storeys taller than the main roof. Lightning or not, a fall from there would kill anyone. No wonder it was closed to the public.

'Then, soon after they buried Hendrick and Simon became the new Viscount, people began to disappear. Locals said they saw Hendrick still walking, and servants kept dying. So, the staff all quit. For two generations nobody would work at Hendale.'

'Thus was born the legend of the Hendale Vampire,' I said. 'A good thing too, in a way. Without that story, George might have had to sell this place off years ago.'

Pri snorted again. 'Are we supposed to believe this vampire has come back and killed Yash because he was

Indian? I've heard some racist things in my time, but come on.'

'Why not?' said Angela. 'There are more things in heaven and earth than are dreamt of in your philosophy, Priya. Ever since we came here, I've felt an evil shadow upon us.'

'That's the northern chill, darling,' said Ruby. 'You get used to it eventually.'

Angela levelled her gaze at the older actress. 'I'm from Norway.'

'Yes, well, that explains a lot.'

'Enough, ladies,' I said. 'Pri is right. As I said, this is an attempt by the killer to divert attention away from what really happened.'

Ruby turned back at the trailer. 'Is there a ceiling hatch?'

Juliette looked at her like she'd asked if it had wings. 'Why in God's name would my trailer have a ceiling hatch?'

'I don't know, I just thought whoever killed Yash might have escaped that way. Does it?'

'No! Anyway, this is a case of mistaken identity. Obviously, I was the killer's intended target.'

Everyone turned to look at Juliette in silence. Finally, Needles spoke up.

'So . . . our vampire really was blind as a bat?'

'No, dammit, it was dark!' she yelled. 'Or they panicked, whatever, I don't know. But it's my trailer, so why in hell would anyone sit there and wait for Yash Rani of all people to come through? I hardly knew the kid.' She held up her phone and walked away. 'Now if you'll excuse me, I need to call my agent.'

It occurred to me that she shouldn't really have been using the phone, considering it had been inside her trailer when Yash was killed. But that battle was a lost cause.

Besides, as ridiculous as Juliette's theory sounded, she had a point. If anyone had waited in her trailer it would surely be for her, not Yash . . . unless the killer hadn't been waiting, but followed him inside? But that didn't explain why he was there to begin with, or why he didn't seem to have put up a fight. Had Yash been drugged? Asleep? No, not asleep. Notwithstanding the question of why he'd use Juliette's trailer to take a nap, there was no blood on the furniture. Only on the floor.

Lily barked twice then let out a soft, high-pitched howl. A moment later I heard the distant sound of sirens matching her tone.

'Hopefully the police can find whatever it is we're missing about this,' I said. 'In the meantime, Juliette has the right idea. I'm going to call my agent.'

CHAPTER NINE

I wandered round to the back of the house, for privacy and to get Lily's sensitive nose away from the awful smells around Juliette's trailer. While we walked through the shrubs and bushes I dialled my agent, Bostin Jim.

'Gwinny,' he answered in his thick Brummie accent. 'Everything all right on set?' He wasn't psychic; it's a standard question when a client calls their agent in the middle of a shoot.

'As it happens, Jim, no . . .'

I explained what had happened, and that the police were now on the scene. He listened while emitting a series of grunts that alternated between surprise, horror and disappointment.

'So much for *Draculania*, then. Bloody hell, and this was going to be your first step back into bigger parts. That's real bad luck.'

'Not so fast. Steven McDonald seems determined to press on and recast the Luke role. He's even going to try and spin this into publicity for the film.'

'I don't know why he wouldn't take the insurance and move on,' said Jim, surprised. 'He's done it before.'

'I'm not entirely sure he can. I heard him on the phone earlier complaining to someone about a lack of insurance. Could he be swindling the financiers?'

'That'd be risky. No decent financier's going to fund a picture without insurance in place. If he lied to them . . .'

'I'll ask him. Either way, I don't think it's really a motive. On the other hand, if he *is* insured and Juliette is right that she was the target—'

'Hold your horses, Sherlock,' Jim interrupted. 'Didn't you just say the police had arrived? Do me a favour and focus on your performance, all right? Not on running around investigating.'

Jim was a good agent, but no fun at all. 'I'm not investigating; I was merely thinking aloud. I'm sure the police will get to the bottom of things — *Lily*!'

The terrier was trying to burrow underneath a shrubbery with bright yellow flowers, and currently flinging soil onto the hem of my costume dress. 'Sorry, I'm walking the dog. Long story.'

'When is it not?' he said, laughing. 'Let me know if anything changes. Gruesome as it is, maybe McDonald's right. The publicity from this could turn *Draculania* into a hit, so give everything your best shot.'

I promised him I would and ended the call. Then I reached down to pull Lily out of the shrubbery by her thick, solid tail, like a working terrier from a rabbit warren. With her now on a short lead, I was trying to casually kick the soil back onto the bed when I heard the approaching voices of two men. Several bushes hid the speakers from my sight, but I recognised one as George, and I didn't need to see the other to recognise the speech mannerisms of a police officer.

'. . . investigate to the fullest extent, Your Lordship, don't worry about that. No stone will be left unturned in our enquiries.'

'To be honest, Inspector, I'd prefer you did leave a few unturned,' George replied. 'If people stop renting the house because they think there are murderous ghosts abroad, it'll be the end of Hendale Hall.'

'Not to make light of a terrible situation, but wouldn't a little notoriety increase your tourist numbers?'

'Don't be impertinent, man. Need I remind you that I count the police commissioner as a good friend, and when he asks me about your performance—'

I never found out the full extent of George's threat because Lily chose that moment to bark loudly and give us away. I stepped out from behind the bushes, doing my best to pretend that we'd been walking the whole time.

'Ah, Gwinny,' said George. 'This is Detective Chief Inspector Pierce. He's here to find out what happened to the young man.'

The inspector was a large man in every dimension, with a dour expression. He nodded curtly at me. 'We'll be speaking to the estate staff in good time, lass. Find one of the uniforms and make yourself known.'

George and I exchanged glances, then he laughed

while I reddened. 'This is a costume, Inspector,' I explained. 'I'm Gwinny Tuffel, an actor in the film. Surely you don't think the Viscount's staff wear Victorian period dress?'

DCI Pierce took a roll of extra-strong mints from his pocket and popped one in his mouth. 'Don't go in for it much myself,' he said while sucking. 'Why make stuff up when there's a real world right in front of your face?'

I hadn't anticipated the need to improvise a speech on the cultural value and importance of storytelling, but thankfully I was saved by Juliette Shine. Still in full Draculania costume, she marched over to the men with a determined expression.

'About damn time,' she said. 'Now listen, Detective. I have to tell you there were a lot of folks walking around the body, OK? I mean, you can't blame them. But nothing was removed from the trailer, and we already checked all the cupboards and hiding spaces, so we know nobody else was inside. Oh yeah, and the door was locked when—'

Pierce raised a hand to stop Juliette in her tracks, and looked her up and down. Then he said, 'You're another actor, aren't you?'

She blinked, looking from me to him to me again. 'Is this guy for real?'

'He really is DCI Pierce,' I said with a note of apology. Why I should apologise for the police I wasn't sure, but it felt the right thing to do.

'Don't you know who I am?'

'I'm afraid not, madam.'

'Don't you "madam" me. I swear, this country is like living in the Dark Ages. Do you people even have Netflix?'

'The inspector doesn't see the value of films, apparently,' I explained. Juliette sputtered, unable to comprehend such an opinion, so I pressed on. 'Inspector, this is our leading lady, Juliette Shine. As she was saying, the door to the trailer where Yash died was locked – from the inside – and there was nobody else present. Would you like me to show you?'

'My officers have already secured the trailer, Ms Tuffel. In fact, we'll be securing all of this area for the time being, until we've examined the scene.'

Sure enough, over his shoulder I saw uniformed police officers sealing off unit base with incident tape.

'Now hold on,' Juliette protested, 'you can't keep us out of there. Look at us, for God's sake. We have to get back into our normal clothes.'

'Don't worry, ladies,' said Pierce, walking back towards the car park. 'We'll sort this out in no time. Sounds like a terrible accident, right enough—'

'Hey, copper! There you are!'

Chloe ran out of the rear of the house with a face like thunder. 'I'm the director,' she explained. 'I need access to those trailers. You can't shut us out of them.'

Juliette nodded. 'That's what I said.'

Pierce adopted what he probably thought was a sympathetic expression but made him look like he had stomach cramps.

'We won't be here long. Twenty-four hours at the

most, I should think. You'll have to cope until then.'

'Twenty-four hours to solve a murder?' I said, surprised. 'You seem very confident.'

The inspector turned to me. 'Murder? I was told this was an accident.'

He didn't need to say who'd put this idea in his head. I noticed Steven was nowhere to be seen.

'I very much doubt that,' I said. 'Juliette's already convinced she was the real target.'

'Hold up,' said Pierce. 'It doesn't help anyone to start flying off with half-cocked theories. Didn't you say he was locked in there by himself? How could it not be an accident?'

'I don't know, but the man has a resin stunt stake rammed into his chest. I very much doubt he tripped and fell on it.'

DCI Pierce frowned. 'We'll see about that. But if you're right, we might have to maintain the integrity of this area for several days or even a week.'

Chloe began protesting again. She was soon joined by Needles, who'd been ejected from inside unit base and wanted to state his own case. Juliette threw up her hands and stalked off back to the house.

I followed, leaving the others arguing with DCI Pierce, and took Lily upstairs to my room. The clothes I'd been wearing that morning were trapped in Needles' wardrobe trailer, along with Juliette's and Ruby's, so I found a fresh outfit and changed into it, placing all the items of my costume carefully on the bed while the terrier curled up for a nap.

My thoughts drifted to the blustering DCI Pierce. Simultaneously oleaginous and brusque, he hadn't given a good first impression. If I'd told Birch that Yash was killed by a 'stunt stake', for example, he would have immediately asked me to explain what that was. Pierce showed no such inclination, and given his ignorance of films it was safe to assume he didn't already know.

I decided it couldn't hurt to ask a few questions of my own. I might even be able to help the police. Despite Bostin Jim's ribbing, and the murders I've solved in the past, I don't think of myself a detective. But I do have a talent for puzzles, and everything I'd seen so far suggested this was a tricky one.

I'd recognised the murder weapon as a stunt stake when we all crowded around the body in the trailer. All the prop stakes were resin painted to look like wood (we avoided real wood so actors wouldn't get splinters) but most were hollow and blunted, so they could be handled easily and safely in scenes where they merely had to look good. When we needed to perform an action – like, say, hammer a stake into a vampire's chest – we used a stunt stake, made of solid resin that wouldn't break.

There were two scenes where that would happen. One was the climactic staking of Draculania herself in the finale, scheduled to be shot next week on a soundstage outside London. The other was the scene where Van Helsing and Seward dispatch Luke Westenra in the family crypt. That was to be filmed here, on the set being built by the old gatehouse.

To make it look real, both scenes would employ fake bodies and camera trickery: tried and tested methods that had been used in film for decades. Nevertheless, the stunt coordinator and special effects supervisor had insisted everyone involved in those scenes familiarise ourselves with how it would work. That was standard procedure, as asking an actor to do anything besides stand on a mark and deliver their lines carries some element of risk.

So, even though we hadn't yet shot the staking scene here at Hendale, everyone had handled those props. Juliette, Ruby, Yash and I – plus the stand-ins, Angela and Zayn – had spent thirty minutes picking them up and waving them around, getting used to handling them . . . and learning to tell the difference between the plain hollow prop stakes and the solid stunt stakes.

Yash's killer had known the difference. Unless this was all a horrible joke gone very wrong, they'd deliberately used a stunt stake with murder in mind.

Puzzle pieces began to form in my mind's eye. They were indistinct, and there was no picture to assemble yet, but eventually there would be. Imagining a jigsaw helped me make sense of the disparate snippets of information.

One of the first pieces I wanted to establish was who could have got their hands on a stunt stake. The most likely person to know that was Bill, the special effects supervisor. I didn't know where he was, and couldn't risk leaving Lily in the room with an entire expensive costume lying on the bed, so I clipped her lead back on and took her downstairs. She grumbled, understandably annoyed that I'd interrupted her sleep, but natural curiosity got the better of her.

In the entrance hallway I heard Steven's voice. He paced up and down in one of the reception rooms off the main hall, arguing with someone on the phone again.

'Can't you backdate it?' he shouted. 'Just find someone, for Christ's sake . . . I swear, if I'd known I wouldn't have—'

At that he turned, saw me watching and closed the door. Lily barked indignantly, but I couldn't blame Steven for wanting privacy.

Before I could reach the front door, it was flung open by Zayn Patel, who stormed inside.

'Where's Steven?' he demanded. 'I've looked all over for him.'

'Small reception. But he's on the phone,' I called after his already-disappearing back. Zayn was evidently on a mission and didn't care.

Sorely tempted as I was to stick around and eavesdrop, at that moment one of the special effects crew happened by and, when asked, informed me Bill was at the crypt set by the gatehouse. I led Lily outside, through the larch wood and past the lake.

CHAPTER TEN

Despite the large number of people working on the film, the estate was big enough that I didn't have to walk far before I was completely alone. Feeling suddenly vulnerable, what with a killer on the loose, I decided to call Birch.

'Afternoon,' he answered cheerily. From his background I could see he was still at home. 'Finished filming already?'

'Yes, but not in the way you mean.' I told him what had happened to Yash, and about the police arriving. 'Do you know DCI Pierce, or his reputation?'

'Doesn't ring a bell. The Met and Yorkshire don't always get along, truth be told. How does he seem?'

'Hard to say after such a short time. Perhaps a little too keen to please the Viscount, but I suppose politics and policing inevitably mix in a place like this.'

Birch leant back on his sofa, fussing Ronnie, who was curled up by his side. 'Must say, bit peeved I'm missing it down here. You told me filming was boring.'

'It is,' I protested. 'Most of the time we sit around all day, waiting for the ten minutes when we get to do our job. Actors being murdered is hardly commonplace.'

'Maybe I should drive up. Could be there by tomorrow.'

The suggestion set off a cascade of mixed emotions in me. On the one hand, I hadn't seen Birch in person for several weeks due to filming. On the other hand, he was old-fashioned enough to probably think I needed to be protected, which irked me. And on the third hand . . .

'Was that Tina I saw with you earlier, when I was in make-up?'

'No, no,' he said, perhaps too quickly. 'Perish the thought. Trick of the light.'

Being a former policeman, Birch was a practised liar. Not as good as an actor like me, but not bad. There was nothing in his manner or expression that told me he was definitely lying here, but my doubts remained.

'Better if you stay there,' I said, making up my mind. 'The set has already been thrown into chaos, and we don't know for sure if we'll continue filming. Your presence would only cause more confusion.'

'Right you are.' I couldn't tell if he was put out or quietly relieved. 'All the same, sounds like a rum do. I'm always here to talk about the case, if you want.'

'It really is a mystery,' I said. 'There was definitely nobody in the trailer with Yash. Security had to prise the door open with a crowbar, and Juliette's own keys were still in the inside lock. We even opened all the cabinets, wardrobe and so on. There was nobody in there.'

'What about that message on the mirror? *Hendrick Lives*. Could Yash have written it himself?'

'It's possible. His body was lying in the kitchen area, and most of his blood also appeared to be there, but with everyone stamping around I couldn't be sure. I should have stopped them, but it was rather overwhelming.'

I wished I could show Birch photos of the scene, then remembered that I'd admonished Needles for taking his own pictures. Perhaps I'd been too hasty. If I asked nicely, maybe he'd send me copies.

'Mustn't blame yourself,' said Birch. 'Any chance Yash was still alive when you opened the door?'

'With a ten-inch resin stake rammed into his chest? I think not.'

'Not what I mean. I was thinking he might have been injured, or unconscious. Whoever got to the body first could have finished him off, then claimed he was already dead.'

'Oh, I see.' This was unusually lateral thinking for Birch, who was normally of a more linear mind. 'I don't think so, though. Yash was some distance from the door, and before anyone entered we all got a good look at him. He was very clearly dead, with the stake already, um . . . in place.'

'Only one thing for it, then. Killer must have escaped before you all got there, somehow leaving the door locked—' He looked up at the sound of his doorbell, but didn't move.

'Aren't you going to answer that?'

'Oh – yes, but – of course – hold on . . .' Flustered, he put the phone down on the coffee table so all I could see was his ceiling. I heard him leave the room and close the door, followed by a muffled sound, which I assumed was him answering the front door. Then nothing.

By now Lily and I were almost at the gatehouse. Someone had told these crew members the show was indeed going on, because the crypt was complete and now their attention had turned to finishing the graveyard.

A minute later Birch returned to his phone, still flustered.

'Everything OK?' I asked.

'Absolutely, all tickety-boo. Just the, um, dog groomer.'

This was such a blatant lie that even Birch's police training couldn't disguise it.

'For Ronnie? Since when?'

'What do you mean?' he said, offended. 'Good-looking dog, Ronnie. Why wouldn't I have him groomed?'

I laughed. 'He's beautiful, Birch, but you've never once mentioned a groomer before.'

He reddened, looking even more offended. 'Sorry, have to go. Deal with the . . . groomer.' And with that, he ended the call.

Of course, what I'd wanted to ask was whether his mystery caller was really Tina. I could phone her now, to check where she was . . .

Don't be silly, woman. I took a deep breath to calm my paranoia and gave myself a good talking-to for letting my imagination run away with itself. Even if Tina was there, so what? Birch had known her as long as he'd known me. Surely there was a perfectly innocent reason why, while I was away for several weeks, this handsome, eligible widower might secretly spend time with my best friend, who also happened to be a beautiful, wealthy and very single actress . . .

No, this was no good. If I let my thoughts go down that road I'd drive myself mad. Instead I picked up Lily, in order to carry her safely through the set, and called out for Bill. A carpenter gestured to the crypt, and the special effects supervisor stepped out to face me with a gloomy expression.

CHAPTER ELEVEN

'It's unbelievable,' said Bill, his shoulders slumped. 'Absolutely unbelievable. How could this happen?'

'That's what the police are trying to find out,' I said, carefully stepping through the set. 'DCI Pierce is hoping it was an accident so he can pack up and go home, but I can't see it. An accident like this seems impossible.'

I didn't voice my fears that a murder like this also seemed impossible. No need to spread panic among the crew.

'Bill, how did someone get hold of a stunt stake in the first place? Did you notice it was missing?'

He shook his head. 'To be honest with you, I didn't. We don't keep them under lock and key, and until we actually shoot scene thirty-six there's no need for anyone to go near them.'

'Assuming we do shoot it. Steven's keen to carry on, but at the very least it'll take time to re-cast Luke.'

'Yeah, he called everyone earlier and told us to

maintain schedule for now. Maybe they'll finally cast Zayn instead.'

'Zayn? Yash's stand-in? Why would they cast him?'

'Didn't you know?' Bill asked, surprised. 'Zayn was on the shortlist to play Luke, until Yash came along. He got bumped, but seeing as they're about the same build they gave him stand-in as a consolation.'

I'd had no idea. But it did cast things in a new light, especially as minutes before Zayn had been angrily looking for Steven. Would Zayn Patel kill Yash Rani just to take his role? Could it mean that much to him?

Or could he have been the target? Bill was right that Zayn and Yash were of similar build, and as Juliette had pointed out it would have been dark in her trailer with all the blinds down. Had the killer mistaken Yash for Zayn? It was certainly more likely than mistaking him for Juliette.

'Whatever they decide, at least the set will be ready,' said Bill, rousing me from my thoughts. 'What do you think?'

I took it in, impressed. Old, weathered gravestones lined the grass next to the old gatehouse, connected to which was a crypt of grey stone. A heavy wooden door, braced with large iron hinges and a formidable lock, beckoned us inside. Stepping through brought us into the cold, gloomy embrace of a dusty crypt carpeted with dry autumn leaves. Stone shelves lined the walls, and coffins lined the shelves . . . except for one. On the room's central dais lay a single wooden coffin, the resting place of a recently dead family member. But there was no body inside; its lid was propped against the dais, revealing an empty space where Luke Westenra should have been.

'How will you fit cameras in here?' I asked.

Bill smiled and walked to the rear of the crypt. 'Slide-away wall,' he said, reaching up to grip an iron sconce. With a heave, he pulled on it and the stone wall slid aside. Beyond lay an empty space, twice as large, of plain timbers and sawdust. 'Chloe wants a transitional tracking shot of you coming from the graveyard into the crypt, with the rear wall in place. Then we'll remove it for the staking gag, so cameras can shoot from this angle.'

I could now see that the wall was only two inches thick and on rollers, its surface covered with painted foam and polystyrene to look like old, grey stone. The same was true of the other walls in the crypt, and everything else in sight apart from the old gatehouse itself. The iron sconces were plastic, painted black. The shelves and coffins were made of lightweight balsa wood. The heavy door and its iron hinges were painted plywood, while the headstones outside were hollow resin. The creeping vines smothering the stones were plastic, and even the autumn leaves underfoot were made of paper.

The set was to be the location of a scene familiar to anyone who knows the story of *Dracula* – albeit done in *Draculania*'s unique fashion.

Drs Abigail Van Helsing and Jacqueline Seward, having chased the vampiric Luke Westenra to his crypt through the night, enter shortly after sunrise and find him sleeping in his coffin. To rid the world of this accursed vampire, and redeem Luke's immortal soul, Van Helsing takes a wooden stake and hammers it into the sleeping creature's chest. Luke screams, and stolen blood gushes forth from his body, but Van Helsing hammers again and again and again . . . until the ghastly deed is done.

At least, that's how it would appear on film. The truth was more prosaic and, like the crypt itself, mere movie fakery.

The secret, if it even deserved that moniker, was similar to the magician's trick of sawing a woman in half. The coffin had a head-sized hole cut near the top of its base, which was in fact a false floor. The actor (formerly Yash, now whoever replaced him) would lie with most of his body underneath that false floor, his head angled to protrude through the hole. Resting in the coffin was a fake body, also built by Bill and his crew, which was dressed to look like the vampire. The body would be attached to the actor's neck with prosthetic make-up to cover the join. This is one reason why many movie vampires sleep in full dress, often with elaborate collars or ruffs.

Ruby, as Van Helsing, would take the stunt stake, position it in a particular spot over the fake chest, and use the hammer to strike it down. The prosthetic body was built with a small pre-drilled hole in the right spot, hidden by clothing, which allowed the stake to easily enter the body. Meanwhile an off-screen technician would manipulate a pump connected to a small hose filled with fake blood, the end of which was placed inside the false chest. With each hammer blow blood would pump out of the hose, over 'Luke's' chest and shirt.

The stake and hammer were both made of solid resin: lightweight, so nobody was at risk of dropping something heavy on a body part, but solid enough to withstand the necessary hammer strikes. The action was perfectly safe, because at no point would anything be in contact with Yash's body. The coffin's false floor included a layer of metal sheeting, which the resin stake couldn't possibly penetrate.

This kind of fake body 'gag' is one of the oldest in the special effects book, used in thousands of films. I've never been the body in question myself, but I'm told that the biggest danger to any actor in such scenes is death by boredom as they lie there waiting for the prosthetics to be laboriously applied.

But Yash hadn't been wearing a fake body, or a bag of stage blood. Someone hammered a stake through his chest for real. I shuddered at the thought.

Bill's set radio crackled. '*Cast and crew gather in the house's entrance hall in ten minutes. Repeat, all cast and crew to the entrance hall in ten minutes. No exceptions.*'

The voice belonged to one of the runners, those energetic juniors who cat-herd cast and crew during production, but the message was obviously from on high. Probably Steven himself.

We set off back to the house together, and I put Lily down to let her walk. She immediately went for Bill's ankle, but he was ready for her and dodged out of the way.

'Had a Jack Russell myself, once,' he said with a smile. 'Nippy little buggers. So, what do you think this gathering is about?'

'Perhaps DCI Pierce has realised he won't be getting his supper tonight.'

CHAPTER TWELVE

Being right isn't always a good thing.

The whole cast and crew crowded into the entrance hall, and I noticed the Hendale staff were present too. Everyone had guessed this summons was related to Yash's death, but nobody was sure how.

Then Steven and Chloe entered through the front door, calling for quiet.

'What's going on?' Needles asked. 'Are we being shut down?'

'No,' Steven insisted. 'We'll figure it out. For now, you all have to listen to the police.'

DCI Pierce entered as if taking a cue, accompanied by two uniformed officers.

'Can't we do this in the ballroom?' asked Ruby, who was still in costume. 'It's big enough, and at least it's got chairs.'

DCI Pierce fixed her with a glare that he probably thought would cow her into submission, but if so, he didn't know Ruby very well. Nevertheless, she shrugged and waited for him to continue.

If I'd hoped the inspector might be humbled by learning he'd jumped to conclusions in declaring Yash's death an accident, I was in for disappointment. He took long strides up and down the hall, pausing to pop an extra-strong mint in his mouth. Lily watched him, her head turning like she was courtside at Wimbledon.

'We now believe Mr Rani's death wasn't an accident at all, but that someone deliberately killed him.' Pierce paused for effect. 'In other words: it was murder.'

Gasps sounded around the room, and Lily barked in response. Everyone started whispering – except, I noticed, those who'd been at the trailer when we found the body. Juliette, Ruby, Chloe, Steven, Angela, Needles . . . we were all equally unsurprised.

'Who's your main suspect?' asked Juliette. 'Because it was obviously someone on set. Nobody else is allowed on the estate while we're shooting.'

'He wasn't shot, he was stabbed,' said Pierce, confused. 'Do you mean to tell me there are firearms in this house?'

Viscount Henning spoke up from the back. 'Actually, there aren't. We stopped sport in the grounds some years ago, after . . . well, you know.' I didn't know, and judging by their faces neither did most of the people here. But the inspector nodded and the Viscount continued, 'Regardless, we know that's not how the young man was killed. What we don't know is, who did it?'

'If I had that information I'd make an arrest. We

98

assume, as the lady said, that it was someone involved with either the house or film.'

Juliette smiled smugly.

'Saying that, the boundary walls are hardly Mount Everest, so we can't rule out the idea that someone unauthorised entered the scene.'

Juliette's smile faded.

'I must ask you all to remain in the vicinity so we can interview you and conduct the investigation.'

'We're not going anywhere,' said Steven. 'There are other scenes we can shoot while we're re-casting Luke.'

Needles turned on him. 'Are you having a laugh? There's a psycho running around, and you want us to carry on like nothing's happened? What if one of us is next?'

'That depends on why Yash was killed,' said Juliette, beating me to it. Irritating, but at least she was asking the right questions. 'The motive could be unconnected to the film.'

'He was staked through the heart while filming *Dracula*! How much more of a clue do you need? Bats flying in through the window?'

'*Draculania*, Needles, it's totally different,' Chloe corrected him. 'We'll do it in Yash's memory, and dedicate the picture to him.'

'Should we at least take a day off?' I suggested. 'We can't shoot anyway without hair, make-up and wardrobe. Perhaps the police will let us retrieve the equipment and set up somewhere in the house, instead. Unless you're finished with the trailers . . . ?' I looked at DCI Pierce hopefully, but he shook his head.

'You can go about your business as you like,' he said. 'But the area around the crime scene remains off-limits without an escort. We'll also need to take everyone's fingerprints.'

'That won't help,' I said. 'There were half a dozen of us who found Yash, and we've all been in and out of Juliette's trailer in the past week anyway. Everyone's prints will be all over the place.'

'Including on the murder weapon?'

Of that I wasn't sure. I hadn't touched it, but in the scrum and shock of finding the body, I couldn't swear nobody else had.

'It's not just about the people in the trailer,' I explained. 'That stake has been handled by a dozen or more people, both crew and cast, long before it was used to kill Yash.'

'We've commandeered one of your office trailers to use as an incident room,' said Pierce, ignoring me. 'I'll expect everyone here to present themselves at their earliest opportunity to be fingerprinted. We'll then coordinate moving your equipment in here, once forensics has cleared it.'

He turned on his heel and walked out, followed by the uniformed officers.

'Where *is* your costume?' Ruby asked me. 'How'd you get changed?'

'In my room. I wasn't about to walk Lily through the woods in full Victorian bustle. By the way, did you know Zayn was originally going to play Luke?'

Ruby had been booked before me, but she shook her

head. 'All I remember is that Luke remained uncast for ages, then suddenly it was Yash, and everyone jumped for joy.' She grimaced. 'If only we'd known. Shall we go and get fingerprinted, then? Maybe they've already got an idea of who did it.'

I doubted that, but there was no sense in hanging back. We made our way outside and approached the police cordon around unit base. A constable offered warily to take Lily, reaching for her, but backed off when she barked at him. I insisted the dog would be fine and kept her on a short lead as the constable escorted us to what had formerly been the production trailer, now transformed into a police incident room.

Juliette had beaten us to it. It was something of an absurd sight, as she still wore full Draculania costume, and at first I didn't understand why she was standing there with one hand pressed to a sheet of glass. Then I saw she was being scanned. Fingerprinting had evidently come a long way since the days of ink rollers. She and DCI Pierce were chatting, and when she saw us enter she said, deliberately loud, 'Yes, Detective, I'd be glad to show you how we found the body in my trailer. I can tell you exactly what happened.'

This annoyed me, as I'm sure she knew it would, because I'd planned to make the same offer to DCI Pierce. Then I remembered something important.

'I'll come with you if you like,' I said. 'After all, Juliette, you didn't arrive until *after* we called security.'

She fixed me with a disdainful glare worthy of Draculania herself.

'Until then nothing important had happened,' she countered. 'You were all standing around outside my trailer.'

'Nonsense. For one thing, there was the gunshot.'

That got Pierce's attention. 'Didn't we establish there are no guns on the estate?' he said, frustrated.

'All right,' I admitted, 'it probably wasn't a gun. But it sounded quite like one. At first I thought it was someone dropping a section of track, but now I wonder if it was connected to Yash's death.'

'How?' Juliette sneered. 'He was stabbed, not shot. You'll have to do better than that, Gwinny.'

Lily snarled at her. Maybe the terrier wasn't such a bad judge of character after all.

'Is this a competition now as well?' Ruby sighed. 'Can we just get on with being fingerprinted and let the police do their job?'

'A fine idea,' said DCI Pierce, cutting off whatever barb Juliette had lined up to respond. Having finished scanning her, he beckoned me forward.

'I'm merely trying to give you all the facts,' I said as he guided my hand over the scanner's glass surface. 'My friend DCI Birch of the Met always says you can never have too much information in a murder case.'

Birch had never said anything of the sort, and strictly speaking he was *formerly* of the Met, but I hoped dropping his name might sway Pierce.

Instead he said, 'We're not the Met, madam. I'm sure DCI Bench is a fine man, but we do things our own way in Yorkshire.'

'I didn't say Birch was a man,' I replied weakly, but he didn't bother to respond. He tapped some keys on the laptop, then dismissed me and waved for Ruby to take my place.

Juliette remained inside the trailer, waiting by the door. As I passed her, she stopped me.

'We should talk. After I'm done showing the cop what happened, I'm gonna get changed and go back to my room. How about you stop by the inn, say at four o'clock?'

'If I'm not busy,' I said, perhaps a bit too snippily, and continued outside.

CHAPTER THIRTEEN

Juliette and I both knew I wasn't busy, of course. But I refused to let her ride roughshod over me.

Besides, there was Lily to consider. The Jack Russell had been a fine companion so far, thank goodness, and was taking in all these new experiences with enthusiasm. But she wasn't a young dog, and I could tell she was tired. At some point I'd have to leave her in my room, but I was wary of it so long as my costume was in there. I wanted to wait until Needles had set up an impromptu wardrobe in the house, even though I had no idea when that would be.

'Penny for your thoughts?' said Ruby, catching up with me after her fingerprints had been taken.

'Thinking about my costume. I daren't leave Lily alone in the room with it.' An idea struck me. 'Could I leave it in your room, perhaps? Until Needles sorts somewhere out, I mean.'

Ruby hesitated, then said, 'I don't think so, sorry. You

know me, I explode all over dressing rooms and hotels. Needles wouldn't thank either of us if I damaged it.'

That was true, so far as it went, but something about Ruby's expression made me wonder if there was another reason – one she didn't want to tell me. Earlier I'd mused on the possibility of Juliette and Yash having an on-set affair, but now I wondered if Ruby might be indulging with someone, too. She'd been divorced for twenty years, and the plastic surgery had to be good for something.

'What about Yash's room?' she said suddenly. 'He won't be needing it.'

'Oh, no, how horrible. Besides, the police will seal it off now they know it was murder. I wonder if the Viscount has another spare room somewhere? A house this size must have rooms we haven't seen yet.'

Ruby yawned. 'Speaking of bedrooms, I'm ready for a nap. Good luck finding somewhere.'

We walked up to the bedrooms together and she went straight into her room, next to mine. I carried on a while, past the locked tower entrance, to peek around the corner. Yash's room was along here, next to Zayn's, and sure enough a uniformed police officer now guarded his door.

I returned to my room, removed Lily's coat at last and encouraged her onto her bed. With all the excitement so far today I hoped she'd want to sleep, and I was right. She curled up in a tight ball and within minutes began to snooze. I quietly gathered up my costume and left, locking the door.

Surely there was somewhere in this enormous house where I could store the costume until Needles sorted out a temporary wardrobe department. Not somewhere we were scheduled to film, though, as then it would be in the way.

What about the Viscount's own area? Would George relax his boundaries a little, in light of what had happened?

Downstairs, I entered the private corridor. For some reason I felt guilty, like a naughty schoolgirl trespassing in a teachers-only area, and after a few steps realised I was walking on tiptoe. *Get a grip, you ridiculous woman.* I did, stood up straight and continued.

'No, you don't belong there, do you?'

I jumped at the sound of George's voice, and dropped the hat from my costume. But as I bent to retrieve it and looked around, he was nowhere to be seen. Then I heard movement from up ahead, and he leant out through a doorway.

'I say, what are you doing here?'

I reddened, still feeling like a trespasser – which I technically was – and said, 'I was, um, hoping you might have somewhere I could store this. My costume. I can't put it in the trailer.' I picked up the hat and waved it, hoping that would explain everything.

'Yes, I hadn't thought of that. Of course, of course. Come in.' He beckoned me into the room.

It was a study, one that might have been preserved in aspic since the nineteenth century if not for the computer on a side desk. Even that had to share space with an old-fashioned blotting pad and mechanical typewriter. Dark wooden shelves filled with cloth-bound books lined three walls. The fourth was a chimney wall, hung with paintings of past Viscounts and Hendale itself above a fireplace that looked recently used, with two easy chairs in front of the hearth. Daylight was afforded by a tall window behind the main desk. I guessed that was where George had been, because he now returned to it and gestured at a high-backed leather chair near the side desk.

'By all means drop your things there.'

I did, gratefully. As I turned back, though, my eye was caught by some literature on the desktop. A glossy brochure extolled the virtues of investing in green energy, its cover photograph a field of wind turbines on a summer's day.

'It'll be perfectly safe,' said George. 'Nobody uses this room except me, and all I'm doing in here at the moment is this damned jigsaw.'

'Jigsaw? What jigsaw?'

I joined him at the desk. On its surface was a large puzzle, and it was immediately clear George wasn't very good.

'My own fault for making it so big,' he said. 'I should have asked for the three-hundred-piece version.'

The lower-left corner (grass) was partially completed, along with a portion of the upper border (sky), but otherwise he'd been trying to form the middle (a house?) from the inside out, which hadn't got him very far. I remembered what I heard in the corridor: 'You don't belong there' hadn't been talking about me at all.

'You're tackling it all wrong,' I said, not unkindly. 'Always complete the border first, because those are the only pieces whose position you can be sure of.'

'How?' he asked, then answered his own question. 'Oh, because they have a flat side. Or two, if it's a corner. So, you're an expert, what?'

It hardly takes an expert to know one begins a jigsaw at the edges. Could George somehow have made it to his age without ever doing one before?

'Merely an enthusiast for puzzles,' I demurred, reaching for the box of remaining pieces. It looked like a two-thousand-piecer, so there was plenty still to do. 'Let's go through the box and find all of those edge pieces. You must begin with whatever you can be sure about, rather than trying to guess where things go in the middle.'

'Not a bad philosophy for life.' He rummaged in the box, extracting edge and corner pieces as he found them.

'Where's the lid?' I asked, searching for it in vain. 'What's this a picture of?'

George chuckled. 'Oh, we haven't got that yet. I'm having these made, you see, to sell to tourists. But you'd think I shouldn't have this much trouble, given I've lived here all my life.' He pointed to a painting of Hendale Hall on the chimney wall, and now I saw that the puzzle was the same picture.

'What a lovely painting,' I said. 'I'll buy one of these to take home with me.'

'Oh, you can't. This is a prototype, you see. First, I

need to open a gift shop, to sell souvenirs and what have you. All raising funds for the legacy, you see?'

For a moment we looked at each other, similarly confused. Me because I didn't know what he was talking about; him because he couldn't conceive that anyone wouldn't.

Then his expression changed to one of great sadness, his shoulders slumped, and he seemed to age many years in a single moment.

'But why would you?' he said. 'You're not from around here.'

'No, and I confess I'm awfully confused.'

He nodded. 'I forget sometimes. I'm the last, you understand. No more viscounts after me. I had a son, Charlie, but he . . . we lost him in a shooting accident. Here on the estate. Many years ago, now.'

'That's why there are no guns,' I said, finally understanding the earlier exchange between him and DCI Pierce. 'I'm so sorry.'

This also explained why such an eligible gentleman was cooped up in this house all by himself. The loss of their only child must have driven him and his wife apart, presumably leaving him too wracked with grief to marry again.

'Water under the bridge,' he said, putting on a brave face. 'When I'm gone, Hendale will fall to the National Trust. A memorial for Charlie, one likes to think. That's why I hire it out to chaps like you. It's never too early to fundraise.'

I wondered if that was the only reason, or if having

people constantly around the Hall also helped keep solitude at bay.

'Presumably lineage is a sore point for you all around, then,' I said, placing several grass edge pieces in the lower left of the puzzle. 'What with the Hendale Vampire, too? No wonder you were shocked to see that writing on the mirror.'

He grimaced. 'To be honest, I don't much enjoy cashing in old Hendrick for tourists. But it's a part of one's history, so one can't escape it.'

I looked at the wall of paintings again. 'Is he up there? Hendrick?'

'Heavens, no. Simon, the fourteenth Viscount, destroyed every portrait. All that remains is Hendrick's military record and the usual certificates: birth, marriage, death.'

'When he fell from the tower after being cursed by a dead Indian,' I said, remembering the tale. 'I must say I'm not surprised the story draws tourists. How much of it is actually true?'

George busied himself in the jigsaw box, avoiding eye contact. 'The nonsense about a curse, and undead Hendrick killing villagers, is obviously rot. Beyond that it's largely factual, as far as we know. The Hennings have a long history with India, and both Hendrick and Helena spent time there. Hendrick really did fall from the tower.'

'Is that why you don't allow people up there? Does it not have safety railings?'

'Railings are the least of it. Loose stonework, broken

steps, rotten floorboards. We'd be sued into oblivion within a week.'

'So, what do you think *Hendrick Lives* means? Why would someone write that on the mirror?'

'I really don't know, but I do resent the implication that your chap might have been killed by our vampire. It's really beyond the pale.'

He was visibly upset by the subject, and instinctively I placed my hand over his. It felt delicate, with long, slim fingers – most unlike Birch's firm, solid digits. That thought brought me to my senses, and I quickly removed my hand. Now it was my turn to busy myself looking for pieces, avoiding George's eyes.

'I'm sure the police will get to the bottom of it,' I said.

'No doubt,' he agreed. 'The local commissioner is an old friend, and I'm sure he sent his best man. Sad to say, he should probably start with that star of yours.'

'You mean Juliette? Why?'

'I saw her with the young fella, the night before. Over at the old gamekeeper's cottage.'

'There's a cottage? Where?'

'Near the lake. It's a complete ruin, hasn't been used in years, but visitors like it so I left it standing. Juliette and what's his name, Rash . . . ?'

'Yash. Yash Rani.'

'That's him. They were arguing about something. I couldn't hear what, and didn't think it was any of my business.'

This could be a huge piece of evidence. 'When did this happen? What time?'

'Around midnight, I think. They had torches, so I could see them well enough. I meant to ask her about it.'

'I'd recommend against that, George. Tell the police, and let them question Juliette. If you ask her, she'll know it was you who saw them.'

He looked almost amused. 'Surely you don't think I'm in danger?'

'There might be an entirely innocent explanation, but you can't be too careful. Trust me, I have some experience of these things. My . . . friend is a retired Met detective.'

George took my hand. 'Then I'll do as you say. Mum's the word, eh?'

Why had I called Birch my 'friend'? Why hadn't I said 'boyfriend' or 'partner'? Why hadn't I removed my hand yet? Why—

'Georgie, I want to ask you some questions,' said Juliette Shine, sweeping into the room. 'So pull up – oh! I didn't realise I was interrupting.'

George immediately let go of my hand and we both stood in embarrassed silence. Juliette had removed her costume and make-up, and was now in everyday clothes.

'Have you already been to the inn and back?' I asked, wondering where she'd stored her costume.

'What? No, I'm going there in a bit.' She noticed the jigsaw and snorted with derision. 'You know what, I never saw the point. It's not like you took the picture yourself, right? So why bother?'

I took that moment to place a piece of the tree line on the right-hand side, attached to the border. 'This will start you off, *Georgie*,' I said, smiling. 'Now I'll leave you two to discuss . . . whatever it is Juliette wants to talk about. Remember what I said, won't you?'

For a split-second I caught a panicked expression on his face, as if begging me not to leave him alone with her, but it was quickly replaced by his easy, charming smile as he invited her to sit with him by the fireplace. I felt a bit miffed that I hadn't been made the same offer, then reminded myself I shouldn't care and walked out into the corridor.

George's account of seeing Juliette and Yash made me wonder who else might have seen something last night. I decided to call on Walter, the head of security.

CHAPTER FOURTEEN

I flagged down a passing crew member and asked them to radio Walter. Fortunately, he was nearby, having given the police his fingerprints and an account of what we'd all seen at Juliette's trailer.

'Is it true she never locks her trailer?' I asked him. 'I had no idea.'

'I didn't either, but like she says, why bother? Nobody would dare go in without knocking.'

'Someone did. Didn't any of your people see Yash going inside?'

Walter looked horrified at the implication he might be responsible. 'No, and I told that copper the same thing. You lot are in and out of trailers all day. My job is to make sure nobody from the outside gets into the set, and that's what I've been doing. I can't follow everyone around in case you start killing one another.'

'Nobody's suggesting it's your fault,' I reassured him. 'But if you saw anything odd, or someone going into

Juliette's trailer before Yash's death, the police will want to know.'

'None of my crew were anywhere near the trailer before we broke it open, if that's what you mean.'

Was that what I meant? I thought about the timing, and when exactly Yash had been killed. He was definitely alive an hour before, when I'd seen him smoking with Ruby.

'Oh!' I exclaimed, making Walter jump. 'Maybe that's why he was there.'

'Who was where?'

'Yash. He was at the tradesman's entrance, with Ruby, when I arrived just after noon. Maybe he was waiting to see Juliette leave her trailer so he could sneak in.' I mentally retraced my steps. 'Now that I think about it, he can't have been inside for more than half an hour. Juliette finally left her trailer as I was coming out of wardrobe. Five minutes later we began shooting, five minutes after that it was cut short, then around fifteen to twenty minutes later you opened the trailer door.'

Walter shrugged. 'Nobody from my team had been at unit base since around ten o'clock. I do set rounds at night and dawn, and the rest of the day I'm on call. My people generally watch the perimeter, not the trailers.'

That reminded me why I'd sought him out to begin with. 'How far do your rounds take you at night? Do you go into the woods?'

He looked at me like I'd suggested he wear a tutu and skip through the trees.

'Why would I do that? I'm set security, not a gamekeeper.'

'So you don't know the old cottage in the woods? You didn't see anything unusual on your rounds?'

He hesitated. 'Nothing to do with a cottage, but now that you mention it . . . when I finished my late round last night I saw a light in Ms Shine's trailer, which is a bit unusual.'

'I'll say. She normally goes straight back to her room at the inn when we're finished for the day.'

'I assumed she was working late. You sometimes do that, reading scripts and stuff, don't you?'

That was true, but Juliette wasn't in the habit. Walter's observation suggested George was right: Juliette had stayed late to meet Yash in the old cottage, then returned to her trailer.

'What time was this? Was it definitely Juliette?'

'About one in the morning. I didn't actually see Ms Shine; the blinds were down as usual.'

'So how do you know she was in there?'

'Who else would it be? I saw someone moving; there was a shadow on the blinds.'

Walter's radio crackled, and one of his crew called him away. I thanked him absently, wondering why Juliette and Yash would be arguing at midnight in an old, ruined cottage. If they'd had differences about the film, wouldn't they'd have argued during shooting . . . or in her trailer during the day?

A production car drove past me and away, heading out of the estate. I didn't see if it was carrying Juliette, but it reminded me that I should visit her to see what she wanted to talk about. Was it safe to do so? What if she was Yash's killer? But how could she be, if he'd waited until she left to enter her trailer?

Lily could come with me, for protection. She'd been sleeping upstairs for a while, and could continue napping in the boot of my car. Besides, I couldn't leave her. Nobody else even knew she was in my room.

I gasped as these thoughts collided and combined in my mind, forming a new puzzle piece.

Yash had waited until Juliette left to enter her trailer, hadn't he? But what if he hadn't? What if he was already inside at that point, and nobody else knew . . . apart from Juliette, because she'd killed him?

Climbing the stairs to the first floor, I was suddenly overwhelmed by nightmare visions of doggy destruction. Torn curtains, chewed bedposts, ripped pillows, and at the centre of it all Lily – looking simultaneously resentful she'd been left alone, and blessedly innocent because how could anyone possibly think this was all her doing?

My hands trembled as I unlocked the door, closing my eyes in dreadful anticipation of what I was about to see.

I entered and quickly closed the door behind me, remembering Lily's earlier escape, then finally opened my eyes and was shocked when I saw . . .

Nothing at all. Well, nothing unusual. The Jack Russell lay curled up on her dog bed, awoken by my entrance but seemingly having been fast asleep until this moment. Nothing in the room had been destroyed or moved. She hadn't even touched her water. The excitement of the day really had caught up with her, and to be honest I knew the feeling.

Nevertheless, it was now half past three and I didn't want to miss my appointment with Juliette, especially as it was her idea. What could she want to talk to me about? Surely a simple confession wasn't on the cards; she'd go to the police for that. No, it was more likely that she either wanted to confide in me over something secret, or perhaps try to find out what the police already knew.

Was that because she was guilty? I couldn't be certain. My new theory, that she might have killed Yash before she left her trailer, fitted the facts but was pure speculation. The only thing I knew was that she and Yash had met the night before. That would have to be my line of attack.

The moment I reached for Lily's coat and lead, her drowsiness disappeared. She bounded off her bed, lapped up some water, then stood at my feet with her tail wagging and tongue panting. When I clipped the lead onto her collar she shook herself vigorously and immediately turned toward the door.

'Feeling refreshed and ready to defend me from a crazed stake-wielding killer?' I said, laughing nervously.

I was glad I could joke about it now, because I might feel very differently at four o'clock.

CHAPTER FIFTEEN

The Hendale Inn was the sort of place whose one-word summary in a guidebook would be 'charming', an old coaching inn that had been repurposed as a boutique hotel and gastropub. I made sure to toilet Lily in the car park outside before entering. It was still reasonably quiet, the Friday-night crowds not yet in force, so I caught the landlady's eye.

'What can I get you?' she asked.

'Oh, I'm not here for a drink. I'm a friend of Juliette Shine—'

'Here we go. Listen, round here people mind our own business and leave others be, understand? You're not in London now. This is Yorkshire, and we're proud of it.'

Her outburst confused me, but then I guessed she thought I was a fan. Perhaps even a stalker.

'No, no,' I said, forcing a light laugh to try and lighten the mood. 'I'm an actress, too. We're in the same film, over at Hendale Hall.' I decided to try bare-faced flattery. 'Of course, you're too young to recognise me. I haven't been on screen for a while.'

Before I could introduce myself, she did a double-take and gasped, 'Gwinny Tuffel! I didn't recognise you with grey hair.' The flattery had worked, though evidently wouldn't be reciprocated. Ah, well. 'Mind you, I'm not surprised with that young man being killed. Sounds horrible. Now, how come you're not staying here with us too, then?'

'We're all staying at the Hall, but as Juliette's the star she's entitled to a bit of luxury. So they rented a room for her.' I had no idea how luxurious the rooms here might be, but keeping up the flattery couldn't hurt.

'Hmph,' she grumbled. 'You should have asked them as well. Too late now, we're full up, but I wouldn't wish staying with Viscount Vampire on anyone.'

'Oh, um . . . do you know him?'

She pointed at a flyer pinned to one end of the bar. It was a protest flyer, with a picture showing dozens of wind turbines rising from a forest of trees, over which floated a pair of fangs dripping blood. Underneath it read:

Stop the Hendale turbines! Don't let Viscount Vampire get away with it!

'I'm head of the anti-turbine committee,' the landlady said with pride. 'Yes, I know the high-and-mighty Viscount all right. It may be his land, but the view belongs to everyone in Hendale! It's not right, and he won't get away with it!'

This explained the brochure in George's study. Was

he really planning to turn the estate into a wind farm?

'I suppose it's another part of his fundraising scheme,' I said.

'Ruining the landscape scheme, more like. There's no call for it, not round here.'

They do say we live in bubbles nowadays, and I wondered if the landlady's own bubble at the Hendale Inn reflected the wider community. Still, it was really none of my business.

'So about Juliette,' I said, returning to the original subject. 'How do I find her room? She's expecting me.'

The landlady turned her scowl on me and walked away. I thought she was rudely dismissing me, but before I could protest, she stopped at the end of the bar and picked up a phone. She pressed two numbers, waited, then said, 'Ms Shine, are you expecting a visitor? Gwinny Tuffel . . . yes, that's right.' She stood on tiptoe to peer over the bar at . . . my feet? No, at Lily. 'Yes, I'm afraid so. Right, then. I'll send her up.'

Juliette answered barefoot, wearing a voluminous bathrobe and towelling her wet hair. She must have taken a shower as soon as she arrived at the inn, though I couldn't help noticing she'd already re-applied a light layer of make-up.

'Gwinny, come in,' she said with a smile. 'You brought the dog, too. How delightful.' Her forced expression invited an apology, but I declined. As if to justify my thoughts, when Juliette's gaze dropped to the terrier Lily immediately snarled.

'*No*,' I said. 'Behave.'

The room was wood-panelled and quaint, but Juliette wasn't getting that much more than those of us at the Hall. It technically qualified as a suite by having a divider between the bed and lounge areas, but the Hendale Inn was no Four Seasons. I detected a musty note in the air, as if the windows hadn't been opened this century. Juliette had done her best to make it more luxurious by draping gauzy pink cloths over lamps and filling the surfaces with bouquets and cards. While unclipping Lily's lead I noticed a stack of pre-signed headshots on the dresser, ready to hand out to fans.

I tried to think of something complimentary to say and settled on the inevitable, 'How charming.'

'Don't patronise me,' said Juliette wearily. 'It's a dive, but it gets me away from the set – what is she doing?!'

I followed Juliette's gaze to the bed, where Lily's backside stuck out as she scrabbled furiously at something underneath. Terriers do this, and Jack Russells especially; they have a natural instinct to search for rats, rabbits and whatever else might be found lurking in low, dark places.

'Lily, *no*,' I shouted, but she ignored me. Her bottom jiggled from side to side, tail thrashing back and forth as she burrowed herself further into the narrow space. Had she actually found something under there?

There was nothing else for it. I got down on my hands and knees, reached in and grabbed her tail to pull her out. I couldn't imagine Viv had trained her, but like the hunting instinct, a terrier's natural reaction to being pulled by the base of the tail is to go limp and allow themselves to be removed.

Not all of Lily was limp, though. She had something clamped in her jaw, albeit not vermin. It was a box of chocolates.

'Are these yours . . . ?' I asked Juliette, quickly taking the box from Lily and checking she hadn't eaten any. Chocolate and dogs are not a good mix.

'What? No! Someone must have left them there. Honestly, the housekeeping here is terrible.'

A likely story, but I wasn't here for this, and there was no point antagonising her. As Juliette placed the box on her dresser, I picked Lily up and took her with me to a chair by the window. I sat with her on my lap, where she continued to sniff the air.

'No, please, make yourself at home,' said Juliette, still standing. 'Shall I call room service?' I realised I'd taken the room's only chair. Juliette leant against the bathroom door, wrapping the towel around her head into a turban.

'You wanted to talk . . . ?' I said, hoping to move things along.

'Sure. First of all, where were you before everyone crowded around my trailer?'

'What do you mean? I was on set, with you.'

'No, *after* that. While I took a walk to clear my head.'

'I did the same, with Lily, walking around the house.'

She looked sceptical. 'Oh, yeah? I didn't see you.'

'I didn't see you either. Nobody did, in fact. But

other people did see me, including Chloe. I walked with her to your trailer.'

'OK, so who *didn't* you see? I'm trying to figure out who could have got into my trailer and killed Yash.'

We all were, but it was typical of Juliette to assume nobody else had thought of this already. 'More to the point,' I said, 'why was he in your trailer at all? I gather you had an argument . . .'

Juliette looked confused. 'Argument? I hardly knew the kid. We didn't argue.'

'Then why were you with him last night, at the old cottage in the woods?'

Her expression froze. Then she frowned and said, 'I don't know anything about a cottage. Last night I was here, and you can ask my driver if you don't believe me. Who said I was there?'

My phone buzzed. Steven McDonald was calling, and I saw he'd tried to phone me twice while I was driving here, too. I declined the call and switched the phone to silent, as I had more important things to think about . . . such as the fact that I now knew either George or Juliette was lying.

I didn't see any good reason why he might lie, but I could imagine many reasons why she'd deny having a midnight meeting with Yash. But then why was she so confident her driver would vouch for her? I decided to have another chat with the landlady before I left.

'Never mind, I must have misheard,' I said, moving on. 'Who would want to kill Yash, though? Perhaps he had enemies?'

'Who cares?' said Juliette dismissively.

I thought that was harsh. 'Lots of people, not least his family. And if we're going to get to the bottom of things, I believe it's really the most important question.'

She opened her mouth to answer but was interrupted by a buzzing sound from the dresser. It was her phone, vibrating, and from here I could see the caller ID. Steven McDonald.

'He's been trying to get hold of me, too,' I said. 'Maybe you should answer.'

Juliette walked to the dresser, picked up her phone . . . and declined the call. Interesting.

'You don't get it, do you?' she said. 'I was the target, not Yash. It's the only explanation that makes sense. The lights in the trailer were off, and the blinds were down. They waited inside, Yash came in, they thought it was me, and *blam*! Stake through the heart!'

I maintained it was highly unlikely anyone would mistake Yash for Juliette, but decided to humour her. 'Persuade me, then. Who would want you dead? Surely none of your ex-husbands are that mad at you.'

She laughed dismissively. 'They all remarried someone half my age, and last year one of them did the same thing again to wife number two. Hell, that one's even produced pictures of mine since we divorced. There's nothing there.'

'Then what about over here? You've been to England before. Have you made any enemies here?'

'If I have, it's one-sided. I had a bad Jonathan Ross show once, but I hardly think he's been gunning for me ever since.' She paced the room, and her eyes took on a determined glare. 'No, this is someone on set. And I think I might have an idea who.'

'Don't keep me in suspense. Who?'

She tilted her head in the direction of her phone. 'Steven.'

No wonder she hadn't answered his call.

'Why would he sabotage his own film?' I asked. 'As soon as Yash was found, Steven was on to the casting director for a replacement. All day he's been pushing for us to carry on shooting.'

Juliette let out a frustrated sigh. 'I told you, Yash wasn't the target. I had a call with my lawyer last night.'

'OK . . . ? I don't follow.'

'That's because you're not an exec producer,' she snorted. 'But I am, and I bought into the production entity too. Why do you think I'm so determined that everything has to be perfect?'

I hadn't known about this, but it wasn't unusual. Producers usually create a new company specific to each film they make, as a way to protect assets if something goes badly wrong. Juliette buying into that company meant she had a financial stake, no pun intended, in *Draculania*'s success.

She continued, 'After what happened, my lawyer naturally checked the company's insurance position to make sure I'm protected.'

'Naturally,' I agreed, although this was starting to go over my head a little. 'And are you? Protected, I mean.'

'Oh, sure. But not as much as Steven is . . . for a

126

very specific event.' The conspiratorial expression on her face implied a silent *if you know what I mean*, and I did.

'The event of . . . your death?'

'"Ms Shine's inability to complete filming due to unforeseen circumstances", to be precise. Killing me would sure achieve that, wouldn't it?'

'So would breaking your arm.'

She rolled her eyes. 'God save me from amateurs. Think! If I was still alive, I'd know he did it, and the insurers won't pay out for fraud. But if I'm dead, I can't talk, and Steven walks away with a mammoth payout.'

'Hang on, though. I overheard Steven on the phone, earlier, and he was chewing someone's ear off about *not* having insurance.'

'He must have been talking about something else. My lawyer has copies of the paperwork. And Steven's done this before, you know.'

'He's killed an actor to claim on the insurance?'

'No! Keep up, Gwinny. Don't you remember? His last picture fell through, and he was the only producer not to lose his shirt. Who's to say he wouldn't do it again?'

This was brand new information to me. Bostin Jim was always telling me I should pay more attention to industry news.

'But wasn't Steven on set at the time of Yash's death?' I said. 'I saw you talking to him.'

'Before shooting, sure. But not after.'

I thought back and remembered that Juliette was

right. When Chloe had called a break, I'd looked for Steven, but he wasn't there.

'So why wait until now?' I wondered aloud. 'Steven could have shut it down on day one and got the same insurance payout.'

'That would look suspicious, wouldn't it? Instead, like you said, he's doing everything he can to keep production open . . . as far as we know. So if the show *did* shut down tomorrow, nobody would suspect him. Ha!' Juliette looked very pleased with her theory.

By now Lily had curled up asleep on my lap, and I stroked her head while trying to make sense of these strange puzzle pieces. Steven was the one who'd brought this whole project into being, and spent a long time wooing Juliette herself to star. Was it all a ruse, so he could claim a big insurance payout when production closed down? Was that really a motivation for murder?

'Did you mention the insurance to DCI Pierce?' I asked.

'He thinks it's a dead end. What does a flatfoot like that know about movie finance? That's why I've got to solve this myself.'

'. . . I'm sorry, you'll what?'

Juliette peered at me like I was slow on the uptake. Perhaps I was. 'Cracking this case will take smarts and experience. Luckily for you all, I have plenty.'

'Experience?' I thought Juliette had been acting since she was a teenager. 'I don't understand. Were you a police officer before you became an actor?'

Now she looked offended. 'What are you talking

about? No, I played Detective Kingfisher in three features.' She winked and pointed an accusing finger at me. 'You must think I came in here without a hat!'

Dumbfounded, I said nothing.

'God, you people,' she said, exasperated. 'Listen, I didn't win a Golden Globe without gaining insight into the criminal mind, and nobody is more motivated than me to find out who did this. They might try to kill me again! I'm going to figure it out before the cops, and that's a promise. Why'd you think I've been questioning you all this time?'

I shifted in the chair, which woke Lily. She woofed grumpily at nobody in particular. 'Actually, I thought I was questioning you. I agree DCI Pierce seems a little slow, but while I don't think of myself as a detective—'

'Of course you don't,' she interrupted. 'Have you ever even played one?'

'Well, no, but I once had a bit part on *Midsomer Murders*.' I winced at the inadequacy of this comeback even as the words left my mouth.

'Like I said: amateur.' Juliette swept across the room like it was a stage and wrenched open the door. 'Leave now, please. I need to be alone to consider what you've told me.'

I clipped Lily's lead on and let her back down. She immediately pulled towards the open door.

'Perhaps we should try to work together,' I suggested to Juliette as we passed. 'Two heads are better than one.'

Having Birch with me to discuss clues and theories

had been invaluable on the previous occasions I'd found myself searching for a killer. Without him here now, could I still do it?

Juliette was blessedly free of any such self-doubt. 'I don't think that's going to work for me,' she said in a patronising tone. 'Go on back to the Hall, stand aside and watch an expert. You might learn something.'

Resisting the urge to ask if that 'something' was how to lose friends and alienate people, I led Lily downstairs into the bar. It was slowly filling up with Friday-night patrons.

'One for the road?' asked the landlady as I entered.

'No, thank you, but I wonder if you could confirm something. Were you here last night?'

'Of course. I live in the old stables. Full-time job, this.'

'So you remember Juliette being here? She came back in the evening?'

'I do. Why?'

I thought on my feet. 'I wondered if she, um, had a visitor that night. I came back from set to find my husband gone, you see. When he finally returned he said he'd been for a drive, but . . .'

I've never been the world's best improv actor, and it was a ridiculous story. But it was plausible enough for the landlady, who nodded and said, 'Miss Shine was definitely in. I remember seeing the light on in her room. But I can't swear to a visitor.'

'Don't you see everyone coming in and out, through here?'

'There's a late-night entrance round the side and all residents have a key. Saves them waking me up at two in the morning, doesn't it?'

'I see. Thank you anyway.' I turned to go.

'Kick him in the balls for me when you get home!' the landlady cried as I walked Lily out to the car park.

CHAPTER SIXTEEN

Driving back to Hendale Hall, I barely noticed the beautiful sunset over the western moors, the shadows cast by the endless drystone walls, or the sheep busily chewing grass in the steep valleys. I was preoccupied with how Juliette could have slipped out of the inn without being seen.

She could have left a light on, then used the side door to leave, secretly returned to Hendale Hall and met Yash in the old cottage. Privacy is a rare commodity at the best of times on a film set, and clandestine meetings aren't uncommon. If they really had been lovers, she couldn't take him back to her room at the inn. That the landlady was screening visitors suggested locals knew she was staying there, so there'd be no chance of keeping a liaison secret. Perhaps the old cottage presented somewhere more private where they could be alone.

But it still didn't feel right. Juliette couldn't have

known George would see them together, so if she wanted Yash dead, why not kill him there in the cottage? Why wait till daylight, then leave the body in her own trailer? Was it all a big double bluff?

Or was she right to accuse Steven? With the lights off and blinds down he could have lain in wait, intending to kill his Hollywood diva for the insurance money . . . but instead killed Yash by accident.

I was still amazed at Juliette playing whodunit. Detective Kingfisher, indeed! It's true that inhabiting a role gives you insight into the character's mindset, and she would have done 'ride-alongs' with real police as part of her research for those films. But it was a far cry from solving a case herself. I might not have been a screen sleuth, but by this point I'd solved two murders, both of which had baffled the police, thanks to my natural talent for puzzles. I was determined to get to the bottom of this before Juliette.

Approaching the Hall, DCI Pierce's words came to mind: 'the boundary walls are hardly Mount Everest'. I hadn't previously given it much thought, but driving past them now, I saw how right he was. Trees and bushes grew up and over the walls in many places, and some sections weren't even all that high. I decided to check one particular piece of the puzzle.

The security guard at the gate was prepared to wave me through with a nod, but I stopped and lowered the window.

'Could you check something for me? I'm trying to win an argument with Ruby,' I lied.

'What's up?'

'Did Juliette leave late yesterday? Around nine o'clock in the evening?'

He flipped a page over on his clipboard and shook his head. 'Thursday . . . no, she left at seven.'

'Really? You're sure she didn't come back?'

'Positive. You did; we've got you returning at eight-twenty, and some equipment trucks at half-nine, but nothing more for talent. Why, did Ruby think she was still here?'

'No, I did. But I must have been wrong. Thanks.'

I drove on into the estate. It was a bit embarrassing to make up a lie where I was in the wrong, but I couldn't risk Ruby telling him she'd said nothing of the sort.

As I drove under the oaks and around the lake, I further considered Juliette's possible deception. She was still in good physical shape, and I now knew the estate walls were climbable. What if she'd been taken to the inn by her production driver, as the records showed . . . but later snuck out via the unmonitored side entrance and caught an anonymous taxi back to the estate? Then she could climb over the wall to meet Yash, and nobody would be any the wiser.

I squeezed my Volvo into a narrow parking space between two trucks, then let Lily hop down from the boot. On the other side of the police cordon, Needles and his assistant wheeled racks of costumes towards the tradesman's entrance, under the watchful eye of a uniformed officer. Lily barked at them a couple of times, then an angry voice yelled: 'Where have you been? Why is nobody answering their phone? Where's Juliette?'

Steven was in his usual state: with phone in hand. I checked my own and saw more missed calls from him while I'd been driving.

'Sorry, I set it to silent. I've just come from the inn, actually, and I don't think Juliette is taking calls. I'm sure she'll be back tomorrow.'

'She's at the inn? But we need to work out a new schedule! She doesn't have a call sheet!'

'Then text her one, and send her driver over in the morning.' I couldn't help thinking that he wasn't behaving like someone trying to tank the production. 'There are only so many scenes we can film without a Luke, anyway.'

He groaned, and some tension left his shoulders. 'It's not that, it's – well, never mind. You're right, we can sort it out tomorrow and put all this business behind us.'

'I wouldn't go that far. We still don't know who killed Yash, and the police won't leave until they find out. I see they're letting you remove costumes at last, though. Have Fi and Pri been able to get their equipment as well?'

'Soon, they said. The police are going over everything for forensics, though God knows what they expect to find. Everyone's fingerprints and DNA will be everywhere anyway.'

The same thought had occurred to me when DCI Pierce declared his intention to search the trailers. We were all in and out of them so often that I couldn't imagine the investigators finding anything conclusive. Still, the police had to follow procedure.

I didn't, though.

'It's Lily's feeding time,' I said. 'Why don't we go up to my room, and we can talk while I sort her out?'

Actually I had no idea what her regular feeding times were. Previously I'd turned up at Viv's house each morning and evening to walk the dog, leaving everything else to her owner. But Steven didn't know that, so he agreed and we went inside. As we mounted the main stairs I saw Needles stride past in the direction of the tradesman's entrance, presumably returning to fetch more costumes. Past him, though, something else caught my eye: Angela and Zayn, talking by a window. They stood close to one another and looked friendly. Stand-ins naturally hang out together, so it might be perfectly innocent, but I wasn't taking anything at face value.

I didn't have time to think about that now, though. We reached my room, and Steven sat on the bed while I dealt with Lily. I refreshed her water and forked a pouch of wet food into her bowl. She was so eager that I almost had to hold her back with one hand while I did, but a few sharp cries of '*Ah!*' got the message across clearly enough. Viv might not care about controlling her terrier, but I did. Finally I said, 'Good girl, *go on*,' and Lily fell on the bowl like a dog demented.

During all this I tried to think how I could broach the subject of the insurance with Steven, but ultimately decided not to. Not yet, anyway. Even if Juliette's lawyer was right that he'd taken out a large policy against her incapacitation, it didn't prove he'd tried to kill her and he'd brush it off as standard policy. I took a different tack.

'The police asked me if I saw anyone go into Juliette's trailer,' I said, which wasn't true at all. 'Before Yash, I mean. I was on the other side of the house, though. How about you?'

'They never asked me, but I was on set anyway.'

'At video village?'

He nodded. 'But then Juliette screwed it up, didn't she, and stormed off. Honestly, her agent needs to sort her out before she costs us a fortune in overrun. You lot have no idea how close to the edge we are on this show. Every tantrum by Little Miss Sunshine puts us further behind schedule, and meanwhile I've got the financiers constantly on the phone wanting to know why she's being such a problem and how we're going to fix it.'

'You were the one who wanted to cast a big Hollywood star,' I reminded him. 'But you can't recast her now, especially since she bought into the film entity.' I threw in that last to confirm what Juliette had told me, and it worked.

'Too bloody right.' He nodded. 'Like an albatross around my neck. I keep telling myself it'll be worth it in the end.'

'I'm sure it will be,' I said. 'We have to hope someone saw something that gives the police what they need to find the killer.'

Steven snorted. 'They should look at His Nibs, for a start.'

'The Viscount? What do you mean?'

'I saw him arguing with Yash yesterday morning, in the house. No idea what about, before you ask, but it got heated. They were in that private corridor when I walked past. I heard the Viscount say, "Never – over my dead body," and then he poked Yash in the chest.'

'That doesn't make sense,' I said. By now Lily had licked her bowl clean, and was doing circles in her bed before curling up to sleep. 'It's Yash who's dead, not him.'

'Well, that's what I heard. Then the Viscount stormed off, and Yash went upstairs. They didn't see me,' he added, slightly smug.

'Have you told the police?' I asked, wondering if George might have told them himself. Probably not, as it sounded quite damning.

Steven scoffed. 'I'm not going to accuse the man whose house we're filming in. If it got back to him, he'd throw us out on our ear. Bad enough we've lost one of the biggest names on the show. We were lucky to get Yash in the first place.'

'I did wonder about that. Your casting director deserves a raise.'

'Why? Nothing to do with her. Yash and I had been discussing a different project, but he wasn't interested in *Draculania*. Then, one day, he suddenly was. Practically begged me for the part of Luke. It was the perfect role for him.'

'What brought on that change of heart?'

'It wasn't long after I secured financing for his next picture,' he said with a shrug. 'One good turn deserves another.'

'A shame you had to bump Zayn, though.'

'Not really a bump. Yes, Zayn was on the shortlist, but so were half a dozen others. In fact, if Yash hadn't taken the part, we wouldn't need an Asian stand-in and Zayn wouldn't even be here. Now he's lobbying for the part again, of course.'

I remembered Zayn storming into the house, demanding to know where Steven was. 'Is that why he was looking for you earlier? He seemed angry.'

'All afternoon he's been on at me about it. He's persistent, even though I told him it's a poisoned chalice and we should probably cast someone who looks nothing like Yash.'

I blinked. 'Darling, that's a terrible idea. Replacing a person of colour with a white actor will have the papers on you before you know it.'

Steven huffed. Evidently this thought hadn't occurred to him. 'You might be right. I'll have to talk to casting about that.'

'In Zayn's favour, he already knows the lines, and everyone on set.' I didn't mention my earlier suspicion that he might have killed Yash to get the part. 'You could do worse.'

Lily was now quietly snoring, so I took her food bowl into the bathroom to wash in the sink. But I was missing an important ingredient.

'Rats,' I said. 'I'll have to borrow some washing-up liquid from the staff. Come on, let's go while she's asleep.'

'I should be supervising Needles and the girls anyway,'

said Steven, standing. 'I swear, this show has aged me ten years. I'll be damned if I let it all go to waste.'

'I'm glad to hear it,' I said. 'Let's hope tomorrow goes better, shall we?' I ushered him out into the corridor and followed, making sure to lock the door.

'Could it go any worse? Don't answer that,' he grumbled and walked ahead of me down the stairs.

I hung back, letting him go on while I considered the two new puzzle pieces I had. I'd need to ask George about that argument, of course. But now I also knew Steven had lied about being on set when Yash was killed.

Neither I nor Juliette had seen him there, but that didn't prove anything. A working film set is loud, chaotic, and full of people. It's easy to miss someone. But Steven's description of what had happened during that scene was all wrong.

Juliette screwed it up and stormed off, he'd said. In ninety-nine per cent of cases where someone messed up a scene in this film, that would be correct. But not today. It was *Ruby* who'd screwed up, causing the break in filming. If Steven had been on set, he'd have known that.

So where was he really?

CHAPTER SEVENTEEN

I reached the foot of the stairs and stopped, having no idea where the kitchen was. I hadn't noticed a green baize door anywhere while I'd been here, and couldn't see any staff around to ask. I wondered if George was still about; the gloom of dusk enveloped the house, but he might still be in his private rooms. As I walked down the corridor, I encountered Needles coming the other way in a hurry.

'Is the Viscount down there?' I asked him. 'Or any house staff?'

'No room for them now,' he said. 'We've taken over, since the police still won't let us in our trailers.'

'Oh, that's generous of him. Next best thing, I suppose.'

'If you say so. Now, if you're looking for staff, why not try the kitchen?'

He dashed off before I could explain the logical conundrum of that suggestion, so I walked on to the study where I'd left my costume. I planned to collect it and take it to wherever Needles had set up his racks.

When I entered, though, I laughed because the racks were already here. This was the very room George had given to Needles for a temporary wardrobe. All I had to do was take the costume from the corner chair and hang it up.

'What's funny?' said Angela, entering behind me. 'I was passing and heard you laugh,' she added, though I didn't think I'd been especially loud.

I explained the coincidence with where I'd left my costume earlier. 'Hardly side-splitting, I know, but we could all do with something to cheer us up at the moment. Including you, I imagine. Your bad omens about this place turned out to be true.'

She nodded glumly. 'I know you all think I'm silly. But ever since we arrived I felt there was something evil about this place. You wouldn't listen to me.'

Angela looked upset and vulnerable, bringing home to me how young she was. As an actor you get so used to sets filled with people of all ages running around doing their job at maximum speed and stress levels, not to mention how young directors seem nowadays, it's easy to forget not everyone is your contemporary. I was a veteran actress in my thirties before Angela was even born.

'What was it you saw in the trees this morning?' I asked. 'You wouldn't tell me at the time.'

She didn't want to tell me now, either. But I let the question hang, as she ran her hands through the racked costumes, and eventually she relented.

'I saw a spirit,' she said quietly. 'Moving in the shadows.'

'Could it have been . . . an animal, or a person?'

She fixed me with a glare. 'Then I would have said so, wouldn't I? I knew you wouldn't believe me.' She turned to go.

'Wait, please,' I said. 'I'm sorry, I – well, given the timing I wonder if you might have seen Yash's killer. It wasn't that long before we found him, remember.'

'How could I forget?' Angela snarled. 'But of course it wasn't his killer. I would have recognised Ruby.'

That knocked me for six. 'You think Ruby killed Yash? Why?'

'Because she's jealous of Juliette, of course.' Seeing my confusion, she explained, 'That's who she was waiting for. But Yash walked in, and she killed him by mistake, like Juliette said.'

'Did you see Ruby go into the trailer?'

'No, but it's obvious. I heard her on the phone, asking how long it would be until Juliette was back.'

This was a bombshell. I had to make certain.

'When was this? Can you remember exactly what she said?'

'Before we started filming. You were in make-up and Chloe called everyone to set, to be ready for whenever Juliette came out of her trailer. It was still foggy, and I don't think Ruby saw me, but she was walking around unit base. I heard her say, "Why can't you just tell me? It's a simple bloody question, I only want to know how long she'll be away." She was whispering, but shouting, if you know what I mean. Is there a word for that?'

'No, that describes it well enough. Do you know who she was talking to? Who would know how long Juliette would be away from her trailer?'

Angela thought about that. 'I don't know. Her agent, maybe? Look, everyone knows Ruby wants to play Draculania, even though she wouldn't be as good. No offence to your friend,' she added, 'but her eyes are filled with jealousy.'

That was true enough. I'd known Ruby for more than thirty years. She was definitely ambitious and even bitchy at times. But would she really murder the leading lady to take her part?

Then again, I'd been prepared to believe Zayn might have done it over the role of Luke. Perhaps it was time to check my own unconscious sexism.

How long she'll be away . . . had Ruby messed up the library scene deliberately? But how could she have known Juliette would take a walk instead of returning to her trailer? Ruby had been as shocked as the rest of us when we found Yash inside. Or was that the fake reaction of a seasoned actress?

My head was working overtime, trying in vain to form all these oddly-shaped puzzle pieces into a picture that made sense.

George accused Juliette, Juliette accused Steven, Steven accused George, and now Angela accused Ruby. I certainly felt more informed about everyone's grievances and dirty laundry, but no closer to knowing what had really happened. What next? Was someone at this very moment accusing me to DCI Pierce?

I tried to put it out of my mind. This wasn't even why I'd come downstairs.

'Do you by any chance know where the kitchen is?' I asked.

Angela nodded. 'Of course. Fi and Pri are setting up there.' She gave me directions, and I left her amongst the costumes in the impromptu wardrobe room. I wondered if George would ever have a chance to finish his jigsaw.

CHAPTER EIGHTEEN

Fi and Pri's temporary workstation was set up in a corner of the main kitchen. It lacked natural light but was brimming with power outlets, so they'd corralled some daylight-temperature lights from the set, diffused them with softboxes, and used those to light their subjects.

'Very impressive,' I said, admiring their handiwork. On the work surface in front of the single chair stood a framed mirror, taken from somewhere else in the house and propped upright. In front of the mirror, hair and make-up kits stood open. 'I'm glad the police let you have your kit back, anyway.'

Fi nodded. 'They inspected them first, but obviously there was nothing to find.'

I had to agree. It was hard to imagine how make-up brushes and hairspray might have helped someone kill Yash. Then again, that very unlikeliness could make it an ingenious scheme. If they didn't know what they were looking for, the police's forensic inspection might have overlooked something important, and now the evidence had been smuggled out from under DCI Pierce's nose.

I suddenly realised I was contemplating whether Fi and Pri might have done the deed, and my mind was beginning to spin again. It had been a long day.

'I hope the police find whoever did it soon,' said Pri. 'I mean, it could be anyone. We might be standing right next to them and never know.' Her hand flew to her mouth. 'It could even be you, Gwinny.'

I opened my mouth to protest, but Fi picked up the train of thought.

'No, Gwinny was walking her dog. Although she might have killed him, then ran back into the house for the dog, then out again with time to spare. You're fit enough,' she added, looking me up and down.

'Actually, I'm not really in the best shape—' I tried to say, but Pri talked over me.

'Nobody would have seen you in the fog,' she said. 'It was really thick earlier.'

Worrying as this new direction of conversation was, she made a good point. The fog had been thick enough that I could only just make out Chloe standing at the door of Juliette's trailer while I'd been talking to Needles. If not for her pink bum bag, I might not have identified her at all.

'You're right,' I said, looking from one to the other. 'The fog was so thick that I couldn't see your trailer, for example.'

'We didn't do anything,' Fi squeaked.

147

'I'm sure you didn't,' I reassured her. 'Let's hope the police agree. Now, if you'll excuse me, I came in for some washing-up liquid.'

I took the stairs again, now with a bottle of Fairy in hand (thanks to a friendly cook) and paranoia in mind (thanks to Fi and Pri). If they could suspect me of being the killer, so could DCI Pierce. It was a matter of time before he questioned me. I ran through my alibi. First, Steven came to my room; then there was George, who caught Lily when she tried to run outside; then I saw Steven again, arguing on the phone (but had he seen me?); next I passed the crew, standing outside the library window; then I ran into Chloe . . .

I opened my bedroom door and walked into a snowstorm.

No, not snow. *Down.*

Feathers filled the air, making it hard to see Lily perched on the bed with the remains of a pillow in her mouth. Caught in the act, she stood frozen to the spot, staring defiantly up at me. Then she dropped the fabric remnant and barked. Whether she was inviting me to join in, or implying this was obviously my fault for leaving her alone, I couldn't tell.

I quickly closed the door to hide what had happened and frowned deeply at Lily. '*Bad girl,*' I said, and thrust a finger in the direction of her bed. She tried to stare me out, but I'm an old hand. Eventually she dropped her head and hopped onto her bed, circling a few times before curling up once again and looking sorry for herself.

'Don't look like that,' I said. 'If nothing else it should be extra comfy now it's covered in feathers.' The damage appeared to be two shredded pillows, tooth marks in my handbag on the bedside table, and – the final insult, now reaching my nostrils – a small poo on the bathroom floor. Frankly it looked so small I wondered if she'd forced it out in protest rather than actually needing to go. At least the bathroom was easy to clean, and I could simply flush the offending pile away.

So, I did just that, then gathered all the feathers into a laundry bag (though I suspected I'd be finding them in unexpected places for a while) and finally washed up Lily's food bowl, the reason I'd left her in the first place.

All the while I told myself off for abandoning a dog in a strange room, in a strange place, surrounded by strange noises and scents. I'd hoped she'd sleep through my absence after eating, but she must have woken up and panicked. Thank goodness I'd already removed my costume. I dreaded to think how much those pillows might cost, but hopefully Steven could be persuaded to cover it from the production coffers. Surely the money he'd saved by putting us all up here instead of in local hotels would be enough for a couple of pillows.

After cleaning, I sat down next to Lily's bed. She gave me a disapproving side-eye and a perfunctory *woof*, but her heart wasn't in it. I told her she was a good girl for staying in her bed and gently stroked her soft, smooth head and ears. Minutes later she was asleep again, and after all that exertion I felt done in myself.

Stifling a yawn, I lay on the bed and propped myself

up on the sole remaining pillow. I pulled out my phone and found myself automatically calling Tina Chapel. I decided I must have been mistaken when I imagined seeing her at Birch's house this morning, which already felt half a lifetime ago. Tina was always good for a funny story about a showbiz party or high-end restaurant outing to make me laugh, and right now I could do with it.

'Sweet pea,' she said, answering. The background told me she was at Hayburn Stead, her country home. Normally that meant she was chilling out, but this evening she looked flustered. 'Can I call you back? Not the best time.'

'There's a lot of it about,' I replied, remembering that Birch had said the same earlier. 'Everything all right?'

She twitched away from something off-screen. 'What? Yes, of course, but I'm . . . busy. Spera! Oh, for goodness' sake. The dogs want to say hello.'

The view dropped as Tina crouched, and the screen was quickly filled with two large twitching black noses. Spera and Fede, her sibling Salukis, sniffed at the screen.

'Hello, you two,' I called out, smiling. 'Are you being good dogs for your mother?'

Spera barked enthusiastically in response while Fede kept sniffing, perhaps hoping to detect treats in my pockets through the screen.

Suddenly Lily sprang up onto the bed and stood with her nose to my phone, furiously wagging her tail at the sight of the Salukis but wise enough not to bother trying to sniff them.

I laughed at this unorthodox doggy encounter, but my amusement turned to baffled surprise when yet another dog joined the fray beside Spera and Fede – a suspiciously familiar black Labrador. It barked along with Spera, at which point the Salukis stopped and turned away haughtily as if their game had been spoilt by the lower classes.

'Ronnie?' I said, knowing it must be him. 'Tina . . . is Birch there with you?'

Tina sighed and turned the phone to reveal Birch standing nearby, waving awkwardly.

'Evening, ma'am,' he called out. 'Just, um, visiting. Let the dogs have some fun together, you know.'

Considering the contempt in which Spera and Fede held Ronnie, I had difficulty picturing much 'fun' being had.

'Are you *sure* there isn't something you should be telling me?' I said, not directed at either Birch or Tina in particular. They both shook their heads and protested innocence.

'No, absolutely not—'

'Sweet pea, how could you—'

'Stopped by, spur of the moment—'

Feeling cheated of my hope that this call would cheer me up, I dismissed their protests.

'Yes, well, have fun then. Love to the dogs, but I must be going.'

I ended the call and sat motionless on the bed. How naive I'd been, to think my own eyes had deceived me when I saw Tina at Birch's. Of course it was her. How could I not recognise my own best friend?

She wasn't acting like much of a best friend now, though. And what about Birch? It had taken him years to move on after his wife's death, finally removing his wedding ring and taking my hand in his, but what had I unleashed? Had he swung too far in the other direction, feeling so footloose and fancy-free that he now flirted with other women?

No, no, this was no good. Tina had known Birch as long as I had, and within days of meeting we'd all been through the wringer together when her groom-to-be was murdered. Why shouldn't friends pop round to see one another . . . at short notice on a Friday night . . . and not mention it until they were caught out . . .

Stop it, Gwinny. I'd drive myself mad at this rate. I no longer felt remotely tired, and what I wanted more than anything was some fresh air.

'Come along, Lily,' I said, reaching for her coat. 'Let's take a walk.'

CHAPTER NINETEEN

Evening mist clung to the ground, grasping at our feet before fading into shadow. The crisp air gave both Lily and I a second wind, and when we first stepped outside she eagerly pulled me into the woods surrounding the lake. This was prime hunting time for a dog like her, so I took out my torch and let the terrier run free to burn off her renewed energy.

The house had been unusually quiet as we left. Now within the woods the only sound was the gentle rustling of trees. I hadn't yet seen another soul, and that was perfectly fine by me.

Lily ran across my path, sniffing furiously, occasionally fetching sticks and dropping them at my feet. I tracked her with my torch beam, watching her dive into the undergrowth, and hoped sticks were all she found. Either way it was good for her to have a free roam like this. I doubted Viv was in the habit of walking through local woods alone in the dark.

Suddenly Lily ran in front of me, stopped, sniffed the air – then shot off directly ahead. I raised my torch beam to find what had caught her attention and gasped when I saw a jagged shadow rising from the ground. Then I moved the light over it and recognised it as a wall, half of its stones having fallen away to leave a broken window pane jutting into the night.

The old ruined cottage.

Lily scampered inside, through an open doorway in which a rotting door hung from rusted hinges. I followed, casting my torch beam around. It really was a ruin, with crumbling stone, creeping moss and crunching glass underfoot. Whole sections of the roof were missing and broken tiles lay on the ground. How long had the cottage stood like this? A long time, surely. I briefly took some comfort in knowing that, no matter how much work my house in Chelsea needed, at least it still had all four walls and a roof to keep out the weather.

Seeing the broken roof tiles also made me think of Lily and her exposed paws. The last thing I wanted was to spend the rest of my night removing glass shards and bandaging her pads.

'Lily, where are you? Lily, *come.*'

I heard her moving in response, but couldn't locate her with my torch.

Seeing the state of the broken, mouldering house up close as the light moved over it, I wondered again why Juliette and Yash had come here. In its favour, the cottage was an easy landmark to find in the dark and they could be sure nobody else would be in the woods at night. Well, nobody except an old woman and her dog. And the estate owner, who'd seen them, which was bad luck for them . . . but good for us.

Did it matter, though? Was there any connection here to Yash's death, or was it merely a midnight tryst that turned into an argument? If I'd been invited out here for a knee-trembler, I'd have complained too when I saw the place.

Or was the argument about something else? Did Yash have a hold over Juliette, or vice versa? Surely he was too young to have accumulated the sort of secrets worth being blackmailed over. Juliette had more than enough, but she was already considered a diva. It was hard to imagine what might be so bad she was willing to kill to keep it secret.

My second wind had quickly died down. I yawned, thinking I should stop going around in circles and sleep on it. But when I swung the torch around to find and retrieve Lily, there was still no sign of her.

'Lily,' I called out, hoping she hadn't run off. It was one thing to wander through trees in the dark with her by my side, but quite another to do it alone. *Though she be but little she is fierce*; Jack Russells often suffer from delusions of size, behaving and barking like they're enormous wolfhounds rather than diminutive terriers.

Something rustled. A twig snapped somewhere in the trees.

'Lily, is that you? *Come here*, girl.'

No response, not even a bark. Small stones clattered somewhere in a corner of the cottage. Were there rats in here? I shuddered at the thought, but it would be better than another person skulking out there in the woods, watching. Hunting.

I held my breath, listening to the rapid thud of my heartbeat.

Stones crashed to the ground. I whirled round, letting out a yelp. Something moved in the shadow of my torchlight—

Lily scampered out from behind a loose pile of stones with something gripped between her teeth. I exhaled with relief, crouching to meet her.

'What's that you've got, girl? Come on, let's see. *Lily, drop.*' At the last firm command, she finally did.

I'd feared a rodent, but in fact it was a photograph . . . or half of one. The right-hand edge was ragged and burnt. Shining my torch on it revealed a picture taken at night, of a besuited man with grey hair. I didn't recognise him. He smiled, and from the position of his body it seemed he was posing with his arm around someone. I say seemed because they were no longer visible; the burn had obliterated the other person from the image, making it impossible to even tell if it was a man or woman.

Was this what Yash and Juliette had been arguing about? Scratching Lily's ears, I wondered at the photo's origins.

I tucked it into my coat pocket and clipped on her lead, ready to return to the house. This had been enough investigating in the dark for both of us. But then I saw something else from the corner of my eye, small and bright on the ground.

A discarded cigarette.

Not a butt, used and extinguished under heel. It was a whole unlit Marlboro, damp but surprisingly clean. It didn't take a forensic expert to guess that the lack of moss and dirt meant the cigarette hadn't been here long.

Did Yash smoke this brand? I didn't know, but Ruby might. I added it to the burnt photo in my pocket, wondering what it could mean. It might confirm Yash's recent presence, which put Juliette in a tight spot. She'd denied they met here, but how could she explain this? Perhaps Yash had dropped a cigarette while they fought. But the photo had been in a different place. If he'd dropped that too, wouldn't he have noticed it was gone? Or did he only realise later, and thought he'd dropped it somewhere else?

Like, say, Juliette's trailer.

Another twig snapped, closer this time. Something, or someone, was in the woods . . . and drawing nearer.

CHAPTER TWENTY

'Hello?' I called out. 'Who's there? Show yourself!'

If I'd had keys with me I would have held them between my fingers, the lifelong habit of women alone at night. But they were in my bag, and my bag was in my room. Instead I bent down and picked up a piece of rotten wood, embedded with several rusty nails, holding it ready to strike. Then I raised the torch above my head to point straight ahead of me. Anyone looking wouldn't be able to identify me behind the light, and would also hopefully think I was a lot taller.

Then again, I'd called out to them without even trying to disguise my voice.

Unless they were prepared to climb over a half-fallen wall or through a broken window, the doorway through which I'd entered was the only way in. I kept my torch trained firmly on it while Lily strained at her lead, coiled like a spring.

A figure stepped into the doorway, wielding their

own torch with its blinding beam turned on me. Feeling significantly less brave than I had five seconds ago I staggered back, dropping the piece of wood. Lily barked, sounding like the wolfhound she imagined she was, but the figure advanced, and as the breeze changed I caught the sharp, acute scent of . . .

Extra-strong mints.

'Ms Tuffel? What are you doing out here?'

I peered into the darkness. 'DCI Pierce? I could ask you the same question.'

'You could,' he replied, 'but I asked first.'

I lowered my torch and shone the light on Lily. 'Dogs need walks, Inspector.'

'Not in a ruined old cottage in the dark, they don't,' he said, unimpressed. 'Let me guess, you once played a famous detective as well?'

Tempted as I was to say 'yes' for the hell of it, I opted for truth. 'No, but I assume you've been talking to Juliette.'

'The constabulary takes a dim view of amateurs involving themselves in police matters, Ms Tuffel. I told Ms Shine the same thing, and got an earful for my troubles.'

That sounded about right. 'I assure you, I'm not trying to obstruct or interfere with your investigation. I came out here because George – the Viscount, I mean – mentioned he saw Juliette arguing with Yash in this cottage late last night.'

'So rather than informing me of this, you decided to come out here yourself because . . . ?'

'It's late, and I didn't want to wake you up for something that might turn out to be nothing,' I said, improvising. He gave me a sceptical look, but he couldn't prove otherwise, could he? Then a thought struck me. 'Hang on, did he tell you the same thing? Or perhaps Juliette mentioned it? Is that why you're here?'

'Ms Tuffel, need I remind you that you're also a suspect in this matter? We're as certain as we can be it was someone involved with the film, and you and Ms Shine have been seen to argue.'

'Says who? When?'

'Do you deny it?'

'No,' I admitted, 'but Juliette argues with everyone from Chloe to the clapper loader. I sometimes think she does it deliberately to maintain her diva reputation. So you can't suspect me just because we've had the odd word, or you'd have to haul in the entire crew for questioning.'

He said nothing, which made me realise that was precisely what he would do.

'Now look here,' I said, feeling a sudden urge to prove my innocence. 'From the moment I arrived on set today to the time we found Yash I was never alone. First I was in hair and make-up, then wardrobe, then I ran to set with Ruby. When we took a break I saw Angela, then moved Lily's things upstairs, where Steven found me. Next, I ran into the Viscount downstairs, then I passed some crew outside the library window, and finally I met Chloe as she came out of the house's rear. We walked to unit base together, where I chatted with Needles before

160

joining Chloe outside the trailer. So, you see, I couldn't possibly have killed Yash.'

DCI Pierce listened intently, but took no notes, which didn't bode particularly well. I decided to try one last gambit and reached into my pocket.

'This was on the ground over there,' I said, showing him the unlit cigarette. The inspector removed a handkerchief from his pocket to take it from me. I hoped he didn't see my guilty expression as I remembered picking it up with my bare hands.

'Looks fairly recent,' he said. 'But what's the significance?'

'I think it belonged to Yash Rani,' I said, with confidence surpassing my conviction. 'It suggests that George was right, and Yash was out here arguing with Juliette.'

'You said she argues with everyone,' Pierce pointed out.

'Not at midnight, in a ruined old cottage, the night before that same person is killed.'

'Fair enough,' he said, pocketing the handkerchief and cigarette. 'I'll get this checked out.'

'Don't you think it's curious that it's unsmoked? Why would anyone discard an unused cigarette?'

'If this was indeed Mr Rani's, and he was out here at midnight, he may have dropped it in the dark. No point speculating yet.'

'Isn't now exactly the time to speculate?'

He didn't reply, and for a moment all was deathly quiet in the woods. Then he tilted his head and chuckled. 'You were the one who explained why we'd find everyone's fingerprints at the crime scene, weren't you? You were right, by the way. Now you've found this cigarette . . .' With one hand he deftly removed an extra-strong mint from its packet, popped it in his mouth, then held out the packet to me. I declined the offer. 'Your alibi is strong, Ms Tuffel. Some of the people you mentioned have already corroborated your whereabouts. You're clearly observant, and you have access to the people involved in the film in ways that I don't. So here's a thought: you carry on snooping around, and I won't stop you . . . so long as you tell me everything.'

'I wouldn't call it *snooping*,' I protested.

'That's really not the salient part,' he said, sucking loudly on the mint. 'What's important is that you pass on anything you find or overhear to me. Understand?'

'Inspector, my friend Alan Birch was a DCI in the Met for many years.' I weighed up whether or not to tell him Birch and I had caught killers before, but given the police's attitude in those cases I doubted any of them would give me a glowing reference. At least this one was holding out an olive branch. 'I wouldn't dream of withholding evidence. Whatever I find, I'll let you know.'

'Good,' said DCI Pierce, satisfied. 'Now let me walk you back to the house, and we can all get a good night's sleep.'

He did, taking a more direct route that first took us past the lake, then through the trees and back to the house.

'You haven't given your statement yet,' he said. 'Would

you care to tell me what happened this morning, from your perspective?'

I did, from Ruby messing up the scene to finding Yash in the trailer, once again emphasising all the people who'd seen me as I walked Lily. 'Then George pushed us all back outside, and you arrived shortly afterwards,' I finished.

'So the only person alone at the trailer, that you saw, was Ms Churchill.'

'Now that you mention it, yes, but Chloe didn't go inside because she couldn't open the door. That was entirely the problem. Besides, *Draculania* is her big break – a stepping-stone to bigger and better films. She wouldn't risk that by getting the production shut down.'

'Stranger things have happened,' he said, crunching the last of his mint. As we approached the house in silence its imposing, jagged silhouette loomed against the night sky as if to reinforce how right he was.

I felt vaguely guilty for discussing the case with Pierce and agreeing to help him, as if I was somehow cheating on Birch. That feeling was assuaged, though, by knowing that Birch himself was keeping something from me. Two wrongs may not make a right, but they do wonders for the conscience.

That was just as well, because as the DCI bade me goodnight and drove away, to a final round of barks from Lily, I remembered that despite my claims of honesty and reliability, the burnt photograph was still in my pocket.

I told myself it might be unconnected to Yash's death. It could have been out there in the cottage for weeks or months, dropped by anyone. But I didn't really believe that. Some instinct told me it was important.

Why had someone made a printout of this particular photograph? Who was the silver-haired man shown in it? And who was the unknown person he'd been so friendly with, now violently deleted?

Back in my room I removed Lily's coat, laid a towel from the bathroom on the bed, then placed the dog belly-up on it to check her paws for glass. She was very patient, bless her, and while I found a few tiny fragments stuck to her pads, nothing had been large enough to break the skin. I brushed them off and gave each toe a gentle reassuring rub with my fingers. Then I put her on the floor while I shook out the towel over the toilet. By the time I returned she was on her bed, licking her paws.

The moment I removed my own coat and shoes and lay down, though, Lily abandoned her grooming and hopped up with me. I stroked her soft, short fur absent-mindedly while I considered the multitude of puzzles this week had presented and remembered the warmth of George's hand earlier. Then I remembered the look on Juliette's face as he invited her to sit with him by the fireplace. Had it been . . . *triumph*?

Well, the shoe was on the other foot now. DCI Pierce had recognised my talent for spotting evidence, not hers. It would take more than a Golden Globe to uncover the truth of this case. Clearly, I'd misjudged the inspector upon first sight. Not every policeman could be Birch, after all.

I cursed my own overactive brain. Less than an hour ago, in this exact position, my two best friends had blatantly lied to me. But what right did I have to get worked up about Birch spending time alone with Tina, if I was going to moon over a lonely minor noble who smiled at me?

'Come on, Lily. *Bedtime.*' I stood and placed her back on her dog bed. She kept one eye on me as I changed into my pyjamas, brushed my teeth and pulled back the sheets.

Three down feathers stared back at me, remnants from Lily's earlier escapades. As I removed them, she sprang to her feet and once again leapt onto the bed. She stood there, staring at me with her tail wagging back and forth, and when I didn't move – waiting to see what she would do next – she scampered up to the sole remaining pillow and flopped down with her head on it, like a human. Her tail continued to wag lazily as she looked up at me.

I laughed and climbed in beside her, pulling the sheets over us both.

'So this is how you sleep at home, is it? I shouldn't be surprised, with Viv being on her own.'

Lily replied with a contented grumble and waggled her stocky body, burrowing herself deeper under the covers. I certainly wasn't going to complain, as the warmth radiating from her was most welcome and comforting in the brisk night. Despite the dearth of pillows, we were both asleep in minutes.

CHAPTER TWENTY-ONE

The next morning, someone had slipped a sheet of paper under my door.

Was it a clue? An anonymous message from someone with a guilty conscience? Perhaps even . . . a confession?

No. It was a call sheet, hastily assembled, informing everyone that we would resume filming this afternoon with Scene Twenty-Eight: the hallway confrontation scene, where Drs Van Helsing and Seward witness Draculania's dark powers with their own eyes for the first time. Most importantly, it didn't involve Luke. Neither did the library scene we'd abandoned yesterday, but I could understand why Chloe wouldn't want to revisit that yet.

It was hard to believe it had been less than twenty-four hours since we found Yash's body. So much had happened since then, and despite a night of deep sleep I was exhausted.

Still, I now had several hours before I was needed in

make-up and wardrobe. Plenty of time to get caffeinated and wake myself up. It was a bright and brisk morning, with no sign of yesterday's fog, so I decided I'd take another look at the old cottage, in daylight this time.

After brushing my teeth and dressing, I put Lily in her coat and led her downstairs. There was a chance I might run into Ruby, too, on her morning jog through the grounds. I'd often seen her running first thing as I drove to Viv's place.

Imagine my surprise, then, when I exited the Hall in time to see Ruby climb out of a production car, covered in mud and with a bandaged hand.

'What on earth happened?' I called out to her. 'I thought you normally ran around the estate.'

Ruby turned, startled to see me. 'Oh, it's you. This is your fault, in a way. You've been talking about how lovely the Dales are, and . . . well, after what happened to Yash . . . I got one of the drivers to take me out to the moor for a jog instead of going around this place again. What do you know, ten minutes from the end I tripped over and gashed my hand on a stone.'

'Ouch,' I said in sympathy. 'I'm sorry that happened, but I hardly think you can blame me. Was it a good run?'

'Oh, yes, lovely. I always look forward to a good bout of tetanus.' She unzipped a pocket in her hoodie, fished out a pack of cigarettes and a lighter and sparked up.

'That reminds me,' I said, ignoring her sarcasm. 'Do you know if Yash smoked Marlboros?'

'Mmm,' she agreed, blowing rings into the cool air. 'I think so, why?'

Something stopped me from telling her what I'd found. I didn't want to believe Angela's theory, that Ruby had killed Yash while intending to do away with Juliette, but I couldn't rule it out.

'Oh, the police found an open pack when they were searching the make-up trailer,' I improvised. 'I knew it wasn't yours, so wondered if it had been his.'

She nodded. 'Unless Zayn's begun copying that too.'

'Copying? What do you mean?'

'Haven't you noticed that he's been imitating Yash more and more since we began filming? First he got his hair done the same way, so he wouldn't have to wear a wig for lighting. Then he bought the same brand of trainers, started wearing the same jeans, and he's been adopting Yash's mannerisms . . . seriously, did all of this pass you by?'

It had. I pride myself on being observant, but principal actors rarely share the set with stand-ins, and their entire job is to hang around the set all day in case they're needed. After a while they become invisible.

A new puzzle piece began to form, vague and shapeless yet insistent.

'Isn't that his job?' I said. 'To look and act like Yash, I mean.'

'Not off-camera,' said Ruby. 'Come to think of it, it might even have been Zayn I saw in the woods yesterday morning, not Yash. I wasn't close enough to tell.'

'In the woods? Was he running, too?'

She sucked on her cigarette. 'No, looking for something. I was jogging, and went by that old cottage not far from the lake. Have you seen it?'

'I know it, yes.'

'And who should I see there but Yash – or maybe it was Zayn, like I say – mooching around, eyes on the ground as if he'd lost something.'

My thoughts returned to the unlit Marlboro, and the burnt photo. Could they have belonged to Zayn, not Yash, after all? The new puzzle piece came into sudden focus, and I wondered: what if it had been *Zayn* that George saw arguing with Juliette, not Yash? The Viscount wouldn't know either man well enough to tell them apart in the dark.

'Yash's trainers were stained with mud, though, weren't they? Much like yours today.' Ruby's entire lower body was spattered with mud, to be honest, but she took my point. 'I remember noticing, when you were stood together at the tradesman's entrance, because he still somehow managed to look elegant.'

'Yes, it's a talent,' she said, preening. I kept my thoughts to myself. 'Maybe I should tell the police. Zayn might have killed Yash to get rid of his competition. Especially if he was up to play Luke before the golden boy came along. They could have had an argument, and Zayn snapped.'

'But why in Juliette's trailer?' I said. 'The rest of us were filming at that time anyway. They could have gone into the woods for a slanging match, where nobody would have heard them.'

'Maybe Juliette was involved in some way. Zayn might have been trying to convince her to back him for the role instead. Steven does whatever she says.'

That was true. For all that the star and producer argued, there was no real question about who was in charge. And that reminded me of something else Angela had told me.

'Speaking of arguments . . .' I said hesitantly, 'who were you shouting at while I was in make-up?'

Ruby looked blank. 'Shouting? What do you mean?'

'On the phone. I gather you were angry at someone, asking "Why can't you just tell me how long she'll be away?" What was that about?'

'Who the hell told you that?'

'It really doesn't matter. But if it had anything to do with Juliette, the police will want to know.'

For a split-second Ruby wore a thousand-yard stare. Then it was gone. 'Oh, that,' she said, waving nonchalantly. 'No, nothing to do with Juliette. My cleaner's gone on holiday without arranging cover, and the agency's been useless about finding a sub. My house is gathering dust as we speak.'

Ruby had never struck me as the most domesticated person in the world, although that would explain why she employed a cleaner in the first place.

'Hang on,' she said, grinding her cigarette under her muddy heel. 'Are you insinuating something? You can't think I killed Yash. I barely knew him; he was a child.'

'He was twenty-four,' I pointed out.

'Yes, like I said. For God's sake, what could a boy that age possibly do to make me want to kill him?'

'Not much,' I admitted. 'But if *Juliette* was the real target . . .'

Ruby surprised me by laughing. 'OK, you've got me there. I'd happily throttle her so I could play Draculania, and you know I'd be ten times better in the role. But before you go running to DCI Pierce about it, remember that I was on set with you beforehand, then smoking at the tradesman's entrance afterwards. I didn't go anywhere near Juliette's trailer, and nobody can say otherwise.'

She turned on her heel and walked into the Hall. Lily barked after her, then turned and pulled me in the direction of the trees.

CHAPTER TWENTY-TWO

Lily darted through the trees and undergrowth, no less motivated in daylight than she had been in the dark, dropping sticks at my feet from time to time. It occurred to me that I hadn't thought about Birch and Tina once since waking. In the cold light of day, my paranoid midnight musings felt silly. I was getting myself in a tizz about nothing.

I decided to call Birch. He was a creature of habit, and at this early hour on a Saturday would normally be walking Ronnie. Sure enough, when he answered I could see he was outside, with blue skies overhead.

'Morning,' he said cheerfully. 'Lovely day for it down here. We're on Shepherd's Bush Green. How is it up there?'

'Chilly but bright,' I said. 'If it had been like this yesterday, Yash might still be alive. I can't help but think his killer took advantage of the fog.'

'Very possible,' he agreed, pausing to pick up and

throw a stick for Ronnie. 'Any closer to figuring out who did it? Does DCI Pierce have anyone's scent?'

'If he does, he hasn't said anything to me.'

I decided not to tell Birch about Pierce's offer of *détente* last night. He might get jealous of me teaming up with another policeman, and he'd definitely tell me off for walking alone at night through the woods with a killer on the loose.

Instead, I told him what I'd learnt so far. Zayn being gazumped for the role of Luke by Yash; the Viscount (I didn't call him George in front of Birch) seeing Juliette and Yash meeting on Thursday night in the cottage; her denial of it, and the landlady's mention of the side entrance; Walter spotting a light in Juliette's trailer that same night, and someone moving around; Juliette's accusation of Steven, trying to kill her for the insurance; Steven's own accusation of the Viscount, whom he saw arguing with Yash; Angela believing Ruby wanted to kill Juliette and take her role; and the cigarette and burnt photo I'd found in the cottage (which I told Birch I'd visited during daylight, so he wouldn't worry). I sent him a picture of the photo, hoping he might recognise the grey-haired man, but he didn't.

'Rum do,' he said, twitching his moustache. 'Too many potential suspects to get a grip. Need to whittle it down. You can rule Ruby out, surely?'

'I don't know. I think she lied to me when I asked her about the phone call Angela overheard. That story about the cleaner is plausible, but I've known Ruby a long time. Something about the way she delivered the line felt . . . well, like a delivery. Acting for an audience of one.'

'Police could check her phone records, you know.'

'Yes, but they'd need a good reason. I doubt "I can't explain why, but I think she's lying" will be enough to persuade DCI Pierce.'

By now Lily and I had reached the lake, after following a stream that burbled up from the ground among the trees. I stood on the shore and took it in. It was several hundred metres across in both directions, surrounded by trees, with a few wooden jetties reaching out over the water and spots reserved for fishing. Reeds and rushes clumped around the edges, and in some places further out as well. Ducks, geese and swans swam lazily on the surface.

'This is lovely,' I said, and held up my phone so Birch could see it.

'Very nice,' he agreed. 'Lily seems to think so, too.'

'What do you—'

I heard a *splash*, and looked over to see Lily dive into the lake.

'Lily, *no*! *Come here!*' I ran to the water, shouting like a madwoman. I didn't even know if Lily could swim, though most terriers do take well to water. 'Birch, I'll have to call you back, sorry.'

He laughed. 'Best of luck.'

Lily had decided some nearby swans looked enticing and was paddling towards them. That worried me. Not on the swans' behalf, because they could fly away if they felt threatened, but the adults were almost twice

174

Lily's size. If they turned on her they could do some real damage.

'Lily, *come*!' I called, standing on the lake shore. She either didn't hear me or couldn't care less. The swans had seen her, slowly turning to watch this small bundle of wet fur splashing towards them. Beset by visions of swan-on-dog violence, I wracked my brains for an answer.

Swimming was out of the question. Even if I could, I wouldn't reach her in time. But I had nothing to tempt Lily back to shore; waving a treat at this distance wouldn't register, not when she was fixated on the swans. I'd have more luck throwing it at her and trying to bonk her on the head.

That was it!

Not bonking her on the head, but throwing something. I could do that. A branch or stick of some kind. Lily had found plenty of them along the way here; how hard could it be? Famous last words, because there was nothing at the shore. I'd have to trek back a good twenty yards to the tree line. Did I have time?

'I say, thinking of a swim?' George walked through the trees, from the direction of the Hall.

'George! Throw me a stick!'

He stopped, confused.

'Quickly! To scare off the swans!'

'Oh, I see,' he said, grasping the situation. He picked up a sizeable stick and tossed it to me. I didn't even try to catch it out of the air, but let it fall at my feet, then picked it up and flung it with all my strength in between

Lily and the swans, a gap growing ever smaller by the moment.

I knew it had worked, because I heard loud splashing followed by the sight of swans flying overhead. That was all I could see, because it turns out throwing a stick for all you're worth while standing on a wet shore is a precarious affair unless you're holding on to something, which I was not. My foot slipped out from under me, dropping me backside-first into the muddy water and knocking the wind from my lungs. The next thing I knew a very wet Lily was standing over me and sniffing at my face, soon joined by George, who thankfully refrained from the sniffing part.

'Need a hand?' He held his out, and I gratefully took it so he could pull me upright.

Trying to maintain my dignity, I took a tissue from my handbag and wiped my hands. 'Thank you, George. How are you?'

'As well as can be, all things considered. I'm used to having people all over the place. Has to be more upsetting for you film people, what? Especially as he was one of your own.'

He placed a friendly hand on my shoulder. Perhaps a little forward, but then yesterday we'd almost held hands. I smiled up at him.

'Let me walk you round the place while you dry off,' he said, the lines on his cheeks deepening as he returned the smile. 'Unless you'd rather come inside, and I'll build you a fire.'

Suddenly I remembered him sitting with Juliette in the

study the day before, and wondered how many different cast members he had his eye on. I took half a step back and said, 'Why don't you show me where you're planning to build all those wind turbines, instead?'

'All the what?' he said, his composure rattled. 'Oh, have you been talking to that awful woman at the inn?'

'I saw a protest flyer while I was there with Juliette,' I said, avoiding details.

He sighed. 'Contrary to what the well-meaning but misguided people of Hendale may tell you, I am emphatically not planning to demolish the estate and build a wind farm. The proposal is for a single turbine, discreetly placed near the south bog where no more than a third of visitors will ever see it.'

'Presumably people in the village will, though.'

'True,' he conceded. 'Gwinny, the future is coming whether we like it or not. That turbine will power most of the house on a good day, saving everyone money, including the National Trust when they take over. Really, I'm disappointed you didn't ask me before believing the protestors.'

I reddened a little at this, partly because he was right, but mostly because I hardly knew him, yet he spoke like I was an old friend who'd hurt his feelings. He was a difficult man to fathom, and perhaps that's why I blurted out, 'Then let me disappoint you further by asking what you and Yash Rani were arguing about.'

If the turbine question had surprised George, this one outright shocked him.

'Have you been *spying* on me?' he asked, outraged.

'So, you don't deny it? "Over my dead body", I believe you said to him?'

His eyes narrowed. Through gritted teeth he said, 'He kept trying to buy one of my classics. An original Porsche 911, as it happens. But I wasn't having it.'

'How much?'

'Come again?'

'How much did he offer for the Porsche? Surely you could use the money.'

'Out of the question,' he snorted. 'That car was a twenty-first birthday gift from my father, and I've kept it humming along ever since. I know people think I'm a foppy old twit, but I appreciate a beautiful engine as much as the next man. I could never part with it.'

'I think you should tell the police. About the argument.'

'I don't see why I should do anything of the sort,' he said, turning to leave. 'You may do as you please, but don't expect any further help from me.'

CHAPTER TWENTY-THREE

Still muddy, and feeling I'd achieved very little so far, I decided that was enough investigating for now. I returned to the house, intending to change and review my sides for this afternoon's shoot. Crew members were working in the entrance hallway, moving equipment and preparing the set. Keeping Lily on a short lead, I skirted around them, heading for the stairs.

Passing the small reception room, though, I heard familiar voices and paused to listen. Juliette and Zayn were in there, discussing something.

No, not discussing. Juliette was *questioning* Zayn.

'I wasn't even there when you found him,' said the young actor.

'Exactly,' said Juliette. 'Kind of a convenient alibi, don't you think?'

'What do you mean, convenient? I wasn't due on set until the afternoon. I was in my room when . . . everything happened.'

'So you say, but can anyone back you up? Did you talk to someone?'

Zayn hesitated. 'I . . . no, because I didn't think I'd need to. Look, for heaven's sake, I didn't kill him! Why would I?'

So, Juliette was accusing Zayn. Now that I looked at him properly, I saw that Ruby was right. He really did dress like Yash.

'I think that's obvious, don't you?' said Juliette. 'Especially now. Everyone knows you wanted the part, kid.'

She was much more blunt and forthright in her questioning than I would have been. At least, I hoped so. I was suddenly horrified that I might sound like that to other people. Regardless, she'd gone too far. Zayn turned on his heel and stormed out, almost running over Lily and me in the process.

'Talk some sense into her, will you?' he said to me. 'She thinks this is one of her stupid Detective Kingfisher films.'

Juliette looked smug. 'Did you get all that, Gwinny? Want me to write it down for you, or did you eavesdrop OK?'

'You must have forgotten your hat,' I said, mangling her Kingfisher catchphrase. Damned if I could remember how it went. 'Juliette, leave the poor boy alone. He wouldn't kill Yash just to take his part . . . would you, Zayn?' I neglected to mention that I'd had the same theory, of course.

'No! I mean, yes, OK, I've got it now. But I didn't kill him!'

'Yes, yes. Shocking,' I said, leading him away so Juliette couldn't see or hear my next question. 'I'm glad I ran into you, actually. Did you drop this out in the old cottage?'

I showed him the burnt photograph, watching for his reaction, but Zayn merely looked confused.

'Not me, sorry. What cottage?'

I studied his expression but saw nothing there. If this was his picture, he was doing a first-rate acting job of not showing it.

'It must be someone else's, then. I thought maybe it was something to do with your argument with Juliette.' When he looked back towards the reception room I quickly clarified, 'No, I mean on Thursday night. At the cottage.'

'What cottage?' he repeated. 'I don't know anything about a cottage, or a photo, or an argument. You're all mad!'

Lily barked, though whether in argument or agreement I was unsure.

'Then never mind,' I said. 'I found it on a walk, that's all. I must have misunderstood—' Something Zayn had said a moment ago suddenly hit me. 'Hang on a minute. You said, "I've got it now." What did you mean?'

'The part. I'm playing Luke now. First scene tomorrow, at the crypt.'

'Oh! Congratulations. Horrible circumstances, of course, but Steven's keen to press on.'

'You mean Chloe is. She's desperate to get back to filming and prove she's not cursed.'

181

'Cursed? Whatever do you mean?'

'You know, *Emmerdale*?'

I had no idea what he was talking about. Sometimes, the decade I spent away from showbiz really does leave me in the dark.

'Yash was there,' he continued. 'He told me all about it. The car stunt, remember?' Seeing my blank look he said, 'Ask Needles about it; he was there too, and he's even got photos. I've got to learn my lines.'

Seeing as the only speaking lines for Luke in the crypt scene were a scream and a death rattle I didn't really see the rush, but I was too busy thinking to prevent him leaving.

I'd known Yash had started out as a young actor in soaps, but not that it was the same one Chloe directed. What was this 'curse'? Could it be something Yash held over Chloe . . . and therefore a motive for murder? She was the first of us to approach Juliette's trailer that day, and now that I thought about it, I couldn't swear I'd kept her in sight the whole time. As director, nobody would question her presence in the effects department, and her ever-present bum bag was big enough to hold a stake. Perhaps a hammer, too.

I felt Lily rub against my leg, prompting me to do something. She probably wanted feeding.

'Not yet, Lily. First there's a certain gossip-hungry costumier I need to talk to.'

I found Needles and his assistant at their temporary home in the study, checking and rearranging costumes.

Out of habit I looked at George's jigsaw, but he'd made no further progress. Difficult with people coming in and out to get undressed all the time, no doubt. My gaze drifted to the side desk, where I'd spotted the brochure for the wind farm investment, and saw it was no longer there. Did George really intend to erect only one turbine? Or had he said that to make me stop asking questions?

'I assume nobody's asked you to clean up their blood-soaked clothes?' I asked Needles.

'Chance'd be a fine thing,' he said, not looking up from a clipboard. 'The police examined everything here before they let us have it, too. I don't know what they thought they'd find.'

I looked at the racked costumes and wondered. 'Something hidden in the pockets? Not that most of them have pockets, being period dress.'

'Exactly.' He ticked off a final item and looked at me for the first time, his face falling. 'Oh, I can't do anything with you in that state, duck. You haven't even been to make-up.'

'What? Oh, no. I, um, fell. In the water.'

He said nothing, but raised a judgemental eyebrow.

'Besides, my call time is a while yet. I actually wanted to ask you about what happened on *Emmerdale*. Zayn said you know all about Chloe's supposed curse.'

'Oh, that's just the papers and their nonsense.' Needles scowled. 'I was there, and I'm telling you it wasn't her fault. In fact, I helped prove it in court. Don't you remember? It was all over the news, about five years ago.'

'Five years ago I was retired and spent every hour of the day caring for my father. Showbiz news was the last thing on my mind.'

'But you must remember. The stunt with the car going off the bridge, where that stuntman broke both his legs. He was in a wheelchair for months; it was horrible.'

A faint memory of the news headline finally came to mind. The sort of terrible on-set accident that thankfully is extremely rare nowadays.

'How did that come to reflect on Chloe?' I asked. 'Wouldn't that be the stunt coordinator's responsibility?'

'She had a habit of pushing overtime. I don't remember a single day on that series that we weren't working hours over schedule, and everyone was dead tired. That's how the stunt coordinator tried to shift blame onto her. He said Chloe was pushing everyone too hard, and the papers leapt on it.'

'And it went to court?'

'Yes, the stuntman sued her and the studio. The coordinator egged him on, of course. But it was the coordinator who'd screwed up, and claiming he'd been tired didn't save him. Especially as I had photos that proved it was his error. I'd been snapping away all night.'

I remembered how quick Needles was to take pictures of Yash in the trailer. A ghoulish habit, but if it proved Chloe's innocence, she would have no doubt been very grateful.

'Have you worked on many shows with her since?' I asked.

'I know what you're thinking,' he said. 'Yes, maybe

Chloe hires me out of gratitude. But I also get plenty of work from other directors that I haven't saved from a liability judgement, you know.'

'I wasn't implying anything,' I protested, even though I obviously had been. 'I just wondered if Yash might have had something over her. Something she might want to keep quiet.'

Needles looked shocked. 'I'll pretend I didn't hear that, and don't let Chloe hear you say it either or she might recast more roles than Luke.' He leant in and lowered his voice. 'None of us are saints, Gwinny. You've been around long enough to know that as well as me. But if there was anything going on between Yash and Chloe, it wasn't connected to what happened on *Emmerdale*. The tabloids had their pound of flesh, but that story's over.'

I left them to it and returned upstairs, thinking about that unfinished jigsaw. As I'd explained to George, experienced puzzlers start with corners and edges because they're unquestionably 'true'. If you start with the interior, speculative areas, it's easy to spend hours following the wrong path and getting nowhere. Once you secure the true pieces, though, you can fill in the gaps.

Almost nothing I'd learnt about Yash's death was unquestionably true. How long would I spend following the wrong path?

CHAPTER TWENTY-FOUR

In my bedroom I gave Lily fresh water and breakfast, which she fell on with a hunger. While she scoffed and chomped I changed my clothes, washed and thought about what Zayn and Needles had said about Chloe's 'curse'. It didn't seem related to Yash's death, but perhaps there was a hidden connection I didn't yet know about.

Did Juliette, I wondered? Had Zayn told her everything? Unlikely, given the way he stormed out on her. It was funny how she'd tried so hard to inveigle herself into the investigation without success. I'd done it without really trying, by simply making good observations and being in the right place at the right time.

I chided myself for treating it like a competition. Surely all that mattered was the truth.

Thinking about Juliette secretly meeting Yash inevitably made me think of the other 'competition' playing on my mind, with Birch and Tina. But perhaps there was something I could learn from Yash and Juliette's secret encounter. They hadn't realised someone had seen them. Someone unexpected . . .

I called Katie Crabtree, an old journalist friend. Katie and I had met when she was a young showbiz correspondent, and we'd kept in touch over the years. If Tina was the supportive and loving friend we all need to help us soar, Katie was the blunt and forthright pal we all need to keep our feet on the ground.

More importantly, she knew how to snoop.

'Katie, darling, it's Gwinny,' I said when she answered the voice call. We were friends, but not on the level of video chats. 'How are you?'

She hesitated, then said, 'Do you really want to know?'

'Of course,' I said, wondering what I was letting myself in for.

'Let's see . . . my editor is threatening to spike a story I've been working on for months if I don't produce an impossible number of people to corroborate the exposé. My husband is having a meltdown because one of his authors refuses to sign a huge deal over some petty contract nonsense.' (Katie's husband was a literary agent. I was never sure which of them deserved the long-suffering moniker more.) 'Our plumber is ghosting me, after failing to show up and fix our boiler last week like he promised. I've had to reschedule my next mammogram. And now my actress friend, who never calls me unless she wants something, is on the phone to ask a favour. How does that sound?'

I winced, unable to deny it. But I soldiered on.

'I'm truly sorry. It's amazing how busy one can get with a broken old house to repair, and now I'm away filming in Yorkshire for a while. Even that's gone pear-shaped, with a death on set.'

'Oh my God,' she gasped, rapidly switching to journalist mode. 'Yash Rani? Is that where you're working? Tell me everything.' I heard the unmistakeable tapping of a keyboard.

'I really can't,' I protested. 'There's a policeman here, DCI Pierce. I'm sure he'd be happy to—'

'Gwinny.' Katie interrupted. 'You obviously called because you want something from me, so in return I want something from you. That's how it works.'

Like I said, blunt and forthright. Not to mention relentless and wily. It was those very qualities I hoped she could put to use for me.

So I told her about Yash's death, in sanitised form. I left out the more salacious aspects (saying only that he'd been 'stabbed', in case the police hadn't told anyone about the stake) and my own speculations. I also didn't mention Juliette's attempts to conduct a ham-fisted investigation, much as I was tempted.

Katie was wise to my omissions, of course. 'Gwinny, you haven't told me much that hasn't already been reported. Don't you even know who found the body?'

'I don't want to go on the record with any of this,' I said. I knew the way to satisfy Katie was to let her feel she'd squeezed something out of me unwillingly.

'One hundred per cent anonymous,' she promised.

'"A source close to the production", as we say. Go on.'

'All right. The truth is that we all found him together. Juliette's trailer was locked from the inside, and everyone was stood around trying to get in. When security opened the door . . . well, there was Yash. Lying on the floor, and quite dead.'

'Hold on. How do you know it was locked from the inside?'

'The keys were still in the door. And before you ask, there's no chance he stabbed himself, or that it was an accident. The . . . weapon was embedded much too deeply.'

'So the killer must have climbed out through a window?'

'If they did, they were not only invisible but also somehow locked the window behind them.'

Another pause as I heard rapid typing. Then Katie said, 'This is bonkers. Thank you, Gwinny. Now what is it you want from me?'

I hesitated, and considered hanging up. I hadn't taken the time to properly consider what I was asking. If I had I would never have worked up the courage to call . . . but I had to know. Katie was my sole realistic hope.

'There's a man – that is, a friend of mine, his name is Birch – we've sort of been seeing one another – well, I mean, we see one another fairly often, but—'

'The ex-copper?' she interrupted, and to be honest I was grateful, though somewhat less grateful when she continued, 'Yes, Tina told me about him.'

'Did she? Well, Tina's the problem. No, wait, that's

not what I mean. What I mean is, it's because of Tina that I'm calling. Do you see?'

Katie snorted. 'Not in the slightest. Spit it out, Gwinny.'

'While I've been away, every time I call Birch he's with Tina. And vice versa. I'm worried they might be . . . doing something. In secret.'

I cringed. Saying it out loud made it absurd, ridiculous, laughable. Tina was a timeless beauty, four times married, a glamorous magnet for millionaire playboys and leading men. Why would she waste her time with a middle-class ex-copper? A middle-class, handsome, funny, dependable, trustworthy, dog-loving . . . oh, fiddlesticks.

'It wouldn't be the first time,' said Katie. 'Remember the producer? The one her publicist hushed up.'

'Oh, God. I'd forgotten about that.'

Years ago while starring in a film, Tina had engaged in an affair with one of the producers . . . despite his wife being right there on set because she was also a producer. Said wife threatened to sink the film and divorce him unless Tina backed off, *and* donated most of her fee to charity, *and* helped them make sure the press never got wind of it. Katie and I only knew because Tina herself had told us about it one night after several bottles of red.

'So, what do you want me to do about it? I don't mean to burst your bubble, Gwinny, but it's hardly front-page news. Barely even page eleven.'

'What? No! I don't want it to be in the news at all. I

want the opposite of that. I want to know if it's true, or if I'm imagining things. I'm fond of Birch, you see.'

'Yes, Tina told me that.' Presumably this was an attempt to reassure me, but it had the opposite effect. 'What are you asking me to do? Spy on her?'

'Probably simpler to follow him, actually.' I gave her Birch's address in Shepherd's Bush. 'Normally he only leaves the house for shopping, or to walk his dog.'

She snorted. 'Or help you solve murders. Pity he's not with you in Yorkshire.'

'Yes, for several reasons. But will you do it?'

'I will, but I think you're working yourself up about nothing. He may be your boyfriend, but he's friends with Tina as well, isn't he? Maybe they spend the whole time talking about you.'

'That's what I'm worried about! Look, it's not just that they seem to be joined at the hip, it's that they don't *tell* me unless I work it out for myself, and then they act like children caught red-handed. I hate to think badly of them, but Birch does get starry-eyed around showbiz people . . .'

'And Tina has form for jumping on another woman's catch,' said Katie, completing the thought. 'I get it. Leave it with me and I'll text you.'

'Not with details. Save that for a voice call.'

'Why? Do you think he's hacking your text messages?'

'Of course not. I mean, I don't think so. But still.'

She rang off with a sigh, leaving me alone with my thoughts. It did sound absurd . . . but Tina really did have form for this sort of thing . . . though never with friends, as far as I knew . . . and it had been obvious from the moment we first met in Kensington Gardens that Birch found Tina attractive . . . but then so did every man with a pulse . . .

Lily had finished her breakfast, leaving the bowl as clean as if it had never been used. I washed it anyway, while she snoozed on her bed.

I was due in make-up soon, but not yet. If I was quick, I could still talk to Chloe about her 'curse'. I cajoled Lily off her bed and clipped on her lead. She was grumpy about it, but I wasn't falling for that again.

CHAPTER TWENTY-FIVE

In the entrance hallway, the crew continued to prepare Scene Twenty-Eight. Grips moved lights and built dolly tracks while special effects people rigged up the main door. Chloe stood by her chair, watching everyone but leaving the crew and department heads to do their jobs. They knew what she wanted. The director would step in if she changed her mind or saw something she didn't like.

Which meant I could grab her for five minutes.

'How are you holding up?' I asked. 'Only twenty-four hours since . . . well, you know.'

'All the more reason to get on with it. Yash wouldn't have wanted us to shut down. He believed in *Draculania*.'

'So I've heard. Not to be indelicate, but do you know why? Granted we're all doing our best with the material, but you must admit it's a step down from Prince Hal at the RSC.'

'It certainly will be now he's gone.'

Taken aback, I said, 'Zayn told me it was you who pushed for him to assume the role. Do you regret it?'

'No, not really. He's perfectly capable, he'd already shot plenty of body doubling for Yash and he's here. Sometimes the best actor is the one you can actually lay your hands on, isn't it?'

I wondered if I was included in that less-than-illustrious grouping, but said nothing. Instead, I asked, 'During the library scene, where Ruby messed up, before we all took a break and, um, found Yash . . . do you remember seeing Steven on set? He was at video village to begin with, but then vanished.'

'I don't think I spoke to him at all. He knows where to find me if there's something to discuss. Why?'

I hesitated, and that was enough for her to guess.

'Oh, no,' she said. 'Come on, you can't think Steven would sabotage his own film. He's the biggest cheerleader after me, and he was already planning to work with Yash again after this.'

'Yes, but he also took out a large insurance policy. Specifically against Juliette's inability to complete filming.'

'Juliette's fine.'

'But she's convinced she was the real target.' I still wasn't convinced of that myself, but I couldn't dismiss the idea out of hand.

'This film isn't just a comeback for Juliette,' said Chloe. 'It's also a step up for Steven, and me, and you, and Ruby. Everyone here has too much riding on *Draculania* to want to shut it down. Well, almost everyone.' Chloe lowered her voice. 'I'll tell you who the police should be looking at: Angela.'

'Angela Viste? The stand-in?'

'I saw her arguing with Yash a couple of days ago. He wanted to talk to her about something, but she gave him a serious brush-off. I don't know what it was about, but I heard her say, "Not here, later!" before she walked away. She looked furious.'

'Goodness. You know, Angela told me she saw something in the trees not long before we found Yash. "A spirit moving in the shadows," she said. I've been wondering if it might have been the killer.'

Chloe looked surprised. 'You mean she didn't do it, but might know who did?'

'Possibly. Or the Cassandra thing could be an act to divert attention away from herself. That *Hendrick Lives* message on the mirror isn't helping. But I can't think what reason Angela would have to kill either Yash or Juliette.'

'Maybe she wants to do a Zayn and step into the lead role. Not that she would, because our distribution sales guarantee Juliette as Draculania. No Juliette, no film.'

'But a tidy insurance payout for Steven.'

'No, *no!*' she shouted suddenly. I jumped, thinking she was disagreeing with me, but she walked away in the direction of the key grip. She turned around as she went, walking backwards to face me while simultaneously retrieving a roll of tape from her pink bum bag. 'Residuals, Gwinny,' she said. 'No insurance is going to pay more than we'll earn from actually releasing on time.' Then she was gone, to argue about lighting.

Residuals are the film equivalent of royalties: extra money paid out according to success at the box office, DVD sales and so on. Each residual is small, but if you sell millions of tickets . . .

Steven was right that the notoriety of Yash's death would increase interest in the film, whether we liked it or not. Such increased interest could seriously boost ticket sales and therefore earnings. Was that a motive for murder? A way to goose the film's box office without jeopardising the entire production? It was grisly, but not impossible, and many people on set stood to gain.

It also suggested Yash really was the target, not Juliette. Which once again raised the question of what he was doing in Juliette's trailer, and—

'Ms Tuffel, five minutes to make-up,' said a breathless voice beside me. I turned to see a harassed-looking runner (there is no other kind) wearing a headset radio and ticking me off her clipboard. 'You weren't in your room,' she said between breaths.

Lily barked a warning a split-second before another voice said, 'I'm afraid Ms Tuffel will be delayed.'

DCI Pierce stood on my other side, with a stern expression. 'Come with me, please,' he said.

The runner whispered frantically into her headset as the inspector led me away. As if that wasn't bad enough, we passed Juliette when we exited the house, and she looked very smug.

* * *

DCI Pierce led me under the police cordon and into the production trailer his team had commandeered. Those trailers aren't designed with internal doors or room dividers, so he marched me to the far end, and we sat facing one another at what would normally have been a coordinator's desk. I picked up Lily and sat her on my lap.

'What progress have you made?' Pierce asked quietly.

I breathed a sigh of relief, understanding that I wasn't really in trouble. It had been a pretence so we could compare notes. 'You could have waited till I was on my own before dragging me in. Between Juliette and that runner, now half the set thinks I'm a suspect.'

'You are,' he reminded me, unwrapping an extra-strong mint. 'Everyone is. So, what have you found?'

'Mostly that everyone is pointing the finger at everyone else,' I said, and repeated the multiple accusations I'd already heard. 'The problem as I see it is that it's difficult to eliminate anyone without first knowing three things.' I counted them off on my fingers. 'One: was Yash really the target, or was he killed by someone who actually wanted to kill Juliette? Two: what was he doing in her trailer? And three: if he was the target, how did the killer know he'd be in there?'

'All very good questions,' Pierce agreed. 'Do you have any answers?'

'I'm afraid not. I did wonder if there might be some blackmail going on.'

Pierce shook his head. 'Our preliminary investigation of Mr Rani's finances has found nothing irregular.'

'But what if it wasn't about money? What if the killer couldn't risk him speaking out about something? Like the mere fact the killer was in Juliette's trailer, perhaps?'

'That might make sense, or could have been a secondary motive. Plenty of you lot have secrets, I imagine.'

'Showbiz secrets aren't normally the kind worth killing over, Inspector.'

'Perhaps not, but what about identity? For example, did you know that Angela Viste's real name is Astrid Nordberg?'

I shrugged. 'Stage names aren't unusual in our line of work. Ask Norma Jeane Baker. Nobody would kill over that.' We fell into silence for a moment. 'What did your forensics team find in the trailer, anyway? I know we all trampled through it like a herd of wildebeest, but was there anything useful left?'

'Very little. We can't track Mr Rani's movements accurately because of all the activity following his death, and there's no discernible blood spatter on any clothing or costumes that we've examined.'

'How many have you examined?'

'As many as possible. Mr Lloyd has been helpful, and those people who weren't in costume voluntarily submitted their clothing. Aside from blood on people's shoes, though, we've found nothing.'

'But unless the killer was naked, they must have been covered in blood. So where is that clothing?' Frustration threatened to overwhelm me.

'We'll keep looking. In the meantime, there are two

forensic oddities in the trailer. The first is the writing on the mirror, which was done using one of Ms Shine's lipsticks. The second is an oily residue we found under the sink.'

'Residue?'

'That's the only way I can describe it. Like what we'd expect from a gunshot, except there's no evidence of a shot being fired or any damage to the surroundings. It's all mixed up with the blood at the scene, though, so identifying it is slow going.'

'What about in his bedroom in the house? Was there anything useful there?'

'I'm afraid not. Now, would you say Mr Rani was well-liked on set?'

'Generally, yes. He wasn't particularly close with anyone, apart from Steven McDonald of course, but there were no problems that I know of.'

'All the more puzzling. I'm inclined to think that Ms Shine really was the intended target, even though as you say that raises all sorts of other questions.'

'Not least that they didn't succeed.' I put Lily on the floor and stood up. 'I'm needed on set, and I suggest you need more officers. If you're right about Juliette, there's a killer out there with unfinished business.'

CHAPTER TWENTY-SIX

I dashed over to Fi and Pri's temporary hair and make-up station in the kitchen, where they fixed me up while fussing over Lily and interrogating me about why DCI Pierce had dragged me away. I told them he'd wanted to go over my witness statement again.

Then I rushed to Needles' temporary wardrobe in the study, where he dressed me while avoiding Lily as much as possible and complaining about Juliette having the gall to interrogate him when she'd been through here ten minutes ago.

'I said to her, "I'm sorry, duck, but I can't concentrate on what exactly I was doing at 1.15 p.m. on the day in question when I'm busy trying to pin your blouse, unless you want me to pin it right onto your corselette, that is, and I don't think you do," and that told her.'

Now fully in character, I returned to the house's entrance hallway and found it ready for the big scene. After confronting Drs Van Helsing and Seward in the

200

library, Draculania tries to leave the house:

28 INT. WESTENRA MANOR HALLWAY - DAY

Draculania STRIDES through the hall, intending to leave -- but Van Helsing has been one step ahead of her all along.

GARLIC and CRUCIFIXES hang around the MAIN DOOR.

Draculania RECOILS in horror, and turns to face the doctors.

                    VAN HELSING

    You're not the only one with allies,
    Countess. I gave Doctor Seward's staff clear
    instructions, should you enter this place.

Dr Seward ADVANCES, holding up her own crucifix. DRIVING Draculania back towards the door.

Draculania HISSES, caught between the repellent objects...

Then she LAUGHS, mocking the doctors.

                    DRACULANIA

    Children. You truly do not know that which
                    you face.

CLOSE ON her as she TREMBLES with internal effort -- SUMMONING her demonic power.

Her EYES burn red with hellfire as something builds, and builds, and BUILDS...

She SWEEPS her cape in a grand gesture -- the garlic and crucifixes around the door EXPLODE!

Seward FALLS BACK, stunned by Draculania's power. Van Helsing STARES in awe.

Farewell, ladies. I trust we shall not meet
again, for the gaze of Draculania will surely
mean your doom!

She WALKS OUT through the main door and into
the mist.

There are a variety of ways to shoot a scene like this. Chloe's choice required a good deal of preparation and care by the special effects crew. Rather than cut away to a separate shot of the garlic and crosses exploding, she wanted the camera to be on Draculania while the explosions happened behind her, effectively framing the character in the shot.

It would be a wonderful, dramatic image. But it meant the star of the show would be standing less than ten feet from a variety of exploding props, which is the sort of thing that makes everyone nervous.

Bill, the special effects supervisor, had put a great deal of planning into the shot and spent all morning rigging up the small explosives and breakaway props. He was now arguing with Steven about how long things were taking.

'Every minute we're not shooting is a minute that costs us money!' said Steven. 'We're already delayed and over budget, for God's sake.'

Bill fixed him with a steady eye. 'How long do you think we'll be delayed if Juliette gets hit by a squib or burnt by gunpowder? It'll be a damn sight longer than the extra hour we're taking today to make sure that doesn't happen.'

Angela stood patiently on a cross of blue marking tape while the cinematographer used her to prepare the shot. She really did look like a young Juliette. Time and tide wait for no diva, but Little Miss Sunshine still possessed the bone structure that had helped earn her fame and fortune when she was Angela's age.

I waited for the stand-in to finish, then asked if she'd take care of Lily again while I filmed. I knew the terrier wouldn't appreciate the explosions that were to come.

'No problem.' Angela crouched to let Lily sniff and lick her hand again. I'd have to get the name of that moisturiser; it was like Jack Russell catnip. 'You can be my protection against evil spirits,' she said to the dog. I wasn't sure exactly how that would work, but if it meant Angela was happy to walk her, I wasn't arguing.

As I watched them leave, George caught my eye. He stood in the archway leading to what had previously been his private area and beckoned me over. I hesitated, considering we'd parted this morning on less than stellar terms, but he was all smiles now, so I approached him.

'George, let me apologise. I was in a foul mood this morning, and I took it out on you—'

'No, I won't hear it,' he said, smiling. 'It's me who should apologise. You're trying to get to the bottom of what happened to your friend, and nobody should be above suspicion. I do enjoy your company, Gwinny. I'd hate to fall out over a tiff. Bygones?'

My gaze lingered on him for a moment longer than was perhaps sensible, but he really was easy to look at. I also enjoyed being the one apologised to for once, rather than doing the apologising as usual.

'Bygones,' I agreed.

'Excellent. Now, I must say this is all very exciting. They've assured me the devices won't damage anything, and the force of the blast is to be directed away from the surfaces. Apparently, it's very precise.'

'That's right,' I said. 'These are the same explosives we use for blood squibs, like when someone gets shot. If they're safe for a person to wear, you can be sure they won't damage a door frame.'

'What the hell do you think you're doing?!' came a cry from the direction of the set.

It was Chloe, yelling at DCI Pierce. Oblivious to the scene preparations going on around him and focused on reading his notebook, the lumbering policeman had returned to wander through the set.

'I'm looking for Mr Patel,' he said.

'Then kindly look elsewhere, because he's not in this scene.'

Pierce refused to budge. 'Where can I find him?'

I grabbed the nearest runner. 'Locate Zayn and tell him to go immediately to the police cordon, would you?' She nodded and spoke into her headset while I called out to Pierce. 'He'll be with you in a moment, Inspector. Please wait for him—'

'A-ha! No need. Mr Patel, would you come with me?'

Zayn stood halfway down the stairs, presumably coming to watch the scene be filmed. When Pierce addressed him, he looked confused, then slightly afraid.

For a tense moment I wondered if he might turn and run, but then his shoulders slumped.

'Your Lordship,' said Pierce, practically tugging his forelock at George as he passed us to mount the steps.

'Why's he not interviewing Juliette, that's what I don't understand,' George whispered as the inspector led Zayn out of the house.

Ruby came out of wardrobe, ready to work. I noticed Fi and Pri had covered the cut on her hand with a smaller, thinner bandage and lots of make-up. It wouldn't be in shot much anyway, as it was Seward who wielded a crucifix in this scene.

I said goodbye to George and joined Ruby. We threaded our way between light stands to enter the set. Juliette was nowhere to be seen.

'Don't tell me she's late again,' said Ruby, annoyed.

As if on cue, the ambient chatter and noise stopped.

Juliette emerged from a side reception room in full Draculania costume and fangs, looking regal and stately. A wardrobe assistant scurried alongside her. The star swept past us, so focused she didn't even spare George a glance.

'Listen up, everyone,' Chloe called out. 'Because of the squibs we're going to shoot in order. So first we'll do everything up to the demonic power, in coverage and close. Then it's the squibs for as many times as we can stand to reset, and finally reactions and "Farewell, ladies" among the debris. Ready?'

'Of course,' said Juliette haughtily, already immersed in her character. She fixed Ruby and I with a baleful

205

stare. A prop assistant handed me a crucifix to brandish, and Chloe retreated behind the camera.

'Rolling.'

'Sound.'

'Draculania, scene twenty-eight, take one.'

'*Action!*'

We ran through the first part of the scene, up until the explosive cape-sweeping, a dozen times from different angles. Perhaps due to everything that had happened, the atmosphere was intense, and everyone gave it their all. Neither Ruby nor Juliette messed up any dialogue this time, and my job was easy – no lines, just some business with the crucifix while gasping and recoiling in the right places. Juliette did a wonderful job 'summoning her demonic power', reminding everyone why she was given so much leeway and got away with behaviour that would have seen anyone else fired. In this business, what you do in front of a lens really is all that matters.

At last, we were ready for the big moment. Everyone waited while Chloe, Bill and Juliette went over the shot one more time for safety's sake.

Ruby and I weren't in the shot, but we'd be needed for the aftermath, and having us present would give Juliette something to focus on. So, we stood beside the camera rig, still in costume.

When Chloe called '*Action,*' Juliette picked up where she'd left off with the demonic power, focusing all her character's hatred on me and Ruby. Then she swept her cape around herself, and on cue Chloe yelled, 'Bang!'

Out of shot, Bill fired off the squibs positioned around

the door. The garlic and crucifixes exploded around Draculania while she stood perfectly still, perfectly arrogant in her infernal power—

Crash!

A light stand toppled over and smashed on the floor right beside Juliette. She recoiled as glass shards exploded in the air. Even though I stood metres away, I let out an undignified shriek and stumbled backwards. Ruby did the same, swearing.

Everyone stared at the downed light for a shocked moment. Then grips ran in to retrieve it and check the remaining stands. Studio sets are filled with so many lights that after a while you stop noticing them. Now, looking around with fresh eyes, I felt like I was standing in a forest that could suddenly fall on me.

'Oh, my God, it almost hit me!' Juliette cried, staring at the fallen lamp. 'I *told* you someone is trying to kill me! I told you all!'

'It might have been an accident,' I suggested, then regretted it when the key grip shot me an angry look. It was his job to ensure all the lights and equipment on set were rigged correctly and safely.

'Accident, my ass,' said Juliette. 'Where's that useless cop?'

'He's interviewing Zayn,' I said, but now it seemed he was barking up the wrong tree. If Juliette was right, and this was the killer's second attempt on her life, then how could Zayn have done it when he was with DCI Pierce?

CHAPTER TWENTY-SEVEN

DCI Pierce himself wasn't so sure.

'Perhaps Mr Patel had an accomplice,' he said, after arriving at the scene.

'Oh, so now there are two people trying to kill me?' Juliette protested. 'That's great! Aren't you supposed to protect me?'

Pierce raised his voice to make sure everyone heard him and said, 'If you hadn't all been so very eager to clean up after this incident, we might have retrieved some evidence that could help. Fat chance of that now.'

'I'm starting to wonder if this picture is cursed,' said Ruby.

Chloe caught the word and glared at Ruby, her expression a mixture of anger and fear.

'It's not the film, it's this place,' said Angela, who by now had returned inside with Lily and handed her back to me. 'Remember what it said on the mirror? *Hendrick*

Lives. We're trespassing, and he obviously doesn't want us here.'

'For God's sake, a vampire didn't push over the light stand,' said Juliette. 'It was someone here on set. Who was standing next to it when it fell?'

'Nobody,' said one of the grips. 'It just . . . toppled.'

'You see?!' said Angela.

'So, it was an accident,' said DCI Pierce, but Juliette wasn't having that.

'Or the killer's worried I'm getting too close to the truth and tried to finish me off,' she said defiantly. 'Hell, it could have been anyone here on set, including one of you.' She glared at me and Ruby, and Pierce followed her gaze.

'What possible reason would either of us have?' I said, even though privately I had my own suspicions about Ruby.

Juliette unwittingly fuelled them. 'Who knows? Perhaps you want your pal Ruby to get my job. Or maybe you want it for yourself. Or maybe you're jealous. There's plenty who are.'

'If I went around bumping off everyone more successful than me there'd be nobody left. You'll have to do better than that.' Then I realised what I was saying and quickly added, 'Not that you'll be able to, because I'm not a murderer.'

'I don't need to kill you to prove I'm a better actor, Juliette,' said Ruby. 'How do we know you didn't do this yourself? Garner a bit of extra sympathy, make sure the spotlight's on you.'

She had a point. It wouldn't be the first time a killer had arranged a feint to throw the police off the scent.

'How dare you!' said Juliette. 'I was standing right there, with everyone watching me. There's no way I could have pulled that stand over without you all seeing it.'

That was also true, but the same conundrum applied. If nobody was near the light at the time, how had it moved? It had been weighed down with a sandbag, as all lights are once in position, but that hadn't made any difference. Could it have been an accident? A one-in-a-million coincidence?

I had a sudden feeling that something was missing, something I'd overlooked. The pieces of this puzzle were all jumbled up in my mind, and I still didn't have a full picture to assemble, due to not knowing whether Yash or Juliette had been the real target in the trailer. The falling light, assuming it wasn't an accident, pointed much more conclusively towards Juliette . . .

Steven wasn't here. That's what was missing.

I'd seen him earlier, arguing with Bill about delays, but now, for the second time when something went wrong and filming was delayed, the producer was nowhere to be seen. The producer who'd been most insistent that the show must go on.

Perhaps the man doth protest too much?

I was growing tired of coincidences. While the others continued to argue, I slipped away to find Steven McDonald.

* * *

It wasn't difficult. I followed the sound of angry hissing, or rather Lily did because she heard it long before me, and I followed her.

We found the producer upstairs, pacing back and forth at the corner of the corridor, in front of the locked tower door. I wasn't trying to sneak up on him, but he was so engrossed in a phone call that he didn't see me until we were almost face to face. By then I'd overheard him saying, 'You can't pull out now – we can still make this work – no, the insurance isn't the point – are you stupid? Yash's death will make it bigger than ever, it's a guaranteed—'

At that moment he finally noticed me and hastily ended the call.

'There you are,' I said breezily. 'I'm afraid we had to cut short. Accident on set.'

His face cycled through a maelstrom of expressions, all of which I watched carefully, before he finally settled on simple despair.

'Accident? What now?'

'A light toppled over and almost hit Juliette. Don't worry, I said *almost*. It missed her, and apart from a smashed light and another delay, no real harm done.'

He balled his fists. 'Another delay! I swear, this will kill us. The financiers have been jittery for weeks.'

'Is that who you were talking to just now? I must say that telling someone "Yash's death will make it bigger than ever" doesn't exactly cast you in the best light.'

'What?' He looked genuinely confused, then understood. 'No, no. You've got the wrong end of the stick. I mean, yes, *Draculania* will benefit from the notoriety, assuming we ever get the bloody thing in the can. Leicester Square premiere and box office top five, I shouldn't wonder.'

I certainly wouldn't complain about either of those things, but I'd happily have foregone them in return for Yash being alive.

'But that's not what I was talking about.' Steven looked down both sides of the corridor and lowered his voice. 'Remember I mentioned Yash's next picture? It was a documentary. He'd present and co-produce. And that was enough to persuade him to come on board *Draculania*. So why would I want him dead? He and I were going to make a lot of money together.'

I quickly replayed in my mind what I'd overheard Steven say on the phone, and it fitted his claim. Then I remembered what I'd heard him shouting about yesterday and finally understood.

'Yash's death has the documentary backers threatening to cancel because you've lost your frontman. But you hadn't arranged insurance yet, so if they pull out you're left with nothing.' I recalled something both Juliette and Bostin Jim had mentioned. 'Didn't you shut down your previous film and claim on the insurance?'

'What are you implying?'

'Merely noting a pattern of behaviour.'

Steven fumed. 'Are you stupid? That's exactly why I *wouldn't* do it again here. Closing down two pictures in the space of a year! It's hard enough to get financing without everyone thinking I'm a flake.' He let out a deep breath to calm down. 'I'm telling you, Gwinny, don't ever become a producer. It'll take years off your life.'

'While adding millions to your bank account,' I pointed out, but that didn't seem to sway him. Must be nice. 'Surely you can find another presenter for the documentary. Yash was charming, but plenty of others could do that job.'

There was obviously something about this he was reluctant to tell me, and I wondered again about whether Yash was having an affair. Steven was married with children, but he'd hardly be the first filmmaker to live a life of domestic bliss while also carrying on with a handsome young star.

Eventually he rubbed his hands over his face and said quietly, 'It'll come out one way or another. The last thing I need is you lot spreading rumours.'

So that was it. I had to admit, they'd done a great job of keeping the affair hidden from the rest of the production. Then Steven surprised me by asking, 'Have you heard of the Sentinels of Heaven?'

That wasn't at all where I'd expected the conversation to go.

'I'm sorry, the who? What does this have to do with Yash?'

'Everything. The cult, Sentinels of Heaven? God is angry with the world, the apocalypse is coming, and His soldiers will prevail?'

It still meant nothing to me, but I nodded to encourage him.

He continued, 'Yash's parents were members, but

when he left Margate for RADA he escaped the cult, too. The documentary was going to be an exposé, starting with his personal testimony and then going around interviewing other former members. Some of the stuff he told me would make your blood boil, but getting people on camera has always been impossible.'

'Until Yash came along, willing to go on the record. Presumably as a former member himself he'd also be in a good position to get others talking.'

'Exactly. It was set to be a bombshell, full-on Oscar bait. He was committed, and even insisted I hire a genealogist to work on his family tree. He wanted to see how far back they'd been involved in the cult. Now it's all up in smoke because some psycho tried to kill Juliette, and Yash was in the wrong place at the wrong time.'

I gasped as a new thought occurred to me. 'Do you think perhaps Juliette is a member, too?'

Steven blinked. 'What makes you say that?'

'It might explain why Yash was in her trailer, if he was trying to recruit her for the documentary. Would you know? Is there any way to tell?'

'Quite the opposite. I needed someone like Yash to make the film because the Sentinels are so secretive. It's like the Freemasons times a hundred.'

'But they must have some way to recruit people. You can't proselytise without giving away that you're a believer yourself.'

He shook his head. 'You can, in a way. From what Yash told me it's more like scouting. Let's say I'm a member, out and about living my life, and I find someone who I think could be converted. You, for example. I can't approach you because that would reveal my membership to you, an unbeliever. Instead, I tell my commanding officer, who tells the recruitment division, and they send out a couple of specialists who persuade you to join.

'If it works, I become your mentor within the Sentinels and everyone's a winner. If it doesn't work, well, first they try very hard to change your mind. There are stories of them sabotaging people's lives, anonymously causing trouble at work or with their spouse, so the target eventually runs to the cult for sanctuary. But even if that fails you're none the wiser that I was ever involved. The only members you can identify are the recruiters, and you'll never see them again.'

'Fancy ruining someone's life because they turn you down!' I said, appalled. 'Why do they conceal themselves, if they're so self-righteous?' But as soon as I asked the question I guessed the answer.

'To avoid persecution, they say. The devil is abroad, a great puppet-master controlling their rivals, in preparation for the ultimate heavenly war. Earth is the battlefield, of course. Them versus all the monsters.'

'What do you mean, monsters?'

'Goblins, vampires, werewolves, fairies, imps. The Sentinels of Heaven believe they're all part of Satan's army, walking amongst us in disguise, waiting to be called up for war.'

This put a whole new spin on Yash being staked

through the heart. Could someone have thought he'd left the Sentinels because he'd been turned to Satan? That he wasn't just playing a vampire . . . he truly was an undead servant of evil? Was *Hendrick Lives* a warning that Yash had been converted to evil?

Lily barked, at nothing in particular that I could see. Nobody else had entered the corridor.

'*Quiet*, Lily,' I said. 'I'm trying to talk with Steven.' The Jack Russell ignored me, merrily barking away. Which really was a shame, because this was the longest conversation I'd ever had with Steven and I appeared to finally be getting a glimpse of the human beneath his bluster. It was nice, especially as I knew he'd never show this face to the world at large.

'Do the Sentinels have a hold in the acting community?' I asked, raising my voice to be heard above Lily.

I'd never get an answer to that question, because at that moment the locked door behind us suddenly opened, and I understood what Lily had been barking at.

Someone was descending from the tower.

CHAPTER TWENTY-EIGHT

To my relief the emerging tower denizen wasn't the ghost of Hendrick Henning, or one of Angela's shadowy demons, but George. Which made sense, considering this was his house.

'Heavens, you gave us a fright!' I said, catching my breath. 'I thought the tower was off-limits?'

Steven really had looked shocked, which made me wonder again about his guilty conscience. OK, perhaps he didn't want anyone to get wind of the documentary, but it was hardly a matter of life and death . . . was it?

'Off-limits to the public,' said George, as surprised to see us as we had been to see him. 'One has to know where one's stepping up there. But it still needs attention, what?'

Steven's phone started playing a song I vaguely recognised, something about 'needing a hero'. Apparently this was his ringtone – typical producer ego – because he made his excuses and left, answering the call as he walked away.

'I say, you're not filming here, are you?' George asked.

An understandable question, as I was still in costume. I explained what had happened downstairs, and how filming had been suspended yet again as a result.

'As it happens, there are some things I'd like to discuss with you,' I said. 'Shall we go for a walk? I promise not to accuse you of being in league with Big Turbine.'

He laughed, and offered his arm. 'Capital idea.'

It was apparent that we wouldn't be picking up filming again any time soon. Ruby had already changed out of costume, and she told me Juliette was in the study with Needles doing the same. I asked George if he'd mind waiting while I did too. I swear on my father's grave, the fact that it meant Juliette would see us together was not the main reason I suggested it. Not the *main* reason.

As it happened, the star barely glanced at us as she sauntered out of the temporary wardrobe room. I stood patiently while Needles began to strip me, amused that it took George a minute to realise what was about to happen. He reddened and turned away.

Two minutes later, back in my usual clothes and with my handbag over my shoulder, George and I walked past the remains of the hallway set and out into the woods, where I let Lily off-lead. As she ran among the trees I decided to get straight to the heart of the matter.

'Juliette insists she didn't meet Yash Rani at the cottage on Thursday night,' I said. 'And something Ruby said earlier made me wonder: is it possible you saw Zayn Patel, instead?'

'Zay-who?'

'Zayn. Yash's stand-in, although now he's taken over the role. He really does look like him, you see. That's the point of a stand-in.'

George considered this. 'I'm not sure I've seen this Zayn chap, and it was dark, so I couldn't honestly say either way.'

'But you're sure it was Juliette with him?'

'Oh, yes,' he said, much more certain. 'Easy to recognise her, with her height and the long dark hair. Plus the accent, of course.'

'I thought you said you didn't hear what they were saying.'

At that moment Lily bounded up to George, carrying a stick in her mouth, which she dropped at his feet. He laughed, picked it up and threw it into the trees for her.

'I didn't hear the words,' he said. 'But we have enough American tourists in the house that one gets to know the intonation.'

That was a fair point. But if he'd been wrong about Yash, and it was Zayn that Juliette had met in the cottage, it would explain her insistence that she hadn't met Yash there. Technically it wasn't a lie, but it added another oddly shaped piece to this already complex puzzle. What could *those* two have been arguing about? Surely the Hollywood diva was even less likely to know Zayn than Yash.

Lily returned with the stick, once again dropping it at George's feet rather than mine. She watched him intently, wearing a big grin and helicoptering her tail, as he picked it up.

'You little tart,' I said to her, laughing. She gave me the briefest of glances before returning her full attention to the much more interesting Viscount, then shot off like a rocket when he threw the stick for her.

'I notice you don't keep dogs yourself,' I said as we resumed walking. 'Why is that?'

'Health and safety, mostly. It was fine when the family was here, but for a one-man band it's tricky. I can't watch a dog twenty-four hours a day, and with so many people like yourselves around there's too much potential for a bite or aggression if I'm not there. I'm sure you know how little argument wardens need these days. If a dog even looks at a child funny, they're in like lightning to throw it in the pound. Highly unfair.'

It was a sobering thought, given Lily's propensity to go for people's ankles and bark at her own shadow. That's how terriers are, but explaining such behaviour to people who don't know dogs can be difficult.

My phone buzzed with a call from an unknown number. I almost didn't take it, then remembered the local hospital wouldn't show up on caller ID. I suddenly felt terribly guilty that I hadn't called to check up on Viv.

'Sorry, George, I should take this. It might be about my friend.'

'Not at all, go ahead.'

I did, and a man's voice said, 'Good afternoon. Could I speak to Ms Guinevere Tuffel, please?'

'Speaking. Who's this?' I needn't have asked, to be honest. I'd spent enough time with Birch to immediately recognise the universal policeman's cadence.

'Constable Horton, North Yorkshire Police. I'm calling from Hendale hospital, as it was Vivienne Danforth's wish that you should be informed. I'm afraid I have some bad news.'

My legs buckled, and I clung to George for support.

CHAPTER TWENTY-NINE

I drowned in a sea of possibilities. My mind flailed, desperately searching for a raft of hope to which I could cling.

'But . . . police? I don't understand. If she's – why, why are the police involved?'

'The postman called us first, you see. He noticed the broken window and informed us where we could find Ms Danforth.'

'Postman? Broken window? What?'

'I'm sorry to tell you that Ms Danforth has been the victim of a burglary. As she's unable to leave the hospital she asked us to inform you, as I believe you're currently looking after her dog?'

'You could have led with that!' I yelled in frustration. By now I was practically sitting on the grass while George and Lily, both equally concerned, fussed around me. I took a deep breath and tried to be practical. 'Do you have officers at the house? I'd better come over and see what's been taken.'

'That would be very helpful, Ms Tuffel, thank you. I'll make my way there now.'

George offered his hand, and I pulled myself up.

'Where is it you need to go?' he asked. 'Let me drive you; you don't appear to be in a fit state.'

'Poppycock,' I said, irritated at the suggestion I was a frail woman who needed coddling. Then I calmed down, reminding myself that a moment before he'd watched me crumple to the ground and was trying to help. 'I'm sorry, George, that was harsh. I'm fine, I thought it was . . . the worst news, you know. But it's not, merely enormously inconvenient.' I reminded him of the 'friend in hospital' I'd mentioned the day before.

'No explanation necessary. You had the same look my wife had, when . . . when we lost Charlie.'

'Thank you,' I said, and meant it. Having lost both my parents, I was hardly unfamiliar with death, but until now I'd been lucky enough not to lose close friends. I'd sometimes wondered how that would hit me, and after this taster I was in no hurry to undergo the full experience.

With Lily secured in the boot, I raced my old Volvo as fast as I dared through the winding Dales lanes to Viv's house. On the way I called her at the hospital.

'I'm going to the house now,' I said. 'I'm so sorry, I really don't know what to say. Have you been burgled before?'

'Never, but I suppose an isolated old house will

always be a target.' After a pause Viv added, 'You *did* lock up before coming to the hospital yesterday, didn't you?'

'Of course! Well . . . I'm sure I did. It was a bit of a rush. Oh, heavens, I do hope so.' I felt beset with guilt, until I remembered what the policeman had told me. 'No, wait! The postman reported a broken window. There'd be no need to break in if the door wasn't locked, would there? So, I must have. Not that it's much consolation.'

Viv laughed nervously. 'No, not much. Gwinny, would you do me a huge favour and stay there overnight? In case someone tries to come back.'

'What, so they can wallop me over the head?'

'Oh, I hadn't thought of that.'

Now it was my turn to laugh. 'I'm joking, darling. I've got Lily with me, and her bark alone would scare off a platoon of crooks. Besides, they won't come back and try again with police crawling all over the house. I've arrived. I'll call you again soon.'

If I'd hoped to find a phalanx of police and forensic examiners inspecting the house inch by inch, I was sorely disappointed. In fact, the only person I saw was Constable Horton, waiting patiently by the front door. Sure enough, the windowpane nearest the lock had been broken.

I introduced myself as I took Lily out of the boot and clipped on her lead. Until I knew what had happened inside, I didn't want to risk letting her run free. I anticipated an objection from the constable, so was pleasantly surprised that instead he crouched down to let the Jack Russell give him a good sniffing, then fussed her in return. She spoilt the moment by dropping for a wee on the path.

'Lily!' I admonished her.

Constable Horton laughed. 'Better here than indoors. As you can see, this is how they got in.' He pointed to the broken window. 'Smashed it, reached through and opened the lock from inside. Cut themselves doing it, too.'

He was right; peering at the broken glass around the edges, I saw a smear of blood.

'Can you get that checked? You know, do a DNA test?'

'Already requested,' he said, then grimaced. 'But you should know that non-priority results are currently running at about six weeks' return. Even then, we can't get a match if they're not in the system.'

I sighed. 'What you're saying is, don't get your hopes up.'

'I'm afraid so. Now, please follow me and try to identify if anything's been taken. You might want to carry the dog.'

I picked up Lily as the constable opened the door, and immediately saw what he meant. Shattered glass lay on the floor inside, along with anything loose that had been in the vestibule.

He escorted me around the house, where similar destruction had been wrought in every room. It looked like a whirling dervish had been through, scattering everything that wasn't nailed down in a chaotic frenzy.

After a while, though, I began to wonder why. Drawers and cupboards had been opened, and their contents strewn; chairs were upended; ornaments lay on the floor. But they were *there*, all the same. When Constable Horton asked if anything had been taken, I honestly couldn't tell. I didn't know the house all that well, but the scene nagged at me. It was easy to imagine a thief rummaging through drawers looking for something, but why bother flinging it all on the floor? Why turn over chairs?

Viv's computer lay on the floor next to her desk, amid scattered papers. It wasn't a brand-new model but must be worth a bob or two all the same. That it hadn't been taken suggested the burglar was looking for something specific, not trawling for easy money. Something about the scattered ornaments bothered me, too, but I couldn't put my finger on it.

Finally, I bade the constable goodbye and saw him out the door. 'Don't worry,' I reassured him, 'Lily and I will stay here overnight, so nobody's going to risk coming back.'

'I certainly hope not,' he said, and handed me a card. 'Call the station if you see or hear anything. Ms Danforth is lucky you're on hand while she's in the hospital, I must say. Imagine if this had happened after you finished filming and left her alone again.'

CHAPTER THIRTY

I watched Constable Horton drive away, his final words echoing in my head. Yes, the timing was lucky in more ways than one. Not only that I was here, but that the burglary just happened to take place a day after Viv was rushed into hospital. Had thieves been watching the house, waiting for a night that nobody was home?

But if so, why take so little – if in fact they'd stolen anything at all?

I let Lily down so I could sweep up the glass in the vestibule. I'd seen no shattered ceramics, or kitchen knives lying around, so it was safe for her to wander.

When I'd finished, I took out my phone and snapped photos to show Viv. Seeing this would upset her, but I knew she'd want to.

I moved through to the bedroom, wondering if the intruders might have been here for valuables. But if Viv had a safe filled with money, I didn't know about it, and unless the thieves had taken great care to re-conceal it afterwards, they hadn't found one either. Her purse was with her at the hospital, so there were no credit cards to steal. Jewellery, then? The dresser had been turned over like everything else, its drawers pulled out and emptied on the bed. But dozens of necklaces, earrings and bracelets remained. Viv would know if anything was missing, so I took more photos.

Was it worth attempting to get a glazier out on a Saturday evening to repair the front door? Probably not, and besides, this was a farmhouse. Surely there was something around here I could use to board up the window.

Lily had by now finished running around the house, sniffing everything and looking in vain for a culprit. I left her there for a moment while I looked in the shed, finding an offcut piece of plywood, a hammer and nails. That would do.

I returned to the house and got to work. Lily barked in reply each time I struck with the hammer, and my mind returned to Yash. To force that stake through his chest must have taken real strength. Who would be so determined? Who had the sheer will to do such a thing, even if Yash had been incapacitated?

When I'd finished, I stood back to admire my handiwork. Hardly a perfect fit, and a thin, insistent whistle of wind blew around the edges of the plywood, but it would suffice. I was about to return the hammer to the shed, then thought maybe I'd keep it handy in case anyone did try to return tonight. So I placed it on the kitchen table, then walked around the house replacing things and tidying up.

I wasn't sure where everything went, but I guessed Viv would rather come home to a tidy house than not, even if things were in the wrong place. I persuaded myself that rearranging everything would give her something to do. It might even take her mind off the burglary.

After calling Viv to let her know that it wasn't nearly as bad as it could have been, I fed and toileted Lily nearby, keeping the house within sight. By the time we retired to the sofa she looked as tired as I felt and promptly fell asleep with her head stretched across my thigh. With little else to do, I took out my phone and searched for information about the Sentinels of Heaven.

I soon saw why Steven believed a proper documentary would be a hit. Online I found just two articles of original reporting, with everything else being either a re-written version of the same pieces, or simply wild speculation.

What I read was illuminating, though. The Sentinels of Heaven were formed shortly after the Second World War in Sweden by 'Father Tomas', who believed that Hitler had dabbled in black magic and opened the gates of Hell on earth. Now Satan and his demons walked among humanity, doing their evil deeds, and only those who'd been blessed with second sight could see the horde in order to fight it, which was every person's sacred duty.

I yawned. I'm no expert in apocalyptic religious cults, but very little here was new. Even the Hitler-black magic connection was an old conspiracy theory. The Sentinels also had their own secret greeting; upon meeting they would cover their eyes to indicate 'seeing' one another with second sight. The main thing that distinguished them from other cults was how their members lived within society, instead of isolating themselves from it. That's why their identities were secret; as Steven had said, it was to protect them from the retribution of Beelzebub. Or 'being mocked in the street', as you or I might put it.

He'd also said they were willing to ruin people's lives if they didn't join. Did that extend to members as well? Perhaps it was how they kept people in line. Along with an old-fashioned charismatic leader capable of persuading his followers to do anything, of course. One of the articles had a rare picture of the current leader, the third man (these types are always men) to hold the position, who styled himself Father Tiberius.

I recognised him.

Forgetting that Lily was asleep on my leg, I jumped up from the sofa. She woke, barking at whatever emergency had prompted such sudden movement, while I retrieved the burnt photo I'd found in the old cottage from my coat pocket.

Father Tiberius.

Surely this photo must have belonged to Yash. A picture of him with Father Tiberius, which he'd burnt to hide his membership in the Sentinels of Heaven. But then why not destroy the whole photo? Why carry it around?

Lily continued barking while these new puzzle pieces jostled for position in my mind. What this told me for certain was that it *had* been Yash in the cottage with Juliette, not Zayn. Unless Zayn was also a Sentinel, but what were the chances of that? The Sentinels were comfortable with violence to achieve their ends, too. Had someone in the cult discovered Yash's plans for the documentary and killed him in retribution? Perhaps, but how did they know where he'd be? Particularly at that moment, when shooting had paused, and Juliette should have been in there herself . . .

'Lily, for heaven's sake,' I said, exasperated by her continued barking. '*That's enough.*'

She wasn't barking in my direction, though. She stood upright on the sofa, every muscle taut as a wire, facing in the direction of the lounge window.

By now it was gone ten o'clock and pitch dark outside. I hadn't drawn the curtains. Perhaps I should? Yes, I definitely should. But my body refused to move. The wind had picked up, howling through the plywood gap in the front door like a banshee's lament. Was that a *scratching* sound I heard . . . ?

Lily's bark turned to a snarling growl, her eyes darting between the window and the vestibule.

I'd been wrong. The burglars had decided to come back after all.

CHAPTER THIRTY-ONE

The police would never get here in time. Instead, I willed my legs to move and rushed to pull the curtains over the lounge window, then the kitchen window. It wouldn't stop anyone breaking the glass, but it would prevent them from seeing me pick up the hammer I'd left on the table. Next, I reached into my other coat pocket, retrieved my torch and turned off lights as I tiptoed to the vestibule.

I didn't see anyone outside the front door, but the view was partly blocked by my makeshift plywood repair. Someone could have been standing right on the doorstep and I wouldn't see them.

Lily stood by my side, quietly snarling. This was her territory, the place she'd lived her whole life, and she wasn't about to surrender it to some thieving yobs. I drew confidence from her, raising both the hammer and torch as I silently approached the door.

Not having a third hand with which to open it,

however, left me with a choice to make. I decided illumination could wait and wrapped the torch's loop around my wrist, letting it dangle.

I reached for the handle, hammer raised high and ready to strike. The wind blew stronger, louder. Every nerve in my body burnt with fear, but I refused to back down. I turned the handle and flung the door open . . .

A wall of cold, swirling fog greeted me. The wind bit through my clothes. Lily fell silent.

Then she ran out into the fog, barking. I took two steps to follow, fumbling to turn on the torch one-handed. The fog reflected the beam back at me, but I ventured out and swept it across the alternating patches of mist and darkness.

There was nobody there. Had there been? Impossible to say. I couldn't hear anyone run away over the sound of Lily barking, or my own galloping heartbeat.

After a full circuit of the farmhouse exterior, finding nobody and nothing amiss, I returned inside. I locked the front door, then checked the back, and all the windows as well. Finally, I took Lily upstairs, lay on top of Viv's bed with her and decided that as I was no longer remotely tired I should get a few things done.

First, I texted Steven:

Do you have a number or email for the genealogist you recommended to Yash? I've been thinking of looking into the German side of my family

In fact, both sides of my family were German, but Steven didn't know that. I couldn't shake the idea that

Yash might have been killed to prevent him revealing the Sentinels' secrets. When Katie Crabtree had said she was having trouble at work, it was because her editor needed more corroboration for a story. Any documentary wanting to be taken seriously, especially on a subject as contentious as a religious cult, would have to do likewise. Had Yash approached the wrong person and suffered the consequences? Could it even have been one of his own family?

Next, I called Birch. Regardless of what I'd said to Katie, I knew seeing him would help me feel more secure in the house. Also, I had a job for him.

He answered from his kitchen at home, where he was preparing food for Ronnie. He placed the phone on the countertop as we talked, so all I could see was the ceiling and his head or hand occasionally popping into view.

'Evening, ma'am. Anything to report?'

'Actually, yes.' I told him about the burglary, my rushing here, and how I was staying the night. I didn't mention my paranoia about someone being outside.

'Woodentop abandoned you?' he said, outraged. 'Not on. Should be someone there with you.'

Birch could be overly protective, with a tendency to assume I was a helpless damsel. Most of the time I objected, but tonight I didn't mind so much. Even if he was two hundred miles away.

'I'm fine,' I insisted. 'I mostly feel bad for Viv. Mind you, in a way it's better that she wasn't here. I dread to think what might have happened.'

'Best not to dwell, I say. Dog still with you?'

'Yes, the best early warning system I could hope for.' I stroked Lily's smooth fur, feeling the compact muscles underneath. 'Birch, you still have friends in the Met, don't you?'

'Of course. Keep my hand in. Never know when they might be useful. Want me to look into something?' He'd always been to the point, an aspect of his personality I greatly appreciated.

'Yes, actually. Have you heard of the Sentinels of Heaven?'

He didn't reply immediately, and I heard the clink of a feeding bowl as he dealt with Ronnie. Then he returned to the phone and stood over it, looming down at the camera.

'Religious cult, isn't it? Think we had one or two run-ins with them over harassment.'

'That sounds about right. How easy do you think it would be to find out if someone was a member? Or even a former member?'

'Tricky. Not really police business unless it's relevant to an investigation. How about that journalist friend of yours? Karen, or something?'

'Katie,' I corrected him, hoping the sudden warmth in my cheeks wasn't visible on camera. 'She's very busy at the moment; I don't think she'd have the time.'

'Fair,' he said. 'Nothing but time on my hands, myself. You think this is connected to Yash's death?'

'I do, but I'm not sure how. He was a former member, and had agreed to make an exposé about them. I wondered if maybe someone else involved with our film is a member, and found out.'

He rubbed his chin, considering the theory. 'Good shout. Yes, wouldn't put it past that lot. Going to need a list, though. Lots of people involved in the film, yes?'

'I'm afraid so. More than fifty here at Hendale. But I think you can probably start with the principals first. Something tells me this wasn't a random crew member.' I gave him a short list of the main players.

Birch smiled. 'You're getting a copper's instinct. Mine never did me wrong.'

I still couldn't bring myself to mention my working with DCI Pierce, despite the guilt I felt about it. Instead I thanked him and ended the call. While we'd been talking Steven had texted me a phone number for the genealogist, a woman named Raven based in Devon. I dialled it, and reached her voicemail.

'Hello,' I said after the beep. 'This is Gwinny Tuffel. I'm an actress, working with Steven McDonald and Yash Rani. I'm sure you've heard what happened on the film set here in Hendale. Steven tells me you were looking into Yash's family tree, and I wondered if you could tell me what you found so I can . . . talk about it at his funeral. Do please call me back as soon as you can on this number. Thank you.' I didn't like lying, but if I told Raven the truth she might be reluctant to share anything.

Finally I felt ready for bed, at which point I remembered I'd brought neither pyjamas nor toiletries. I wasn't about to commandeer Viv's, so I found a quilted dressing gown on the back of the bathroom door, wrapped myself in it fully clothed and climbed into bed. Lily snuggled under with me, once again lending me her heat, and I lay there trying not to think about burglars, murderers, vampires . . . or vengeful cultists.

CHAPTER THIRTY-TWO

I was jolted awake by a cold, wet nose on my cheek. Lily stood over me, one paw on my chest and her nose perilously close to doing it again. She barked, which made my ears ring. I pushed her away blearily.

Then I sat bolt upright in bed. I'd forgotten to set an alarm! Cursing myself, I checked my phone and saw it was gone eight. I stumbled out of bed and downstairs, eagerly pursued by a still-barking Lily. The plywood over the front door had remained in place, and nothing in the house appeared to have been disturbed.

When I opened the back door, Lily rushed past me into the garden to perform her toilet. A layer of brittle frost clung to the ground, and the sky was a clear light blue. Once again, the cold, crisp light of morning cleared away the previous night's paranoia. Feeling better, I let out a deep breath and wondered if I had time for coffee.

I didn't know, because I had no idea what the schedule

was for today. What scenes would we be shooting? I texted Ruby to ask, then fed Lily when she came back inside. Finally, I returned upstairs to brush my teeth and dress properly, before making myself a coffee.

Ruby hadn't replied, so I tried calling instead. This time she answered immediately. 'Where are you? Fi and Pri are ready for you.'

'You're in make-up?'

A chorus of 'coo-ee's sounded in the background. Ruby must have had me on speaker.

'I've not long woken up. I was dealing with Viv's burglary.'

After a pause Ruby said, 'Sorry, what? Not sure I heard that right.'

'Didn't George tell you? Someone broke into Viv's house. I came over to deal with it and stayed for the night.'

'Oh, God. Is she all right?'

'She's still in hospital. I think that might be why it happened yesterday, to be honest. I'll tell you all about it later, but I'm actually calling to ask what we're shooting today.'

'Crypt scene interior, then re-shooting Luke's bedroom. They've given it to Zayn, you see. Chloe announced it last night, but we couldn't find you. I assumed you were walking your dog.'

I couldn't help but compare this lack of concern for my whereabouts to the panic and security alerts that had ensued when we couldn't locate Juliette Shine on Friday.

'Yes, I knew Zayn had got the part. Who'll be his stand-in, I wonder?'

'Probably do it himself and pocket both fees,' Ruby snorted. 'Anyway, look lively. I'll tell Chloe you're on your way.'

The day had barely started and already I was behind. I managed half of the coffee, then donned my coat and shoes and lifted Lily into the boot of the Volvo. Rushing down the country lanes toward Hendale Hall, I tried dialling the number Constable Horton had called from yesterday, but it was diverted to the local police station. I asked if they could send someone out to keep watch over the house until tonight, only to be met with short shrift and assurances that burglars aren't likely to return to the same house less than forty-eight hours later, madam. So much for community policing.

No sooner had I rung off than someone called me. I almost hit Decline without looking, but then saw it was Katie Crabtree and hesitated, my finger hovering over the screen.

I tapped Accept but quickly said, 'Katie, can I call you back in half an hour? I'm driving, and in a hurry. In fact, forget it altogether. I should never have asked you. I don't want to know.'

'Are you sure? Because you don't sound sure.'

'Oh, fiddlesticks. No, of course I'm not sure. But I don't – *bloody hell*!'

I slammed on the brakes in time to avoid hitting a flock of sheep in the middle of the road. A weathered old farmer and his sheepdog stood watch, and now turned to see the city fool with the squealing tyres. Meanwhile oblivious sheep ambled across the tarmac, moving from one field to another. The farmer slowly raised an eyebrow at me and shrugged.

'Actually, it looks like I'm not going anywhere for a few minutes, so you might as well go ahead. Please tell me I'm worrying over nothing.'

Katie's hesitation before responding was all I needed to hear, really. The rest was detail.

'I wish I could, but it's not great news. In fact it looks quite bad, if I'm honest. I was wrong, and you were right.'

'What do you mean? What did you see?'

'Birch and Tina sneaking off to have coffee yesterday, is what. I say sneaking off, but they weren't really hiding it. He took his dog and everything, down into the Tube then up into Soho. Met her outside a café near Leicester Square. They were there for almost an hour, having coffee and cake.'

'Did Tina have Spera and Fede with her? The Salukis? Perhaps they were meeting up before taking them for a walk?' I suggested hopefully.

'No, she was on her own. After they finished – with a kiss on the cheek, I might add – they went their separate ways.'

It was bad enough that Birch hadn't mentioned this at all in our conversation last night, but for some reason knowing Ronnie the black Lab was there stabbed at my heart. I ran what Katie had said back through my mind, clutching at straws.

'A kiss on the cheek, you said? Not on the lips?'

'Bless you, Gwinny, but I wouldn't take that as consolation. At one point they were holding hands across the table.'

Considering how long it had taken before Birch even came close to holding my hand, this felt like a particularly sharp dagger. But . . . it still wasn't proof.

'He's known Tina as long as he's known me. Perhaps they were just being friendly. Did you see them do anything else? A kiss on the cheek and a hand across the table aren't conclusive.'

Katie sighed. 'Gwinny, you asked me to watch him because you thought something was up, so don't defend him now. Dump him and run off with your leading man, I say. Or is he the dead one? The point is, find yourself a toy boy who can still get it up and forget about the copper. Now I've got to go, bye!'

She ended the call and left me staring at the sheep, dazed and confused. Katie was right; I'd asked her to do this because I was suspicious. I shouldn't dismiss what she told me because it wasn't what I wanted to hear.

I *wanted* to dismiss it. Birch had been a loyal, steadfast friend to me from the moment we met, through thick and thin. We'd spent hours walking dogs together; he'd listened patiently while I ranted about sexism and ageism in show business; we'd broken into crime scenes and outfoxed murderers, for heaven's sake. And, yes, not so long ago we'd finally become affectionate, sharing cuddles on the sofa in front of

Escape to the Country. Frankly, it was the closest I'd ever come to married life and nobody was more surprised than me to learn I was enjoying it.

But . . .

Tina was beautiful and elegant, with a *je ne sais quoi* that had men flocking to her. Even now, in her sixties, braying directors became dumbstruck when she walked on set; reporters of a certain age flustered their questions to her on press tours; reviewers recalled how seeing her on screen had revived teenage memories of her poster on their bedroom wall.

She was my best friend, but there was no question which of us was the A-lister and which the sidekick. I didn't even mind, because over the years it had helped draw creeps away from me as they focused all their attention on Tina instead. But Birch was different, and if this were true . . .

I flinched as a car horn blasted behind me. The sheep had finally cleared the road, followed by a second Collie who trailed the flock to keep them in line and pick up stragglers.

'Good on you, boy,' I murmured, pulling away. 'I see you, doing all the thankless work while your colleague gets to sit at the farmer's side.'

Katie might be mistaken. She could have misread the situation. I clung to that slim piece of driftwood in the flood of my emotions. A peck on the cheek? Merely friendly. Holding hands across the table? Sympathy for Birch's late wife, whom he had dearly loved. Meeting in full view of the public? That strengthened the case for innocence. If they were doing something nefarious wouldn't they continue to meet at Birch's house, or Tina's country house, Hayburn Stead?

These thoughts were cold comfort, but at that moment I'd take any I could find.

CHAPTER THIRTY-THREE

I was the last person to go through make-up and costume, so I joined Fi, Pri and Needles as they piled into a production car, which took us to the crypt set. It was barely a two-minute drive to the old gatehouse, but they were carrying their portable work kit bags, and I couldn't walk it for fear of messing up the work they'd all done to get me into character. At least I didn't have to worry about dog fur; Angela wasn't required for this scene, and had once again offered to take Lily for a walk while I filmed. I decided I should buy her a gift of some kind to say thank you.

33 INT. WESTENRA FAMILY CRYPT - CONTINUOUS

Van Helsing and Seward stop before a COFFIN, on a raised dais inside the crypt.

The coffin lid is askew, as if placed there hastily.

Van Helsing NODS to Seward, determined. DAWN

BREAKS through the open crypt door as they LIFT the lid together --

To reveal LUKE WESTENRA, sleeping inside the coffin! His FANGS protrude from his closed mouth, dripping BLOOD.

> DR SEWARD
>
> God protect us.

Van Helsing removes a WOODEN STAKE and HAMMER from her bag.

> VAN HELSING
>
> No, Jacqueline.
> (steels herself)
> Not God.

She positions the stake over Luke's HEART --

And HAMMERS it in!

Luke's EYES OPEN. He SCREAMS as BLOOD SPURTS from his body.

Van Helsing doesn't stop. Grim-faced, she STRIKES AGAIN -- and AGAIN -- and AGAIN --

Finally, exhausted and traumatised, Van Helsing and Seward breathe sighs of relief.

> DR SEWARD
>
> Is it done?

> VAN HELSING
>
> It is done.
> (to the body)

Rest now, sweet Luke. Your soul lies beyond Draculania's evil power.

It was now well past dawn, of course, but that was

easily fixed in post-production. We'd shoot at night for Scene Thirty-Two, the chase through the graveyard into the crypt, but the interior scene required many hours of daylight to keep us going through multiple takes. Every reset would require re-doing Zayn's make-up, re-dressing the fake body, cleaning the stake, re-setting blood squibs and more.

To my surprise Juliette was on set when we arrived, though not in costume.

'Safety in numbers,' she admitted when I asked why. 'After what happened yesterday, I intend to spend as little time alone as possible.'

The back wall of the crypt had been rolled aside, like Bill had shown me when I visited on Friday, and a camera rigged up in the space beyond. He stood alongside the camera crew, manning a remote console that would pump fake blood through hidden tubes to the dummy's chest. Chloe hovered around everyone, making sure that this time nothing could go wrong.

The body had been placed inside the coffin and attached to Zayn's head, which protruded through the hole in its fake floor. He saw me and grinned.

'The glamour of showbiz, eh, Gwinny?' he joked.

'Don't knock it, darling. Get this right and it'll be an iconic image. Sadie Frost won't know what hit her.'

'Who?' he said, making me feel very old.

Fi and Pri gently but firmly barged past me to give Zayn one last touch-up, while Needles busily snapped photos. I retreated to stand beside Ruby, who was being walked through the stake gag for the hundredth time by the stunt coordinator. My nerves jangled, anticipating another terrible mishap.

'That *is* a new stake, isn't it?' I blurted out. 'If you wiped down the old one the police will want to know where their evidence has gone.'

The entire set fell silent as everyone looked at me with a shocked expression.

'You're absolutely right, that was in very bad taste,' I said hastily. 'Sorry, everyone. Trying to keep things light.'

'By making jokes about murder,' said Ruby quietly. 'You're a laugh-a-minute.'

'Yes, all right, I apologised. Sorry. I'm nervous, that's all.' That was unusual. Normally walking onto set calms me down and helps me relax into a scene, but today I was on edge.

There was no logical reason I should be. I knew the stunt was perfectly safe, and everyone involved had checked, double-checked and triple-checked every aspect of the scene. If this had been any other set, I would have breezed through it.

But it wasn't, so a few minutes later when Ruby said that fateful line – 'No, Jacqueline. Not God' – and lined up the stake over the dummy chest, it didn't require much acting for me to tremble with fright.

She brought down the hammer. Zayn screamed in excruciating pain, gasping for breath as blood spurted from his chest. Ruby hammered again, and again, and again.

'Is it done?' I gasped.

'It is done. Rest now, sweet Luke. Your soul lies

beyond Draculania's evil power,' she said, shaking with nervous exhaustion.

We remained there, staring down at Zayn's rictus death mask and wide, unblinking eyes. In some ways this is the hardest part of any scene. Once you've finished your lines and action, the natural inclination is to move away and draw a line under things. But to make the editor's life easier actors pause for a few seconds, silently frozen in place while the camera lingers. You get used to it, but it never stops feeling odd.

'And *cut!*' shouted Chloe. 'Great job, everyone. Let's reset and go again in ten.'

Suddenly a mass of bodies surrounded the coffin, ready to remove all evidence of the scene we'd just performed. I watched as the stunt coordinator leant in to remove the stake from Zayn's chest . . .

Who blinked, smiled at me, and said, 'Gwinny, you look like you've seen an actual ghost.'

I let out a huge breath and returned the smile. 'Acting, eh? You can't beat it.'

Even ten minutes was a short time to reset this scene for a second take. The coffin, fake body and props had to be cleaned of stage blood, while Ruby and I changed into fresh costumes. Meanwhile the squibs were re-rigged, the blood replenished, Zayn's make-up re-applied and the body re-clothed, as Luke-the-vampire's white shirt was now covered in blood and dotted with black squib powder. But a film set in full flow is second only to a well-drilled army, and ten minutes later we ran through the scene again. Then, ten minutes after that, we did it again – this time with close-ups on the staking. Ten minutes later we did close-ups on Ruby, then Zayn, then me.

Without a working watch, it was impossible to track how much time had passed. I knew it had been a while due to the changing light through the open door. We'd finished take eight, and were holding our positions, when I heard the unmistakeable sound of scampering paws and distant cries of 'Lily! Lily, stop!'

I couldn't look round to see what was happening, as that would ruin the shot. So, I remained still while the scampering drew closer, culminating in something hard and solid colliding with my leg.

'Owwww!' I cried, unable to hold my position any longer. I looked down to see Lily, very wet and muddy, excitedly wagging her tail and holding a large stick in her mouth.

'*Cut!*' Chloe yelled, storming onto the set. 'What the hell is the dog doing here? I thought she was in your room!'

'I offered . . . to take her . . . for a walk,' Angela panted between breaths. 'You know, Gwinny . . . for an old girl . . . she can run.'

I laughed. 'So I see. Let's be grateful she wasn't fast enough to get here thirty seconds earlier, when we were busy hammering a stake into Zayn.'

'We've got everything we need, anyway,' said Chloe, turning to address the set. 'Thank you, everyone. Let's wrap and turn around ready for the graveyard transition tomorrow night.'

Angela clipped Lily back on-lead and we walked outside.

'I'm so sorry,' she said. 'I let her off-lead near the lake and she dived in for a swim. Then she found that thing tangled up in some reeds, and dragged it out of the water. I tried to take it from her but she ran away and came straight here to you.'

I looked down at Lily and saw that the thing clamped in her jaws wasn't a stick. It was wooden but obviously constructed, with riveted metal bands.

'Always put a Jack Russell on-lead before you try to take anything from them,' I said, laughing. 'They're firm believers in "finders keepers". Have you got a good hold of her? All right, then. Lily, *drop it*.'

The terrier snarled at me, defending her ill-gotten gains. I knew if I reached for it directly, she'd back away, so instead I snuck a hand around the side, to stroke her back and encourage her to relax.

'Good girl. *Drop it*,' I repeated, staring her down. She tried to back away, but I had a firm grip on her harness and held her in place.

Perhaps sensing she was out of options, Lily finally released the object and let it fall to the ground. I didn't take it immediately, because that would reinforce the idea she'd been tricked. Instead, I gave her my full attention, showing her that the object wasn't important by rewarding her with fuss and praise. She paid me back by shaking vigorously, spraying us with water, then allowed me to give her tummy rubs. Soon she'd forgotten all about the contraption and was happily rolling on her back, so I retrieved it and stood up.

'What on earth *is* this?' I wondered aloud. It was about eight inches long, resembling a wooden cylinder that had been flattened. But it had hinges on the long sides, and when I opened them the slats of wood reformed into a rough tube, encircled by thin metal bands. It almost resembled the sort of foot pump one might use to inflate a car tyre, except without a nozzle or canister, and it was covered in watery slime, which I feared foreshadowed an evening of doggy vomit.

'I wondered if it was an animal trap,' said Angela. 'You know, because they don't use guns.'

'Possibly, but there don't appear to be any jaws or spikes. Besides, why would it be in the lake?' I turned it over in my hand, collapsing it flat then opening it again. 'I don't think it's a clay pigeon launcher, either. Have you ever seen anything like it?'

'Definitely not. And I spent two years in the army, so I've seen lots of ordnance. Nothing like this, though.'

'How strange.' It felt like yet another inexplicable piece in this very confusing puzzle, and I couldn't imagine how it fitted. 'Angela, would you take this to DCI Pierce? Perhaps he can identify it. It might be nothing, but I'm sure he'd rather see it than not.'

She handed me Lily's lead, then took the object and turned to leave. 'Yes, of course—'

But Juliette, still hanging around, stood in her way. 'You served in the military? I didn't know that about you.'

'There's no reason you should,' said Angela. 'It was before I started acting.'

'Still, pretty big secret to keep in the middle of a murder investigation, wouldn't you say?'

'It's not a secret. Now, I'm going to take this to the police. Please get out of my way.'

The women faced off for a moment, then Juliette stood aside and let her stand-in walk away.

'You all forget, I'm the victim here – and I'm investigating. Don't think you can outsmart me!' Juliette yelled as she stormed off.

I was left alone with Lily as raindrops began to fall and clouds gathered overhead.

'There you are,' said Needles, suddenly appearing. 'Come on, I need you all back at the house so I can rescue your costumes. That blood won't clean itself.'

His assistant unfurled an umbrella and held it over me to protect against the rain as we walked to a production car.

A puzzle piece unexpectedly slotted into place, and I knew one thing for certain: I had to get Needles alone.

CHAPTER THIRTY-FOUR

By the time we reached the house, the clouds had turned black and the rain intensified. Everyone was glad to be back inside. In the study I hung back, letting Needles deal with the others before me, then waited until I was changing into my normal clothes to ask him the question.

'Did you send those pictures of Yash to the papers, yet?'

'Not yet,' he said with several safety pins gripped between his teeth as he returned my costume to the racks. 'I'm tending offers. Are you going to lecture me about the immorality of it all?'

'You don't need me to tell you that,' I said. 'But I was actually wondering if I could see them. There's something I want to check.'

He snorted. 'Oh, so now you've changed your tune? Not so immoral after all? All right, you can have a look but I'm not sending you copies.'

Lily barked lazily, but I agreed to Needles' terms and a minute later he called up the photos on his phone.

'What are you looking for, duck?'

'Did you take many of Yash himself?'

'Of course.'

He flicked through the gallery, past pictures of the trailer taken from the doorway, then the interior with everyone crowding around the body, to close-ups of Yash's face and upper body.

'Wait! Go back.'

'You said you wanted to see Yash's body.'

'I do, but . . . there, look.'

Needles stopped on a photo of the trailer interior, taken while people were crowding around the body. On the mirror, the words *Hendrick Lives* were written in red lipstick.

'Ooh, I didn't notice that in the background,' he said. 'But we all saw it eventually, anyway.'

'Yes, but now go back to the start. Remember you took some photos through the door, before we went inside?'

He flicked backwards to the first pictures, stopping at one taken from the doorway.

Inside the trailer, the dresser mirror was clearly visible – and clean.

'Oh, my God,' Needles squeaked. 'It really was written by a ghost!'

'What? No, no. Don't you see? Those words were written by one of the people in the trailer. While everyone else was looking at the body, someone picked up Juliette's lipstick and wrote on the mirror.'

'But why?'

'To distract us. Get us all worried about a vampire ghost, instead of focusing on looking for the flesh-and-blood killer. It's been working, too. Who first noticed the writing . . . ?'

'Chloe did. She said, "What the hell's that?" and pointed at the mirror. Does that mean she put it there? You know, like whoever finds the body is always the prime suspect.'

'I don't know. But I have a strong suspicion that whoever wrote this is the same person who killed Yash.'

Could it have been Needles himself? The photos, and his surprise at what we'd found, could be misdirection and bluff.

'Go back to Yash's body, please.'

He did, moving onward to the close-ups of Yash, his skin spattered with blood and the dark discolouration I'd remembered.

'There you are,' I murmured. 'Let's hear it for forensics. And dogs,' I added, glancing down at Lily. She pricked up her ears and tilted her head at me.

'What is it?' asked Needles. 'I don't see anything.'

'Nothing the tabloids are missing out on, I assure you.' I led Lily away. 'Don't worry, I'll explain later.'

The ballroom overlooked the gardens at the rear of the house, its tall windows granting an unrivalled view of the grounds and hills beyond, although grey rain clouds currently spoilt the vista. Cast and crew had gathered for refreshments, and I spied Ruby sitting on one of the many chairs lining the walls.

For the first time in days the atmosphere was one of optimism, having managed an afternoon's shooting without mishap. Nobody had been injured, nobody had been late, nobody had fluffed their lines. Nothing had gone wrong.

'The bedroom scene's going to be useless for sound if this rain keeps up,' said Ruby as I sat down beside her. 'They'll have to dub the whole thing. What did you think of my staking, by the way? Handy with a hammer.'

'Probably not something you should boast about in the current circumstances,' I pointed out.

She laughed it away. 'Cheer up, you know I didn't do it. Join me for a smoke?'

'I'd better not. Lily's had a long day and needs to sleep.' Dogs are a perfect excuse to leave any social gathering.

Ruby made her way outside. I offered some quick smiles and congratulations to the others, then left to head upstairs. The truth was that I wanted to make some phone calls and, colleagues or not, one of the people in that ballroom was Yash's killer. I couldn't risk them overhearing.

Lily practically pulled me up to the first floor, fully on board with our destination. With all the excitement she'd had and now a storm raging, perhaps she really did want to curl up and sleep.

Walking along the bedroom corridor, though, my thoughts returned to Ruby and how her story didn't sit right. Had she really taken a car out for a jog yesterday morning, instead of going around the estate as usual? No matter how much she claimed to have been inspired by my comments about the Dales, it seemed to have come out of the blue. Then there was the obviously made-up story about her cleaner, to explain away the suspicious phone call Angela had overheard. Ruby made no secret of believing she should play Draculania, and had been quick to point the finger at Zayn when I started asking questions.

Without much conscious thought I found myself walking past my own bedroom to the next door along. Ruby's.

Lily took some coaxing, knowing that her dog bed and favourite cushion were both in my room, but when I opened Ruby's door she scurried in and sniffed the air. I stood still for a moment, in case anyone had followed me upstairs, but it was difficult to hear over the sound of the storm outside. Ruby would be outside smoking for at least a couple more minutes. I stepped inside and pulled the door closed, dropping Lily's lead so she could mooch around while I, well, also mooched around. Hopefully with more purpose.

If you'd asked me what I was looking for, I couldn't have told you. I had a vague notion that something would turn up to explain Ruby's phone call, evasiveness or alleged jogging. Maybe all three? That would be nice.

I began with her handbag. I'm not proud, but it was right there on her bedside table and voluminous enough to hold all manner of evidence. No cigarettes and lighter, as she had those with her, along with her phone. But there was a purse, a card wallet, tissues, a folding hairbrush, an old-fashioned week-to-view paper diary . . . I stopped and removed the diary, flipping to the most recent two weeks. It was mostly blank, featuring reminders about her call times and cutting remarks about Juliette being 'late to set *again* . . .' Friday's entry noted this, alongside 'V' and a phone number I didn't recognise. 'V' for Viscount? I took a photo, as a low whine sounded from somewhere behind me.

Turning to see, I realised there had also been a sort of dull scraping sound going on for the past half-minute that I'd been subconsciously aware of but ignoring. Now I saw the source of both noises was Lily, scratching at the bottom drawer of a standing chest.

'Shh, Lily. *Quiet.*'

She whined louder, the very opposite of what I wanted, so I quickly took hold of her harness and pulled open the drawer. It contained . . . underwear.

'What's got into you?' I whispered.

A dog's nose is orders of magnitude more sensitive than a human's, with hundreds of millions more scent receptors. It's often said they can detect a spoonful of sugar in an Olympic-sized swimming pool. But there must be something to detect in the first place, and I didn't see what was so attractive here. Lily hadn't rooted through my underwear at any point, so why was she eager to sniff out Ruby's?

I picked the dog up with both hands, then lowered her nose-first towards the drawer for a sniff, hoping it would sate her curiosity. We'd been in here too long, and I already regretted my nosy parker impulse. Ruby might return at any moment.

The terrier lunged forward with paws outstretched, scrabbling at the underclothes. I hastily pulled her away and checked she hadn't ripped a hole in anything. At the very least I could try to neaten the mess she'd made, so Ruby wouldn't know anyone had been through the drawer.

But Lily's scrabbling wasn't random. There was purpose to all of it: the whining, scratching, and now scrabbling. She'd pulled aside several pairs of knickers to reveal a necklace, delicate filigree silver with jade insets.

A beautiful piece. Why had Lily been so keen to reach it?

In my mind a puzzle piece clicked into place. Understanding dawned, and I suddenly knew many things I hadn't before. Most importantly: this necklace wasn't Ruby's.

I removed it, smoothed down the knickers, closed the drawer and hurried out of the room with Lily on-lead.

As I opened the door to my own bedroom, I heard footsteps and smelt cigarettes. I turned to see Ruby mount the stairs, puffing from exertion, and knew I'd been very lucky.

'You should try quitting to get your lungs back,' I said, making conversation and hoping my own face wasn't too red from almost being caught.

'I'll quit when I'm dead,' she said, shaking her head.

'Sorry, bad taste. But you know me, Gwinny. What's life without a little danger now and again?'

What indeed?

I slipped into my bedroom, locked the door and unclipped Lily. Instead of going immediately onto her bed she took a long drink of water, then stood looking at me. Was it dinner time already? It had been long enough since breakfast, so I prepared some food and watched her wolf it down. Finally, she climbed on her bed and curled up on her cushion, nose to tail. I envied her.

On my phone, I found the photo I'd taken of Ruby's diary and dialled the number listed next to 'V'. Someone answered . . . and my heart sank. I told them I had the wrong number, then took the silver and jade necklace from my pocket and placed it in my handbag for safekeeping.

A thunderclap startled me. But no, it wasn't thunder; someone was hammering at my door. Lily barked indignantly at this interruption to her post-dinner nap.

'Who is it?' I called out.

'It's me,' said Ruby. 'Come on, get downstairs, quick!'

'Darling, I'm not in the bedroom scene. Neither are you, but if you want to watch then go ahead without me.'

'No, not for filming,' she yelled. 'It's the police! They've caught Yash's killer!'

CHAPTER THIRTY-FIVE

A uniformed officer was waiting to escort us downstairs. Zayn had been summoned too, so we went together and found ourselves ushered back into a ballroom where the celebratory mood had now turned sombre. DCI Pierce stood alongside two more constables, while Juliette (still in full Draculania costume), Chloe, Angela, Steven, Needles, Fi and Pri and Walter from security all waited patiently.

The rain grew heavier still, clattering against the windows and threatening a storm. It almost felt like a scene from the film.

'Good. I think we can begin,' said DCI Pierce, unwrapping an extra-strong mint.

I was a little disappointed that he'd evidently had a breakthrough in the case but hadn't shared it with me. Weren't we supposed to be working together? Then again, I'd learnt plenty since yesterday that I hadn't yet told him. Oh, well. I decided the important thing was to find Yash's killer, no matter who did it, and felt rather pleased with my magnanimity.

That lasted about three seconds until Juliette Shine stepped in front of everyone and said, 'Thank you all for coming. I'm now going to tell you who murdered Yash Rani.'

DCI Pierce offered me a wan smile, and I understood I'd been played for a fool. He'd been working with Juliette as well, without telling either of us. How could I have been so blind? I'd been so ready to accept his approval that I didn't stop to question his motives. Dejected, I took a seat near the windows and lifted Lily onto my lap.

'First, let's establish the timeline of what happened that day,' said, Juliette, pacing back and forth. 'Not long after dawn, Ruby saw Yash acting suspicious around the old ruined cottage out in the woods.'

'It might have been Zayn, actually,' said Ruby. 'I wasn't all that close.'

Zayn glared at her. 'What were you doing in the woods that early?'

'Jogging. Every morning for forty years. What's your excuse?'

'It wasn't me. That's all the "excuse" I need.'

'Zayn's right, it wasn't him,' said Juliette. 'I'll explain later. First, we all went through hair and make-up, got dressed, then waited around for scene start. Apparently Gwinny was late? I didn't notice. I was busy rewriting lines in my trailer.' Ruby snorted derisively, and Juliette turned to her. 'I wouldn't take that attitude if I were you. Angela overheard you on the phone while Gwinny was in make-up, asking about when I'd be out of my trailer.'

All eyes turned to Ruby. 'So *that's* who – well, it doesn't matter. It was nothing to do with you,' she said defiantly.

'But I heard you,' said Angela. 'You were asking how long she'd be away, and when she'd be back.'

'Yes, but not — anyway, this was before Juliette had even come out of her trailer.'

'So, who were you talking about?' asked DCI Pierce. He'd settled at the side of the room, taking a position where he could observe everyone's reactions.

'That's none of your business,' said Ruby. 'It was a private matter.' She reddened, and I smiled inwardly.

'Ruby's right,' I said. 'I'll vouch for her. That phone call had nothing to do with what happened to Yash.'

'How would you know? You were in make-up at the time,' said Juliette.

'Then you'll have to trust me. Surely you weren't going to accuse Ruby of killing Yash, were you?'

Juliette sniffed. 'As it happens, no I wasn't. All she's guilty of is being jealous of my success.'

'Oh, please,' said Ruby, rolling her eyes. 'Why are we listening to you instead of the police, anyway? You're not a detective. You could barely even play one.'

'Shut up!' Juliette's temper flared. 'Dammit, everyone knows you wanted this part, but it's mine, you hear me? Because I'm the star here!'

DCI Pierce looked shocked by this outburst, but the

rest of us had heard it all before.

Ruby laughed. 'For your information, when this terrible schlock wraps and you go back to selling menopause pills on TV, I'll be doing eight months in *The Mousetrap*. And if you seriously think starring in this nonsense is going to remake your career, you should take a good, long look in the mirror.'

'Schlock?' cried Chloe. 'Now hang on a minute—'

'She's deflecting,' said Juliette, cutting her off. 'Don't make this about you, Ruby, because nobody cares. I've found the killer, and none of you can beat that.'

In the silence that followed, DCI Pierce coughed politely, and Ruby stalked out of the room, casting me an angry glare. I was tempted to go after her, but it could wait. Finding out who killed Yash was more important.

'All right,' said Juliette, wrestling back control of the situation. 'So, we finally started shooting Scene Twenty-Six. Ruby, Gwinny and me were on camera. Chloe was directing. Steven was at video village—'

'Actually, he wasn't,' I said, unable to resist scoring a point. 'Nobody saw him, and when I mentioned the scene, he said we took a break because, quote, "Juliette screwed up". But everyone who was there knows it was actually Ruby who made a mess of things.'

Steven scowled at me but said nothing.

'Interesting,' Juliette resumed. 'Needles and Zayn weren't there, either. So—'

'And I wasn't at the trailer,' said Zayn, raising his hand.

'I know!' Juliette yelled impatiently. 'Do you even

understand what a "timeline" is? We haven't got to the trailer yet.'

Zayn lowered his hand, abashed.

'Ruby screwed the pooch, so we took fifteen and I told everyone I was going to my trailer. But then I got outside and saw the fog, and thought, you know what? This is good for me to maintain character. So, I took a walk instead. Everyone with me so far?'

'Just get on with it,' said Chloe in a bored voice.

'Hey, none of you were fast enough to figure this out, so I'm making sure you can keep up. Now, from what I've learnt everyone went in different directions. After about five minutes Steven saw Gwinny taking her dumb dog for a walk, and Gwinny saw him arguing on the phone, yes?'

I nodded. She'd missed some things, like me taking Lily's dog bed upstairs, then chasing her around the house and bumping into George, but otherwise she was correct so far.

'After that there's almost ten minutes where nobody can vouch for anyone else,' Juliette continued. 'We were all separated, and in that time, someone killed Yash. Finally, Chloe met Gwinny at the back of the house and walked to unit base, where everyone gathered round my trailer. You called security, and then I arrived. I knew something was wrong because I never lock my trailer. I have a sixth sense about these things.'

I rolled my eyes. Juliette had displayed no such precognition at the time. It was Lily who'd first scented the blood dripping on the step. But I said nothing, as it would only delay matters further.

'Finally, the security guy broke open the door.'

If Walter was surprised or offended that Juliette didn't even know his name, he didn't show it.

'We found Yash lying dead, with nobody else inside, and the writing on the mirror. We were all there.'

'I told you there was evil in this place,' Angela muttered.

Juliette ignored her. 'So, the big question is obviously, who did it? First let's eliminate the people who didn't. Starting with you, Gwinny.'

I nodded, glad that she hadn't completely lost the plot.

'You're in the clear, because your big secret isn't that you're a killer; you're sleeping with the Viscount.'

A collective gasp went up around the room. Needles smiled at me and said, 'You go, girl.'

'I'm really not,' I protested weakly. 'We're . . . friends.'

'Oh, come on,' said Juliette. 'We've all seen the way you look at one another. You take your dumb dog for walks together, and I even caught you holding hands over that stupid jigsaw. That's why nobody saw you for those ten minutes, until Chloe found you.'

'Actually, I was walking around the house. Some of the crew saw me outside the library.' I searched the room for support, but none came. 'It was barely ten minutes, for heaven's sake. What kind of clinch could we have possibly had in that time?'

Fi sniggered. 'He's no spring chicken.'

'Nobody's judging you,' said Juliette, ignoring my

protests. 'And like I said, it's an alibi. You didn't do it.'

'Yes, I know that, thank you.'

My sarcasm sailed over her head. She turned to Steven.

'Then there's our wonderful producer. Did you all know he took out insurance for millions of dollars in case I can't work? At first I thought that explained everything, because obviously the killer actually wanted me, not Yash. But now I know he's innocent. As innocent as a producer gets, anyway.'

Steven frowned as some giggles were had at his expense.

'He does have a secret, though. I'll come to it in a moment. First, let's talk about Zayn. He wasn't happy being Yash's stand-in, were you? Not after being turned down for the role.'

'I wasn't turned down,' said Zayn sulkily. 'Yash gazumped us all.'

'And with him dead, by golly, you've got it now. But I don't think you killed for it.' Juliette turned back to Steven. 'The secret you've both been keeping is that Zayn was bribing you to fire Yash and cast him as Luke instead, wasn't he? After all, why kill for it when you can pay off the producer? But Steven wouldn't do it, and when Yash turned up dead you both knew it made you look guilty.'

The young actor looked stunned. 'I argued my case, but I didn't bribe him. Where would I get that kind of money?'

'Never mind that,' Steven interrupted, 'what makes

you think I'd take a backhander in the first place? Yash was an asset to this movie, an irreplaceable actor whose involvement elevated the project—'

'Oh, thanks ever so much,' said Zayn.

'You know what I mean. His loss is a real blow to this production. I wouldn't take bribes to replace him, and I certainly wouldn't kill him!'

'Relax, Mac,' said Juliette. 'I already said you didn't do it. Neither did Zayn, because like I said, the killer was targeting me, not Yash. Having him out of the way was pretty good for Zayn, though . . . and for Chloe.'

The director sat up. 'Nonsense. Who told you that?'

'Nobody had to. You think I don't research my director when I take on a role? Your "curse" is well-documented, starting with the accident on that soap.'

'I was cleared of wrongdoing,' said Chloe through gritted teeth. 'It *was* a tragic accident, and I've worked very hard ever since to ensure my sets are safe.'

Angela snorted. 'You mean apart from toppling lights and murdered leading men?'

'I'm not the key grip. I can't be held responsible for a light not being secure. Nor for some madman going around killing actors.'

'Maybe not in a court of law,' said Juliette. 'But that's a lot of coincidences, and some people still feel you should take the rap. Needles, what do you say?'

The wardrobe manager looked stunned to be suddenly included in this conversation.

'No, no, duck. Chloe was cleared of everything. I helped defend her.'

'That's right, and you've been holding it over her ever since. It's why you keep turning up on her sets, isn't it? It isn't the quality of your costumes.'

'What?' he exploded. 'How dare you! Chloe, tell them, I would never—'

'Oh, like either of you would admit it. Anyway, that's enough about who *didn't* kill Yash.'

A flash of lightning illuminated the room. Everyone turned to the windows in time to hear the first crash of thunder, which rattled the windows and made Lily whimper.

Juliette smiled. 'Let's talk about who did.'

CHAPTER THIRTY-SIX

A hush fell across the room, punctuated by the lashing rain outside.

'I already took you through Friday's timeline,' said Juliette, enjoying the moment. I could sympathise with that. It was like standing centre stage in a spotlight. 'But to solve this case we have to go further back, to Thursday night, when the Viscount saw Yash arguing with someone in that old cottage. That's how I know it wasn't you, Zayn.'

Where was she going with this? George had told me it was Juliette herself he saw arguing with Yash.

'Who was he arguing with?' asked Chloe.

'Me, so he says.' Juliette smirked. 'But that's not true. I was in my room at the inn all night. He *thought* it was me, because he's used to seeing me in costume. He forgot that to play Draculania I wear a wig, to cover my natural blonde hair.'

She reached up and tore off her wig of long, dark

hair to demonstrate. Fi and Pri gasped simultaneously, because it would take at least twenty minutes to re-apply.

Steven muttered 'Natural?', but Juliette ignored him.

Hair dye aside, though, she was right. I'd been so fixated on proving Juliette was there – or thinking George had mistaken Zayn for Yash – that I'd ignored the other, now obvious, explanation. Yes, Zayn had been imitating Yash lately, because that was his job. But it was Angela's job to imitate Juliette, too. George had even said to me that he recognised Juliette because of the dark hair and her accent. But, like many Scandinavians, Angela spoke English with a transatlantic accent that could easily be mistaken for American.

The stand-in unconsciously raised a hand to her natural dark hair, and my mind began working overtime. If it was *Angela* who'd argued with Yash in the cottage, that changed everything. The photo, the unlit cigarette, the light in Juliette's trailer . . .

'Oh!' I said suddenly. 'The light in Juliette's trailer! Walter, tell them.'

Walter looked like he wanted the earth to swallow him up. 'After midnight, you see – doing my rounds, that is – on Thursday – I saw a light in your trailer – someone moving around – I assumed it was you . . .'

'But it wasn't,' said Juliette. 'Like I told you already, I was at the inn.' She turned to Angela. 'I think we all know who it really was. Would you care to tell us what you and Yash argued about?'

Angela stiffened. 'No, I wouldn't. Yes, we met that

night in the cottage, but it was a private matter and nothing to do with his death.' She was taking a leaf out of Ruby's book, but this time I couldn't help her. I was still trying to assemble these new puzzle pieces for myself.

'It's OK,' said Juliette with a smile. 'I already know. You were sleeping with him, weren't you? And together you plotted to kill me, so you could take my role and star in the film alongside him. But Yash got cold feet. That's why you were arguing . . . and why you lured him to my trailer to kill him. You must think I came in here without a hat!' Juliette said the last line triumphantly, thrusting a finger at Angela.

'I . . . what?'

Chloe explained. 'It's her catchphrase. You know, from Detective Kingfisher.'

'What kind of catchphrase is that?' said Needles. 'It makes no sense.'

'It does in context,' Juliette protested. 'Whatever, it doesn't matter. Angela did it, and I have proof!'

By now Angela was on her feet. The two women faced one another, and if Juliette hadn't removed her wig, they could have been reflections. Instead, it was weird and unsettling, especially when the leading lady flung back her cape with a flourish and said, 'Inspector Pierce?'

The DCI took his cue and held up a folded piece of paper. 'We found this in Mr Rani's room,' he said. 'It was likely slipped under his door the night before.'

My mouth fell open. He'd told me there was nothing

273

in Yash's room, but that was obviously another lie. I felt sick at how easily Pierce had deceived me.

He read the note aloud: '*Juliette knows about your history. She's helping him conceal it. Evidence is in Trailer 1. Stashed under sink, behind bleach. Go tomorrow, during filming – A friend.*'

It was typewritten, on unmarked paper. 'There's an old typewriter in the Viscount's study,' I said. 'Where Needles is set up now. Anyone could have typed it there.'

'Why didn't she text him?' asked Pri.

'To stay anonymous,' said Juliette. 'Look, see? Trailer One, that's my trailer. It was a set-up.'

Chloe disagreed. 'How does this prove anything? It's too vague, and "a friend" could be anyone.'

'It's not just "a" friend. The "A" is for Angela!'

Or Astrid, I thought to myself. It wasn't looking good for the stand-in.

'Angela lured Yash into my trailer, knowing it was empty while we shot the library scene,' Juliette continued. 'She waited there, and when he came in she attacked him with the stake. She already admitted she's ex-military. She's got the strength and knowledge to kill someone like that. Then she locked the door from the inside and escaped through the window. Case closed.'

'No! None of that is true,' Angela protested.

'Do you deny you have military training?' said DCI Pierce.

'I'm from Norway. We have compulsory national service.' That made him pause, so she pressed her argument. 'I didn't send that note. I didn't attack Yash. How could I lie in wait for him, when I was being lit on set?'

'You left when I stepped in for the take,' said Juliette. 'Plenty of time for you to sneak into my trailer.'

'But she was walking Lily,' I pointed out. The terrier barked in agreement. 'When we broke, I found them outside the front of the house.'

Juliette nodded. 'That's how your dog knew something was wrong. Remember it was trying to get inside the trailer? It knew Yash was in there.'

In my opinion that had more to do with Lily's canine sense of smell than having been witness to a terrible crime.

Zayn spoke up. 'What does it mean about Yash's history? What's the evidence you're keeping in your trailer, Juliette?'

'No, dumbass. I'm not keeping anything. It was a lie, to lure him inside.'

'It might refer to the Sentinels of Heaven cult,' said DCI Pierce. 'As I understand it, Mr Rani was a former member. Not the sort of thing you want everyone on set to find out about.' He popped a fresh extra-strong mint in his mouth and turned to me. 'Ms Tuffel, you couldn't decide if Mr Rani or Ms Shine was the target. It turns out, that's because it was both of them. With Mr Rani out of the way, Ms Shine would have been next. We also now know why he was found in that trailer, and how Ms Viste knew where he'd be – because she lured him there.'

Those were exactly the questions I'd put to DCI Pierce in the production trailer. He'd had no answers then, but instead of helping me find out he'd taken them and solved the case with Juliette. I'd never felt so cheated.

'I didn't do it.' Angela insisted as the uniformed constables led her away. 'I'm being framed!'

DCI Pierce laughed. 'That's what they all say. As you were, ladies and gents. Thanks for your help, Ms Shine.' He turned to me as he followed them out. 'Maybe there's some use in these films, after all.'

Needles applauded, while Fi and Pri rushed to Juliette and fixed her wig. Chloe and Steven joined them, all congratulating her for solving the case. Walter left to return to his duties, still looking bewildered.

I remained seated with Lily by the windows, listening to rain on glass and trying to work out where I'd gone wrong. Angela had been a suspect, of course, like everyone else who'd been at the trailer. But I would never have drawn the conclusions Juliette had. Plotting with her lover Yash to kill Juliette so they could be a *Draculania* power couple? Luring Yash to the trailer with an anonymous letter because he got cold feet? Using her military training to hammer a stake into his chest? I'd drawn different conclusions from the same evidence she'd presented. A lot of what she and DCI Pierce had said didn't seem to add up.

But the inspector was satisfied, and I had another secret to expose anyway. I led Lily out of the ballroom, unheard over the storm and unseen by the others. They

276

were all too busy orbiting the bright star of Little Miss Sunshine to notice.

That suited me. I didn't want an audience when I confronted Ruby about what she'd done.

CHAPTER THIRTY-SEVEN

There was no sign of Ruby downstairs, not even in the previously private areas now being used for production, or on the portico having a smoke. Surely she wouldn't have gone outside in this weather?

I decided to try upstairs, and upon reaching the bedroom corridor saw one of the doors was ajar. My door. Someone was in there, moving around. Lily strained on her lead, and though I held her back I was glad not to be the only one who knew something was wrong.

Approaching the door quietly, the scent of old cigarette smoke confirmed my fears. The *clang* of Lily's water bowl being accidentally kicked, followed by quiet swearing, left no doubt.

'Hello, Ruby,' I said, entering. 'Looking for something?'

She froze. Having been in the same situation myself recently while searching her room, I sympathised. But not much.

Ruby opened her mouth to improvise an excuse, like when she claimed the cut on her hand was from a fall while running. Then she saw the look in my eye and knew that wouldn't do. With slumped shoulders, she sat heavily on the bed next to the upended contents of my handbag.

'How did you know?'

I picked up the handbag and opened its hidden security compartment to reveal the silver and jade necklace.

'What kind of burglar breaks into a house and turns out all the drawers, but leaves most of the jewellery? Who declines to steal a valuable computer? Who upends ornaments onto the floor, but is careful not to break them? I called the phone number you'd written next to "V" in your diary, by the way. I wish I'd been surprised when it connected to Hendale General Hospital.'

Ruby looked indignant that I'd been through her diary, but she was in no position to lecture on morality.

'That's who Angela overheard you calling, wasn't it?' I continued. 'I'd told you Viv had been rushed to hospital, so while I was in with Fi and Pri you tried to find out how long she'd be in for. Then you messed up the library scene because you were too distracted thinking about how you could break into Viv's house, and the next morning you got a production driver to take you to the Dales for a run. You jogged over to her house, broke in – cutting your hand on the glass you smashed – and stole this necklace, while trying to make it look like a normal burglary.'

Despite her silence, I knew I was right. 'Lily caught its scent in your room. To her, the necklace smells like home. Viv's home. Why, Ruby? Help me understand.'

'It's mine,' she said resignedly. 'Or it used to be. It went missing when I was still married to my ex-husband, and I could never understand how I'd lost it. Then I saw Viv bloody Danforth wearing it at the BAFTAs, the year after we'd all done a season at Stratford together. She must have thought he'd bought it for her. Ha!' Ruby scowled. 'As if that cheapskate would spend tuppence when he could recycle instead.'

I sat next to her on the bed. 'You told me about his affairs, when you were going through the divorce. You didn't mention Viv.'

'The others didn't bother me as much. But losing that necklace . . .'

'Perhaps you should keep it,' I said suddenly, offering it to her. 'Viv will assume it was taken by the burglar. Which, I suppose, it was.'

Ruby pushed my hand away. 'When I found it, I felt triumphant. Like I was righting a decades-old wrong. But when I came back here, and had to hide it like a naughty stash, I realised it just reminds me of his betrayal.'

'So what were you doing in here when I found you?'

'I saw you come out of my room earlier. When I checked and saw it was missing, I knew you'd figured things out. I was going to throw it in the lake so you couldn't prove anything.'

I got to my feet. Lily barked, ready for action. 'Then let's do that. Now, together.'

'No, no. It still means something to Viv. Let her have the memory. Let her have him.'

My phone rang, startling us both.

Ruby stood up. 'I leave it in your hands, Gwinny. I'm sure you'll do the right thing,' she said bitterly, striding through the open door. I understood why she was angry, but I wouldn't apologise. As she walked away, I checked the caller ID on my phone and saw it was Birch.

'I was about to call you,' I answered. 'They've arrested Angela for Yash's murder.'

'You don't look too pleased about it, if you don't mind my saying.' He was in his lounge again, with Ronnie's head flopped over on the former policeman's lap. As he talked, he tore a piece of cooked ham into strips and fed them to the Labrador. 'Sounds about right to me, though.'

'What do you mean?'

'Looked into the Sentinels of Heaven like you asked. There's someone else besides Yash Rani with you who used to be a member: Astrid Nordberg, aka Angela Viste. Good thing you gave me her real name.'

'You can thank the local police for that,' I said, without elaborating. 'So Angela was a former Sentinel . . . oh, of course.'

I remembered the way she'd covered her eyes over Yash's body in the trailer. She wasn't shielding herself from the grisly sight; she was performing the Sentinels' recognition gesture I'd read about.

One by one, puzzle pieces slotted into place. At last, I understood what had happened on Thursday night, and why Angela had said her meeting with Yash was a personal matter.

'Picture the scene, Birch. Earlier in the week, Chloe overheard Angela arguing with Yash. She said, "Not here, later!" and walked away. So "later" they met at midnight in the old cottage, where they wouldn't be overheard – because Yash was trying to persuade Angela to take part in his documentary about the Sentinels.'

'Her membership isn't something she likes to shout about. Done a good job keeping it secret. Took some digging to find it myself. Plus the name change, of course.'

'Yash and Angela *were* overheard, though, by George – um, I mean, the Viscount – who was walking through the woods.'

'Hang on,' said Birch. 'Why's the chap out at midnight?'

'Why not? It's his estate. Perhaps he saw people going for a midnight stroll and wondered what they were up to.'

'Bit rum.'

I smiled at the irony of a former detective disapproving of such snooping, and retrieved the burnt picture of Father Tobias from my coat pocket. 'Angela still refused to take part. So, Yash tried to force her hand by showing her this photo of Father Tobias . . . with his arm around Astrid Nordberg. If the papers got hold of that, everyone would know.'

Birch's moustache twitched. 'So how did it get burnt?'

'Remember the damp, unlit cigarette? Imagine Angela

was holding the photo, faced with the prospect of her big secret coming out. But then she had an idea. She asked Yash, who was a smoker, for a cigarette. Feeling like this was her admission of defeat, he gladly obliged. Of course, she also needed a light. He offered, and she took his lighter . . .'

'Then burnt the photo with it. Clever girl.'

'She threw it into a pile of stones while it was still burning, but the ground was so damp it extinguished the flame before the whole photo could be destroyed. Angela had only really wanted the lighter, so she tossed the unlit cigarette on the ground and walked away. First thing next morning, Yash returned to the cottage to search for the photo by daylight. He didn't find it, but he was seen by Ruby on her morning run. Later on, Lily sniffed out the photo because she recognised the scent of Angela's hand cream.' I explained that Lily had been a big fan of the stand-in's moisturiser.

'So, you think she killed Yash to keep her ex-Sentinel status secret?'

'It makes more sense as a motive than plotting to kill Juliette, don't you think? She lured him to Angela's trailer, stabbed him with the stunt stake and wrote *Hendrick Lives* on the mirror to distract us all with stories of vampires and curses.'

'Hmmm,' said Birch. 'I've seen worse for less.'

There were still some pieces that didn't fit neatly. Some seemed to belong to a different puzzle altogether. Why did Angela choose Juliette's trailer in broad (well, foggy) daylight? Why not arrange another secret midnight meeting? What was the 'evidence' he thought he'd find in there? How had she staked Yash without getting herself covered in blood? How did Angela get out of the trailer while leaving it locked from the inside? Why was Yash's skin discoloured?

And what was the wooden contraption Lily had found in the lake? Earlier I'd felt sure it was related to how Yash was killed. But if so, why would Angela walk the dog anywhere near its location—

'Hang on,' I said, looking around. 'Where's Lily?'

I'd been so consumed theorising with Birch that I wasn't paying attention . . . and hadn't closed the door after Ruby left.

Lily was gone.

CHAPTER THIRTY-EIGHT

I rushed out of the room, dreading another chase all over the house or, worse, outside. But for once luck was on my side, and Lily hadn't gone far. In fact, she was at the corner of the corridor, sitting by the locked door to the tower.

'What are you doing there, girl?' I said, casually approaching her as if it was all perfectly normal. If I rushed she might bolt, and if I tiptoed she might sense anxiety, so I tried to act like this sort of thing happened every day. Come to think of it, it almost did.

I hadn't unclipped Lily when I found Ruby in my room, so her lead trailed on the floor. I drew close enough to step on it without making her panic, but even then she didn't try to escape. She sat there, tilting her head occasionally as if looking at something odd. I looked past her, down the other leg of the corridor, but saw nobody. Perhaps her sensitive dog hearing was picking up something I couldn't?

Then I heard it. Someone was crying . . . and the sound came from behind the locked door.

All the things George had said about the tower being hazardous, ruined and unsafe flashed through my mind. But someone was in there, and clearly upset. I couldn't leave them.

Keeping Lily on a short lead, I pushed at the door. It swung open. Inside I found a dusty landing, from which a spiral stone staircase led upwards. The crying came from somewhere above. I closed the door behind me so nobody would be foolish enough to follow and picked my way over detritus on the floor: stone, plaster, dust sheets, old tourist signs that would once have guided visitors inside.

Eye bolts in the staircase's outer wall held a thin rope. I clutched it with one hand, Lily firmly held in the other, and began to climb. Who would have come up here? It was certainly a private place to have a cry, but we all had our own rooms, and besides nobody would think twice about an actor having a breakdown. It was as unremarkable as the sun rising.

Dim light shone through narrow window-slits in the wall, which thankfully had been glazed to keep out the weather. I climbed carefully, watching for loose or missing stones, but hadn't seen any yet.

What did I expect to find up here? I don't honestly know. But when I finally reached the top, what I saw was so unpredictable it took my breath away.

The tower widened out into a small, flat space. On the other side was a door, which, judging by the keening wind, led outside to the balcony. To one side of the space was what could only be described as a shrine. Framed photographs of a young man stood on a makeshift altar draped in cloth, lit by several flickering candles.

Most surprising of all, George knelt in front of the shrine, bent double and crying.

I was about to call his name when my phone pinged with a text message, unreasonably loud in this small, quiet space. Caught by surprise, George stumbled and turned to me with wide, red-rimmed eyes.

'Oh, God, it's you,' he gasped. 'What are you doing here?'

My phone pinged again, and I tried to muffle the sound with my hand. 'Sorry, sorry! Oh, heavens, I'm intruding. I heard someone crying, and – oh, of course. That's Charlie, isn't it?'

The photographs looked very much like how I imagined George as a young man, and at last I understood. This was a shrine to his dead son, in the one place he could be absolutely sure no tourist would ever go so long as everyone believed the tower was unsafe. No tourist except me, that is, barging in with my usual lack of grace. I felt awful.

Lily pulled me towards the door, wanting to see what was on the other side. I struggled to hold her back while also retrieving my phone as it pinged yet again. The sound echoed off the stone walls like a bell tolling.

I finally wrestled it from my pocket, intending to switch it to silent, and saw the text notifications. They were from Raven, the genealogist tracing Yash's family, in reply to the voicemail I'd left.

Reading the message previews, a cold sensation washed over me from head to toe. All those oddly shaped puzzle pieces, the ones that had felt like a different puzzle altogether, finally slotted into place.

Juliette and DCI Pierce had got it completely wrong. Angela hadn't killed Yash. The murderer hadn't escaped the trailer and somehow locked it behind them. Yash's death had nothing to do with the Sentinels of Heaven.

My instincts had been right all along . . . except when they told me to climb this tower, because now I was alone with a killer.

I pocketed my phone and mumbled an apology, trying not to betray what I'd just learnt, but it must have been written all over my face. George moved to block my path back to the stairs. He knew the game was up.

'You served in the army.' I backed away from him as he slowly approached, but was soon brought up short by the balcony door. 'Did you specialise in explosives, by any chance? Or engineering?'

'Munitions,' he said with a smirk. 'Something upon which your chaps in special effects are always happy to expound. People do so enjoy talking about their job to anyone who shows genuine interest, what?'

Lily barked, but it would take more than a terrier with delusions of grandeur to save me now. I fumbled for the door latch and pushed it open against the wind. The storm raged, lashing rain against my back.

'When did he tell you?' I shouted above the noise of the storm, still backing away. The balcony flagstones were wet and slick underfoot. 'Was it the day Steven saw you arguing? That story about trying to buy your Porsche was nonsense, wasn't it?'

'The arrogance of the man!' George yelled back, advancing into the rain. 'He called me the moment he joined the film. I knew I'd have to get rid of him eventually.'

'All those years, cashing in on the legend of the Hendale Vampire. Telling the same old story, over and over. Nobody knows how much of it is true, do they? But now you know one particular part is definitely a lie. Because Helena didn't die of malaria, did she?'

'It's preposterous!' George wiped stinging rain from his eyes. 'That stupid woman filled his head with nonsense. It would have ruined everything! Everything I've done in Charlie's name! Do you know he made me a "generous offer" to allow me to stay here? Generous! As if he bloody well owned the place!'

My back pressed against the tower's crenelated parapet. There was nowhere else for me to go but down. Wind howled around my ears and rain soaked my clothes to the skin. A thunderclap crashed overhead. George's grey hair danced, whipped by the elements as lightning forked the sky.

'You said you're leaving it to the National Trust anyway,' I pointed out.

'As a memorial to my son! A shrine to the legacy of Hendale and the Viscounts Henning! Not a playboy mansion for some money-grubbing, filthy *native*!'

He lunged for me. Thunder boomed. Instinctively I

recoiled, but lost my balance and toppled backwards with Lily's lead still in my hand. My feet left the ground—

Lily barked and leapt at the Viscount, yanking me upright. She sank her teeth into his ankle. He screamed in pain and slipped on a wet flagstone. His head smacked against a crenelated upright with a sickening wet slap, and he collapsed to the ground. The driving rain washed blood from the wound, painting a watery red halo around his body.

'Yash Rani was born in Margate,' I said, not caring if he could hear me.

CHAPTER THIRTY-NINE

Downstairs, Walter guided me to a chair in the ballroom and wrapped me in a thermal heat blanket. Needles found an old tartan blanket to cover Lily, who lay snoozing by my side. The other cast and crew had been corralled into the same room by the police, after they cordoned off the tower.

A runner handed me a cup of tea. I held it in my hands for several minutes without drinking, enjoying sensation returning to my cold hands. Outside, the storm had finally begun to pass and evening light broke through the clouds.

'You shouldn't have tried to confront him alone,' said DCI Pierce, who had now returned with Juliette and a vindicated Angela.

'I didn't go to confront him,' I protested. 'I didn't know he was the killer until I was already up there.'

Juliette snorted. 'So it was dumb luck, huh?'

'Actually, no. It was making sure each piece of the

puzzle fits correctly, rather than trying to jam the lugs together even when they don't.' My jigsaw analogy was lost on her, but I could think of no better way to describe the differences in our approach. Not without a lot of swearing, anyway.

'What do you know about it?' she said. 'I've been investigating this from the moment we found Yash's body.'

'Yet you still got everything wrong. It's almost impressive.'

'I knew he was dodgy,' said Steven with a smug expression.

'You also insisted you wouldn't accuse him so long as we were filming in his house,' I reminded him, 'so don't pat yourself on the back too readily. But the argument you overheard between Yash and George was a crucial puzzle piece.'

'Then please explain what those pieces were, and how they fit,' said DCI Pierce.

I took a sip of tea and began.

'The timeline Juliette laid out earlier, from the day before to us finding Yash in the trailer, is basically correct. But she misunderstood many events and jumped to the wrong conclusions. Not least that the Viscount and I were sleeping together, which I hope you'll now accept was way off the mark. Whether Zayn was bribing Steven I can't say for sure, but it's unlikely he would have the money given he's barely D-list. Sorry, Zayn.'

The young actor shrugged. 'I might have if I could

have, but I doubt fifty quid in loose change would be enough.'

'I also strongly doubt Needles is pressuring Chloe to hire him so he keeps quiet about the accident on *Emmerdale*. As he rightly pointed out to me, he's not short of work with other directors, and his photos were already used to support her in court.'

The wardrobe manager preened.

'There were many other dead ends along the way,' I continued. 'Ruby tried to make me think it was Zayn, but I now know that was to distract me from her own misdemeanours – which had nothing to do with Yash, despite what Angela thought. Zayn thought the killing was connected to Chloe's so-called curse, but it wasn't. Juliette thought it was Steven, because of the large insurance policy he took out on her. But that merely reflects the risk anyone takes when casting a troubled star.'

'Troubled?' Juliette spat. 'I've been sober for a decade. The only "risk" is whether everyone else on this film can keep up with me. Ruby sure can't; we've all seen that.'

I ignored Ruby's eye-roll. 'Chloe thought it was Angela, and Juliette later changed her mind along the same lines. But Angela wasn't plotting with Yash to kill Juliette and take her part; she wasn't sleeping with him; she didn't send him that typewritten note; and she didn't wait for him in Juliette's trailer. In fact, the reason they met and argued in the old cottage on Thursday night is much more prosaic.' I looked at Angela with sympathy. 'I'm sorry to spill your secret, but it has to come out.'

She nodded reluctantly. I told them about Angela being a former Sentinel of Heaven, Yash's planned documentary, the argument in the cottage, burning the photo and Yash returning in the morning to search for it as witnessed by Ruby.

'But crucially, when Yash and Angela argued on Thursday night they were seen by the Viscount.' I made a conscious effort not to call him by name. He didn't deserve it. 'Unable to hear what they said, and mistaking Angela for Juliette, he drastically misunderstood the situation.'

'Told you,' said the diva.

'Not so fast, because you also misunderstood. You see, the Viscount had already decided to kill Yash after arguing with him earlier. When he saw Yash creep out of the house at midnight, he followed – perhaps thinking he could kill him in the woods. But when he witnessed Yash meeting and arguing with someone the Viscount thought was Juliette, he saw another opportunity. If he could connect Yash's death to Juliette in some way, it would confuse the issue and deflect suspicion.'

'I *said* there was evil in this place,' said Angela defiantly. 'I could sense it.'

Zayn put a friendly hand on her shoulder. 'We should have listened to you.'

'I'm not sure it would have helped,' I said. 'The deflecting tactics worked. We were all convinced it was someone involved with the film, and the Viscount's ongoing protests that the mirror writing would damage his reputation by linking the murder to Hendrick

Henning was a double-bluff. That said, Angela did help find the key piece of evidence that helped me understand how Yash was killed. Inspector, do you have the device?'

When he first arrived, I'd asked DCI Pierce to fetch the contraption Lily had brought out of the lake. A constable handed it to him, and he displayed it to the assembled crowd.

I continued, 'When I saw that, I had an idea of how it might have been done but it wasn't until I heard the contents of the typewritten letter that everything truly fell into place. When we found Yash's body the skin on his face was discoloured. I assumed it was a deathly pallor, but then DCI Pierce told me his forensics team had found an oily residue in the cupboard under the sink. Combine that with the note directing Yash to look in that same cupboard, the force needed to plunge a stake into his heart, plus our own situation, and it's all rather obvious, don't you think?'

They didn't, of course. I sipped my tea, making them wait and savouring the moment.

'We all saw how friendly and enthusiastic the Viscount was about our film,' I explained. 'That in itself was a bit odd, given his reputation suggested otherwise.'

'Yeah, but those other movies didn't have me,' said Juliette.

'True. They also didn't have Yash . . . or special effects involving explosive squibs, a subject close to the heart of a man who was a munitions specialist in the army and enjoys maintaining classic sports cars.'

Bill, the special effects coordinator, stood at the back

of the room. Now he groaned, understanding. 'Oh, no. Please tell me you're joking.'

'I'm afraid not. You see, the thing I kept stumbling over was how the killer could have escaped while leaving the trailer locked on the inside. It's impossible. But then I thought about your work, Bill, and how everything is set up remotely, so you needn't be anywhere near blood to pump it . . . or squibs to detonate them. I imagine the Viscount was very interested in that as well, wasn't he? Always hanging around the sets, chatting to you about your set-ups and props. He used that familiarity to steal items from your stock: several powerful squibs and a stunt stake.' I pointed to the cylinder of wood and metal, still in Pierce's hands. 'That device is like a makeshift cannon, powered by squibs. Except instead of a cannonball, it fired a solid resin stake.'

Everyone fell silent, imagining the horrible power of such a contraption.

'Late on Thursday night, Walter saw a light in trailer one. Naturally he assumed it was Juliette, but she truly was in her room at the Hendale Inn. In fact, it was the Viscount, setting his trap in the cupboard under the sink – the one door he could be absolutely certain Juliette herself wouldn't open.'

Ruby laughed, and Juliette glared at her.

I continued, 'He wrote the message on his mechanical typewriter and slipped it under Yash's bedroom door. The next day, he waited till we were filming the library scene, then slipped into the woods. Angela even saw him while she was walking Lily, but didn't realise it.'

'The spirit in the shadows!' she gasped.

'More like the Viscount in the fog. He was waiting for the telltale sound of his device going off. Yash had also waited, as the note instructed him to. When we started filming, he slipped inside Juliette's trailer and opened the cupboard under the sink.'

'Bang,' said Bill unenthusiastically. 'Opening the door pulls a tripwire, which detonates the squibs, and the explosive force rams the stake into Yash's chest.'

People gasped and shuddered.

'Chloe and I even heard it as we walked to unit base,' I said. 'Remember I wondered if a grip had dropped a section of dolly track? It was actually the sound of the squibs detonating inside the cannon. Then, when we opened the trailer, I smelt something acrid. I know now that it wasn't the body, but the lingering scent of explosive.'

Chloe despaired. 'If we'd got there just a minute earlier . . .'

'You mustn't think like that,' said DCI Pierce. 'Only one person was responsible for Mr Rani's death, and he's not in this room.'

'That's right,' I agreed. 'In fact, our presence forced the Viscount's first real mistake. Remember, we should have been filming. He thought he'd have plenty of time after Yash was killed to slip inside the trailer, remove the device and dispose of it long before anyone found the body. But because Ruby screwed up and we took a break, there were too many people milling about. He couldn't risk being seen to go inside the trailer.'

'He wouldn't have been able to anyway,' said Steven. 'It was locked from the inside.'

I nodded. 'Yash locked himself in to ensure he wouldn't be disturbed. That's why the Viscount rushed inside once we forced the door, opening all the closets and cupboards in his supposed search for a killer in hiding. In fact, he was covering up his true action, of retrieving the device from under the sink.' I turned to DCI Pierce. 'The residue and skin discolouration were gunpowder from the squibs at such close range, you see. As for the device, the Viscount collapsed it and tucked it in his coat, waiting for the right moment to smuggle it out.'

'How come we didn't see him do all this?' asked Fi, but she already knew the answer.

'We were too busy gawping at Yash. Just to make sure, though, the Viscount waited until nobody was looking, then used one of Juliette's lipsticks to write *Hendrick Lives* on the mirror. Needles' photos prove the writing wasn't there when we first opened the door.'

'But why?' asked Fi. 'Yash wasn't killed by a vampire.'

'First, it confused the issue. I kept wondering what it meant and what I'd missed, trying to find a connection between Yash's death and the Hendale Vampire legend. Which . . . well, there is, but not in the way we all thought. Second, it caused enough uproar and chaos to quickly get everyone out of the trailer.'

'That's right,' said Ruby. 'As soon as he saw it, the Viscount went mad and shoved us all out. But didn't Chloe see the message first? Why not point it out himself?'

298

'Because then it would be easy to suspect he'd written it. By waiting for someone else to see it, then pretending to be outraged, he evaded suspicion and could justify getting us all to leave. The more confusion as we left, the less likelihood of anyone noticing the device under his coat.'

DCI Pierce nodded. 'Presumably he then tried to dispose of it in the lake?'

'Exactly. I remembered that afterwards, the Viscount was nowhere to be seen. He couldn't risk leaving the spent cannon in the Hall, in case your men found it in a search. Tossing it somewhere in the woods was no good, not with cast and crew roaming all over the estate building graveyards, meeting at midnight in the old cottage and getting up to who knows what else. The lake was a safe option, somewhere it would sink without trace. Except it didn't. It got caught in the reeds, where Lily found what she thought was a big stick.'

The terrier looked up at the mention of her name. I bent down and fussed her head until she lay back down.

'I think the Viscount toppled that light in the hallway scene, too. I can't prove it, but he was hanging around the set beforehand and it fell at the exact moment the squibs around the doorway were detonated. Nobody would have heard or noticed a lone squib under the light stand, positioned to throw it off-balance.'

'So, he *did* try to kill me!' Juliette cried. 'I was getting too close to the truth!'

'No, it was simply another distraction. You were already convinced that you were the target, and the light falling fooled the rest of us into thinking the same thing.'

'But *why?*' Chloe cried, applying a director's mind to the unanswered questions. 'None of this makes sense. Why wasn't Juliette the target? Why had the Viscount already decided to kill Yash? What were they arguing about? What was the "evidence" he mentioned in that letter? And why did he go to the trouble of building an explosive stake-cannon, then distract us with Juliette's trailer and old vampire stories?'

She did all of that in one breath. I almost applauded. Instead, when I was sure she'd finished, I sipped my tea and smiled.

'It's quite simple. Yash was the twenty-third Viscount Henning.'

CHAPTER FORTY

Confusion reigned as the room burst into life with surprised chatter. I raised my voice to be heard, because they needed to hear the explanation.

'Steven,' I said, turning to him. 'You told me Yash originally turned down a role in *Draculania*. That's why you almost cast Zayn instead. But then Yash suddenly changed his mind and lobbied you for the part. Why?'

'He said it was gratitude for going ahead with the documentary on the Sentinels of Heaven. I guess he wanted to make a play for the mainstream.'

'Had you already agreed to film here at Hendale by then?'

'Yes, that was always the plan. Why?'

'Because I think he changed his mind after Raven – the genealogist you hired for him as part of the documentary – had made a search of his family tree.'

'I don't understand,' said Pri. 'How could Yash be a Viscount? He was as brown as me and Zayn.'

'We've all come to know the tale of the Hendale Vampire,' I said. 'Some of it may be true, while much is no doubt embellished. But one crucial part is definitely a lie – a convenient fiction that simultaneously makes the story more romantic, while also neatly heading off questions of inheritance. Helena, the pregnant sister, didn't die of malaria. It's possible her Indian lover didn't either, of course; he might have been murdered by Hendrick. Remember, the thirteenth Viscount had fought in the Indian campaign to establish the British Empire. Perhaps Helena feared her domineering, racist brother might turn on her too. Whatever the reason, she fled England and returned to India. Hendrick put about the official story that she'd died. But she lived, and in India she had a child . . . who had a child . . . who had a child . . .'

Zayn looked aghast. 'So, they lied to keep themselves white. They didn't want to admit part of the family was Indian.'

'That's right, and they did it so thoroughly that after two hundred years the truth was simply forgotten. When Yash told the current Viscount he was descended from Helena it must have been a seismic shock.'

I showed them the texts from Raven on my phone, which had explained Yash's claim to the estate.

'Raven was sure of her work, but much of it relied on records from pre-Independence India. Those documents are no longer considered reliable, so Yash was on the lookout for anything else that would bolster his case. When a note arrived under his door promising "evidence" hidden in Juliette's trailer, he couldn't resist.'

'But why would he think Ms Shine had that evidence?' asked DCI Pierce. 'Did Mr Rani really believe she had an independent interest in his claim?'

'An actor's ego knows no bounds, Inspector. We can be convinced of almost anything when it suits the story we tell ourselves.' I directed this last at Juliette, who finally had the grace to look embarrassed. 'The same goes for the Viscount, in a way. Still grieving that he couldn't pass Hendale to his own son, the revelation about Yash's inheritance drove him to extreme measures.'

Ruby snorted. 'I'll say. Seems madness runs in the family.'

'We should probably be a little more sensitive than that about people's mental health,' I said. 'But still, it's no excuse for what he did.'

A constable entered the room and informed DCI Pierce that the Viscount had woken up and was ready to be formally arrested. The police had rushed him to Hendale hospital after carrying his unconscious body down from the tower, and it had apparently been touch-and-go for a while. But Henry George Fitzroy Samuel de Finistere Henning would live to face justice.

The inspector followed the constable out, nodding in acknowledgement to me as he went. 'Leave it with us from here,' he said. 'We'll make sure he never sees the light of day again.'

Outside, the storm clouds made way for a glorious burning orange sunset over the Dales. Everyone breathed a collective sigh of relief and took a moment to admire the maelstrom of colour.

Well, almost everyone.

'You got lucky,' said Juliette, scowling at me. 'That was all guesswork.'

Lily snarled. I didn't bother telling her to be quiet.

'On the contrary,' I said, 'it was *leg*-work. You were too busy trying to make the evidence fit what you wanted to be true, instead of following where it led.'

'It's a good thing you were here, Gwinny,' said Steven. 'I don't think any of us would have seen through the Viscount like you did. Not even the police.'

'People tend to put their guard up around the police,' I said, smiling. 'Not around people like me, though. He must have thought I came in here without a hat.'

CHAPTER FORTY-ONE

Bright morning light streamed through the windows of Viv's hospital room. She sat upright in bed, already looking healthier and heartier.

'Gwinny,' she said, 'would you do me the favour of sleeping at the house while I'm stuck in here? Rather than staying at the Hall, I mean. In case those burglars come back and try again.'

I'd hoped I might not have to tell her the truth. I'd already replaced the necklace in her jewellery box. But keeping such secrets now felt petty.

'They won't be back. In fact, "they" weren't burglars at all. It was Ruby Westcott who broke in. When I told her you were stuck here for a while, she saw her chance to steal a necklace. Silver filigree and jade . . . ?'

I thought Viv would be angry, but she closed her eyes and nodded.

'I always wondered if she knew. I was in *Twelfth Night* with her husband, and he was quite . . . virile. You know what it's like. It didn't last long, but he bought me that beautiful necklace. He must have told her when they were getting divorced. I was already with David by then, so it was water under the bridge.'

Not to Ruby, I thought, but remained silent. She didn't need to know where the necklace had come from.

'I'd still feel better if you stayed at the house for a few days,' she continued. 'The doctor says I can go home on Thursday. I didn't break anything, but they want to keep an eye on me for a while, perhaps in case I spontaneously combust or drop dead of boredom.'

I laughed. It was good to see Viv back to her old self.

'If you insist, then. We'll be here for the rest of week re-shooting the Luke scenes anyway. At least it won't be long before you can snuggle up in bed with Lily again.'

Viv snorted. 'What do you mean, "again"? The dog has her own perfectly suitable bed.'

'Oh, but . . . whenever I get into bed, she leaps under the covers . . . with her head poking out on the pillow, like a human . . .'

This time Viv's snort became a roar of laughter, followed by wincing cries of pain and regret while she clutched her hip. 'God, don't make me laugh like that. You've been had, Gwinny. She saw you coming a mile away.'

'Do you mean you don't sleep like that with Lily?'

'Certainly not. Sleeping with a dog! Whoever would? Well, I suppose we know the answer to that question.' She raised a disapproving eyebrow at me.

'I found a glazier to repair the front door,' I said

to change the subject. 'He's due this afternoon. Then on Thursday I'll come by to pick you up and take you home.'

She squeezed my hand. 'The director won't like you coming and going from set. I can get a cab home.'

'Considering the Viscount would have got away with it if not for me, they can jolly well make allowances. Besides, there are some scenes where I'm not required. I'll make sure Chloe schedules those while I'm away.'

'All right,' she agreed, smiling. 'What does your policeman boyfriend think of all this?'

I smiled. 'Oh, Birch is used to it. This isn't the first time I've caught a killer, as it happens.'

'Then it's a good thing you were here. All's well that ends well.'

'The King's a beggar, now the play is done,' I recited and kissed her head softly before hurrying out. I didn't want her to see the lie plainly written on my face. In fact, I hadn't spoken to Birch since yesterday, when he told me about Angela being a former Sentinel. Afterwards I texted him to say the Viscount had been arrested, and explained I'd be staying here for longer than originally planned. His reply had been a terse one-word reply *Understood.*

I still didn't know how to bring up the matter of Tina, something that appeared to have happened precisely *because* I was here, rather than at home.

All may have ended well regarding Viv and finding Yash's killer, but when it came to my own life things looked very different.

CHAPTER FORTY-TWO

The glazier had been fast and efficient, so long as I kept him plied with cups of strong Yorkshire tea, and soon had the door fixed. Now, while Lily recovered from the excitement and dozed on the sofa, I stood in the same kitchen where Viv had fallen and understood how much worse it could have been. Solid marble countertops, hard tile flooring, a wooden table and chairs, metal cupboard handles . . .

The room began to feel like a death trap, and I shuddered. Silly old Gwinny! Such needless paranoia.

After all, I had something else to be paranoid about. My phone had been in my hand for the past five minutes, as I tried to bring myself to call Birch and face the truth.

Our relationship had always been unusual. Meeting by chance, getting to know one another over mysterious murders, breaking into crime scenes together while awkwardly suppressing our mutual attraction. Even now, having finally acknowledged it, we were still moving slowly. Was that the problem? Had I been too cautious, so careful not to let Birch think I was trying to displace his late wife that he'd turned to Tina instead?

Did it matter?

That was the real question. So long as I had him to myself in our moments together, did I care if he spent his other moments with another woman? Would it be better if that woman wasn't my best friend? Could I face being with them, all the time thinking that I didn't know? Or would it be simpler if we were all open and honest with each other?

No.

It did matter. I did care. I couldn't face it.

When Birch answered the call I found myself looking at half his face from somewhere below, as if the phone was on his lap, the picture juddering and wobbling. He was driving.

'Afternoon, ma'am. How'd it go?'

'Oh, I – I didn't realise you were driving,' I stammered. 'I'll – I'll call you back.'

'No need, all fine here. Nearly arrived, anyway. His Lordship's arrest was all over the news last night. Rum do. Hope the DCI thanked you.'

'In the end, yes. Not before he played me for a fool and tried to embarrass me in front of everyone, though. Definitely not on my Christmas card list.'

Birch laughed, which made everything inside me feel worse. I steeled myself to ask the question.

'Listen, Birch . . . that time I called, and you were at Tina's house . . . and the so-called dog groomer . . .'

'Ah! Yes, time to come clean. Sorry. Hoped to keep it under wraps until you came back to London, but the old subterfuge is a bit rusty. Slipped up, as you saw. Better to tell you now than draw things out.'

Perhaps doing this via video call hadn't been such a good idea. I could barely look at him on the screen, for fear I might cry.

'Tina and I . . . well, first I should say it was me who started it. You mustn't blame her. All my doing, you see.'

'Oh, for heaven's sake, Birch, out with it!'

He coughed. 'Yes, sorry. Anyway, truth is we've been arranging a birthday party. For you. At Hayburn Stead. Plan was I'd drive you there Wednesday, on pretence of Tina wanting advice re the Salukis. Walk through the door, big surprise, lots of balloons. You know the drill. Problem is, staying on to film means you'll be in the Dales for your birthday. Might as well spill the beans.'

I couldn't speak. Confusion, surprise and relief washed over my body like ocean waves smoothing beach sands.

'Ma'am? You still there?'

'Yes—' I croaked, cleared my throat and started again. 'Yes, I'm here. It's . . . a surprise, that's all.' I've always been more likely to spend my birthday with a glass of wine and a jigsaw than hiring a venue, and with one thing and another I'd had more pressing matters on my mind for the past few days.

'Whole thing's off now, of course,' said Birch. 'Doesn't seem much point.'

'What? No, no. You've gone to all this trouble . . . it'll just be delayed, that's all.'

'But you know, now. Can't have a surprise party if it's not a surprise.'

I laughed. 'Darling, I'm an actress. I'll *act* surprised, and it can be our little secret.'

'Our little secret. I like that.' His screen stopped wobbling, and through the camera I heard the ratchet of his handbrake. He smiled. 'Destination achieved. Apologies again for the secrecy, but I'm sure you understand.'

He stepped out of the car and did something I couldn't see. Then I heard Ronnie's *woof*, and realised he was letting the Lab out of the boot. He must have been driving them to take a walk somewhere.

'I wish you'd told me.' I was *less* annoyed now that I knew the truth, but not completely *un*-annoyed. 'I can keep a secret, you know. Lord knows I've—' Before I could finish, the front door chime sounded. 'Hold on, there's someone at the door. Probably the postman. I'll call you back.'

Lily ran into the vestibule and stood barking at the door. Through the newly installed frosted glass I saw a silhouetted figure and wondered if the glazier had forgotten something. Or perhaps Viv had placed an online order from her hospital bed.

'Thank you, Lily, that's enough,' I said in vain as I opened the door. 'I'm sure whoever it is doesn't need deafening while they—'

'Special delivery,' said DCI Alan Birch, retired, his

bright blue eyes flashing mischievously. Ronnie the black Lab stood eagerly by his side on the doorstep. Birch clutched a bouquet of flowers, still bearing their motorway service station price tag. I didn't care. He could have brought me a drooping dandelion from the neighbour's garden, and I'd still have loved him for it.

On impulse I flung my arms around his broad frame and hugged him tightly. To my delight he returned the gesture, enveloping me with his arms. Lily and Ronnie took that as a signal to circle one another, panting and sniffing while threatening to cut our legs out from under us. We were used to it.

'One last secret,' he explained with a smile. 'Ms Danforth called me this morning; said I can use the spare room for a couple of days until the doc lets her come home. She thought you'd like some company.'

'You have no idea,' I said, finally realising how much I'd missed him these last few weeks while filming.

'Booked us dinner at the local pub,' he said, his voice muffled slightly by my hair. 'Don't worry, dogs welcome. Checked ahead. Eight o'clock sharp.'

That was surprisingly forward for Birch, and I was still holding on to him, so it took a moment before I thought to ask, 'Wait, local pub? Which one?'

'Hendale Inn, it's called. Sounds very traditional, good food reviews. Something wrong?'

I shook my head, trying not to laugh, and looked up into those lovely eyes. 'No, nothing's wrong. Nothing at all.'

We stood like that for a while. If there was one

thing I'd learnt about Birch, it was that he wasn't a man of great initiative. Intelligent, loyal, upstanding, righteous . . . these qualities he possessed in spades. But all things being equal, he wouldn't be the first to take a leap.

So I kissed him.

He froze, surprised, and for a split-second I worried I'd made a terrible mistake. But then he relaxed, pulled me closer and returned the kiss. It was delightful . . . until Ronnie and Lily decided they wanted to join in, barking furiously and leaping up at us to paw for attention.

We separated, laughing. Birch's cheeks flushed, which only made my heart melt more.

'Come on, you can unpack while I change for dinner,' I said, ushering everyone through the vestibule. 'As for the spare room, well. I think we can do better than that . . .'

ACKNOWLEDGEMENTS

If you're wondering whether you can visit Hendale, Hendale Hall, and the Henning family, the answer is no; they're fictitious. Given the nature of the story, I didn't want to besmirch the name of a real family and manor house.

However, you can and should visit the real Yorkshire Dales if you have the opportunity, not least because what both Gwinny and George say is true: England is filled with grand old houses – some of which can be found in the Dales – that are open to the public, have centuries of fascinating, often bloody, history and feature a chilling ghost story or two. As a bonus, the Dales are rightfully regarded as one of the UK's most beautiful regions. I've lived a stone's throw away for the last twenty years, and I never get tired of it. Just watch out for the vampires.

I'm indebted to the people and tourist offices of the Yorkshire Dales for providing a wealth of information and history about the area, and to James Moran and Julian Simpson for doing the same regarding life on a film set. I have some experience in that area thanks to *Atomic Blonde*, but those guys have been there, done it, and got the wonkily printed crew T-shirt many times over. Even so, much of the set life in this book is heavily fictionalised and simplified for the sake of drama, and that's all on me.

Thanks to the Mid-Atlantic Writers for invaluable support, notes, and discussion ('In with pages,' at last!) and to my ever-faithful beta readers for helping keep me on the straight and narrow. Once again, my friend Fiona Veitch Smith (whose own Poppy Denby and Clara Vale mysteries I highly recommend) provided especially valuable feedback.

In a funny way I feel I should also thank Bram Stoker. My being both a lifelong horror fan and old-school goth is partly traceable to reading *Dracula* at a young age, and the gender-swapped production *Draculania* is an idea I've been tinkering with for some time. When I realised I'd need to invent a screenplay for this book, the Carpathian Countess seemed a fitting choice.

Thank you to my fellow crime authors, in particular those of the 'modern cosy' community, who are without a doubt some of the kindest and most supportive people I know.

Speaking of support, I couldn't ask for a better publisher than Allison & Busby to spread the good word. My thanks go to all of the wonderful staff and freelancers who help shepherd Gwinny's adventures through the unseen but vitally important process of actually getting books out into the world, not to mention saving me from embarrassing tyops.

My agent Sarah Such continues to work wonders, and my partner Marcia continues not to stake out my undead form in the blistering dawn light. For which I'm grateful.

ANTONY JOHNSTON's career has spanned books, award-winning video games and graphic novels including collaborations with Anthony Horowitz and Alan Moore. He wrote the *New York Times* bestseller *Daredevil Season One* for Marvel Comics and is the creator of *Atomic Blonde* which grossed over $100 million at the box office. The first book featuring Gwinny Tuffel, *The Dog Sitter Detective*, was the winner of the Barker Fiction Award. Johnston can often be found writing at home in Lancashire with a snoozing hound for company.

antonyjohnston.com
dogsitterdetective.com
@AntonyJohnston